DEVIL'S FOOD

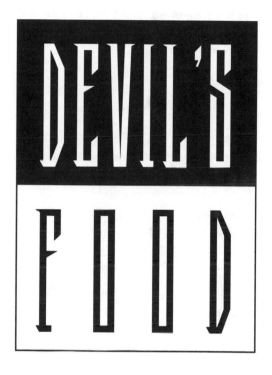

DEVIL'S FOOD

ANTHONY BRUNO

A TOM DOHERTY ASSOCIATES BOOK / NEW YORK

DEVIL'S FOOD

This book is printed on acid-free paper.

A Forge Book
Published by Tom Doherty Associates, Inc.
175 Fifth Avenue
New York, NY 10010

Forge® is a registered trademark of Tom Doherty Associates, Inc.

Library of Congress Cataloging-in-Publication Data

Bruno, Anthony.
　　　Devil's food / Anthony Bruno.—1st ed.
　　　　　p. cm.
　　　"A Tom Doherty Associates book."
　　　ISBN 0-312-85990-2 (acid-free paper)
　　　I. Title.
　　　PS3552.R82D48 1997
　　　813'.54—dc20　　　　　　　　　　　96-30730
　　　　　　　　　　　　　　　　　　　　　　　CIP

First Edition: February 1997

Printed in the United States of America

0　9　8　7　6　5　4　3　2　1

For Lauren and Kristen

DEVIL'S FOOD

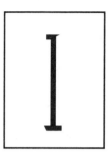

1

Loretta Kovacs stood out in the hallway and stared at the black lettering on the thick glass pane in the door.

State of New Jersey
Department of Corrections
Bureau of Parole
Parole Violators Search Unit

Mentally she added the words that should've been painted underneath:

aka PVSU
aka the Jump Squad
aka the End of the Line

She sighed. *Bad attitude,* she thought. This time she wasn't going to start off on the wrong foot. No more bad attitudes. She was determined to make this work. She had no choice really. There was nowhere else to go in Corrections after the Jump

Squad. Truth be told, this was the bottom, the place where the screwups got their last chance, the end of the line.

Suddenly, out of the blue, that old black mantra started chanting in her head, droning in her ears like a swarm of killer bees coming over the horizon: *I'm fat; I'm single; my career is in the toilet. . . . I'm fat; I'm single; my career is in the toilet. . . . I'm fat; I'm single; my career is in the toilet. . . .*

She cleared her throat to chase it away before it worsened her already bleak frame of mind. Besides, that stupid mantra wasn't entirely true, she told herself. Her life wasn't that bad. All right, so her career was in the toilet—but no one had flushed it yet. And yes, she was single and had no prospects, but she wasn't over the hill; she could still meet someone. And she wasn't *that* fat. It wasn't as if she were obese. One hundred and sixty-seven pounds, five foot six and a half. That's not fat. That's zaftig, Rubenesque, big-boned.

A Milky Way wrapper rustled in the pocket of her jacket as she reached for the doorknob, and her face drooped. Who was she trying to kid? She was fat. But so what if she was? Only stupid people got hung up on looks. And fat people can always lose weight; stupid people can't grow brains. Given a choice, she'd rather be smart than skinny. That's what her father the lawyer always used to tell her. It's what you know that counts, not what you look like. Unfortunately, she hadn't learned enough to please him, though. To this day he was still deeply disappointed in her because she hadn't gone to law school, and Dad was never very good at hiding his feelings. Unfortunately.

Her father's stern face with its constantly constipated expression loomed over her like a ghost. She was thirty-four years old, living her own life, and she knew it was stupid to feel this way, but still, just once, she'd like to please him. Just once before he died.

She opened the Jump Squad door, knowing her father wouldn't approve of this. But as soon as she walked in, a wonderfully familiar smell wrinkled her nose and displaced the cranky spirit of her dear old dad. It was cinnamon. Buttery cinnamon.

Powerful cinnamon. Like at those hot cinnamon bun places, the ones that seemed to be at all the malls whenever she was trying to buy clothes. She snapped her head back and tossed a cloud of wavy dirty blond hair over her shoulder, determined to ignore the aroma because she'd just had a candy bar, which she really shouldn't have had in the first place. She took in the big room instead.

The place was deserted. Eight battered metal desks were positioned back-to-back in pairs, but there was no one sitting at them. Small basement windows covered with security gates lined the top of one wall. The opposite wall held a long row of scratched gray file cabinets. Thick files were stacked on top, the piles leaning against each other like a bunch of drunks.

Loretta was about to close the door behind her when she spotted the source of the cinnamon smell. On a typing table behind the door where an electric coffeemaker was set up there were two aluminum trays of cinnamon buns—one full, the other with just two left. She furrowed her brows over her green eyes, then one brow slowly arched above the other. Were these here for the taking? she wondered. Or did they belong to someone? She was tempted to help herself, but the mantra started playing in her head again. *I'm fat; I'm single; my career is in the toilet.* . . . There was a definite correlation between being fat and being single, and cinnamon buns were one of her seventy-seven deadly sins—right between eclairs and Devil Dogs.

She started to close the door, but paused for a moment to stare at the lettering on the glass again. The Jump Squad. Never in a million years did she think she'd ever wind up here. Her father would die if he ever found out. The parole officers who worked here were no better than skip tracers, bounty hunters for the state. Since parole violators are the same as prison escapees under the law, they have none of the rights of due process that regular citizens have, which means that PVSU officers can do anything to bring in a jumper. *Anything.* No wonder this unit had such a bad rep.

Loretta let out a long sigh and started talking to herself over the mantra before she really got depressed, telling herself that this couldn't be as bad as it seemed and that anyway, it was only temporary. This wasn't going to be the rest of her life, because she had a plan. She'd spend six months with the Jump Squad, then apply for a staff counselor job, which paid better and had regular nine-to-five hours. In the meantime she'd take the law boards and apply to law school. If everything worked out, she could go nights and have her degree in five years, and then she could go into practice with her sister, which is what she'd originally intended to do ten years ago when she'd graduated from college. That was before she had gotten sidetracked with social work and a career in corrections. But it's never too late to salvage your dreams, she kept telling herself. Kovacs and Kovacs was still a definite possibility, and if that happened, her sourpuss old man would have to find something else to be disappointed about. If everything went right, she could definitely make it happen. Because you can always make the best of a crappy situation if you just try hard enough.

She looked down at the cinnamon buns and sighed. "Yeah, and someday I'll be a size six," she muttered under her breath.

"Coming through! Outta the way, please. Coming through!"

Loretta glanced up and quickly stepped out of the way as a wrecking ball of tangled bodies banged into the door and crashed into the room. She caught the flying door before it slammed into the typing table and glass shattered all over the cinnamon buns.

A roar of pain and sorrow trailed behind the two passing bodies like smoke from a locomotive. The lead body was the cowcatcher, his face the screaming whistle. The man was as big as a buffalo and just as shaggy, with reddish-brown hair down to the middle of his back and a scraggly beard that covered his chest. He was at least six foot six, with a powerful, topheavy build—slim in the hips but huge in the chest. He wore a black leather vest with some sort of biker insignia sewn on the back, a black T-shirt, and frayed blue jeans with holes in the knees. Tattoos covered every visible inch of both arms.

The other guy, who had this monster in an armlock, forcing

him forward from behind, was no more than average in size, with dark, slicked-back hair, a round face, and sloped-back eyes. Loretta would almost have said it was a kind face except for the fact that the big biker was screaming bloody murder, desperately pleading with the man not to break his arm. Actually, he was kind of cute, Loretta thought, except for the greaseball haircut.

As the smaller man tried to guide the unruly buffalo through the office, the big man suddenly dug his heels in and shouldered his captor into the file cabinets. The biker started ramming his back against the smaller man, rattling the cabinets and spilling files all over the floor until the place looked and sounded like a demolition site. But the smaller man didn't seem terribly fazed by the brutal hammering. In fact, he looked bored. Loretta could see that he still had the big man trapped in the armlock.

After about two minutes of this, the biker stopped to catch his breath.

The smaller man peered over the biker's shoulder. "You through yet, Joe? You get it out of your system yet?"

The buffalo snarled. "Eat shi—oooww!"

With what seemed like a simple flick of the wrist, the smaller man torqued up the pressure on the biker's arm and brought him to his knees. Loretta winced in sympathy.

The smaller man stood over the fallen beast, shaking his head. "You're acting like a big baby, Joe. You know that? I'm ashamed of you."

"You're breaking my friggin' arm, Marvelli."

"Whattaya want me to do? Give you a hug? All right, Joe. C'mon. I'll give you a big hug if it'll make you feel better. Here."

The man named Marvelli released the biker and opened his arms like Luciano Pavarotti, tilting his head and grinning as if he were perfectly willing to let bygones be bygones.

Joe slowly dragged himself to his feet, shaking his weary head, but then suddenly he spun around, scowling like a mad dog. He lunged headfirst, diving into Marvelli's midsection, propelling him backward into the nearest desk. The desk slid several feet with Marvelli on his back on the desktop, Joe face down on top of him. It slammed into another desk, and the momentum—or maybe it was Marvelli; Loretta couldn't tell which—flipped Joe up and over onto his back on top of the next desk, like a great big flapjack. Marvelli quickly scrambled to his knees and trapped the biker's head between them, then started to massage the bridge of his nose. Joe reached up to grab Marvelli's head, but Marvelli rested the pads of his thumbs on Joe's eyelids.

"You like your eyes, Joe?"

Joe instantly dropped his arms to his side.

"Good boy, Joe." Marvelli continued to massage the big man's forehead, circling his eye sockets now and then to remind him not to get cute. "Just relax, Joe. Take deep breaths. Think about the shore. Waves coming in on an empty beach. Just you and the waves on this nice beach—"

Joe started to reach up again, but Marvelli's thumbs were quicker. "They don't do eye transplants, Joe."

Joe let his arms fall.

Marvelli took his thumbs off and massaged the biker's temples some more. "Just go with it, Joe. Let yourself drift. Watch the waves. If you listen, you can hear them. Isn't it nice? Of course, it is. See, I can feel you starting to relax already."

Loretta couldn't believe what she was seeing. Who was this guy? He was incredible.

"Okay, now that you're calm, Joe," Marvelli said, "let's talk about your life, your future."

"Frig you, Mar—"

"Uh-uh!" The thumbs returned to Joe's eyes.

Joe went limp.

"Good boy. Now just listen to me and don't talk. Talking gets people into trouble. Believe me, I know. There aren't that many people in this world who can kept their mouths shut, but those are the only ones who stay out of trouble. Believe me."

The biker snorted. "*You* never shut up, Marvelli."

"That's true, but I'm different."

"Why's that?"

" 'Cause I'm always in trouble, and it doesn't seem to matter whether I shut up or not, so I may as well keep talking. Anyway, I know more than most people, so I sorta got a license to talk."

"Bullsh—"

"Hey!" Thumbs on eyes again. "Watch your friggin' mouth, Joe. There's a lady here." Marvelli looked over his shoulder and smiled at Loretta. "How ya doin'?"

"Fine," Loretta said. He had a nice smile. But that hair . . . yuk!

"You didn't get hurt or anything?" Marvelli asked. "When we came in, I mean."

"No, I'm okay. Don't worry about me." In truth, Loretta's heartbeat was just starting to calm down.

"You sure you're okay?"

"Yeah, I'm fine."

"Good." He turned back to Joe, adjusting his knee clamp on the biker's shaggy head and settling into a more comfortable position as he continued the face massage. "Now, Joe, what were we talking about?"

"My future."

"Oh, yeah. Well, what can I tell you, Joe? You violated the terms of your parole, pal."

"Yeah, but I been trying to tell you, man. My bike broke down out in Ohio. I was stuck."

"For five months you were stuck? Can't get Harley parts in Ohio? They don't have phones in Ohio? You couldn't have called your PO and let him know where you were?"

"He's an assho—"

Thumbs on eyes. "I said watch your mouth." Marvelli turned to Loretta. "Sorry."

"Don't worry about it," she said. "You should hear *me* sometimes."

He laughed. He had a nice laugh. A little hoarse, like Gene Kelly's.

"So, Marvelli, what happens to me now, man?" Joe asked. "I gotta go back to the joint, right?"

Marvelli rubbed the biker's chubby cheeks. "It's not up to me, Joe. You gotta go before the parole board, see what they say. Who knows? Maybe they'll buy your Ohio story and give you another chance with parole."

"Or?"

"Or they'll send you back to prison."

"For how long?"

"That's up to them. I just bring you guys in."

"Friggin' bounty hunter, that's all you are, Marvelli."

"Joe! You hurt my feelings. I'm insulted. How could you call me such a thing? I'm a trained professional and a public servant. You make me sound like some kind of cattle rustler."

"You're worse, man. You're crazy. *You're* the one who oughta be locked up."

Marvelli considered it for a moment. "Maybe I should. You know, you're not the first one to say that."

All the while Marvelli never stopped kneading the biker's face. Loretta just stood there, staring at the two of them. She'd never heard of a parole officer who operated like this. Some POs coddle their cases, others bully them, but she'd never seen anyone who could do both at the same time.

"All right, Joe, fun time is over," Marvelli said. "I'm gonna let go of your head now, and we're gonna go straight back through that hallway to the lockup, so I can process you. Okay?"

Joe nodded between Marvelli's knees.

"You calm now?"

Joe nodded.

"You're not gonna try something stupid?"

Joe shook his head.

Marvelli spread his knees, and the biker sat up on the desk, chin on his chest in defeat. Marvelli hopped off and rubbed his knees, wincing with pain. "Knees ain't what they used to be," he said to no one in particular.

"Ah, excuse me—" Loretta was just about to ask him where she could find the supervisor's office when she suddenly spotted Joe's hulking form coming up behind Marvelli like a Kodiak bear up on its hind legs. The big man had a desk chair hoisted over his head.

Loretta opened her mouth, but she couldn't get the words out as the old fear overtook her. She panicked, thinking for a split second that *she* was Joe's intended victim. She had to force herself to point and shout, "Heads up!"

Marvelli turned his head toward Joe, and without even standing up from his bent over position, he moved into the big man's gut, staying low and getting under him just as the chair came crashing down. Joe missed his target, and the momentum of the blow combined with a little lift from Marvelli's standing up flipped the big man over onto his back. He hit the floor like a natural disaster.

Marvelli stood over him, shaking his head in disappointment. "God*dam*mit, Joe! When're you gonna learn?"

Joe's eyes were out of focus. He was in a daze.

Marvelli picked up the chair and put it back on its wheels, then grabbed Joe by the hair and hauled him up into a sitting position. He pinned the big man's arm back behind him and forced him to his feet with the armlock again. Joe groaned and cursed, then made a half-hearted effort at breaking loose, but Marvelli torqued his wrist another notch and got him back under control.

"C'mon, Joe. Let's go."

Panting hard, Joe nodded at the tray of cinnamon buns. "Think I could get me one of those, Marvelli? I'm kinda hungry."

Marvelli frowned down at the buns and shook his head. "You got enough problems, Joe. You don't need sugar. Now that I think about it, that's probably where all your problems started. Too much refined sugar when you were a kid. I bet you were one of those hyperactive kids. That comes from too much sugar. That's probably when your weight problem started, too."

"Frig you, Marvelli."

Yeah, frig you, Marvelli! Loretta thought, instantly changing her mind about him. She hated it when skinny people shot their mouths off about how other people should lose weight. What gave them the right? These were the same little skinny-

minnie shit-asses who used to make fun of her in school when
she was a kid. They had no idea how much hurt and misery they
caused. All of a sudden Loretta felt sorry for Joe. The skinny kids
probably used to make fun of him, too, when he was in school.
Before he dropped out and became a full-time scumbag, that is.

"C'mon, Joe, move," Marvelli said. "Holding cell's all the
way in the back. You get settled in and I'll make you a nice cup
of herb tea. It'll mellow you right out. I guarantee."

"Don't bother."

"Might help your attitude, too. Give it a try. You'll be surprised."

Marvelli maneuvered the biker to the rear of the office where
they disappeared down a narrow hallway. Loretta stared blankly
at their departing backs, eyes wide, not blinking. Then out of the
blue her heart started to do a merengue in her chest as she flashed
back on big Joe with that chair up over his head. It all came back
in a rush, and she had to grip the straps of the handbag slung over
her shoulder with both hands to control the trembling. The old
fear came crashing down over her—the panic, the terror, the
anger and humiliation of being trapped and helpless. She had
been looking at Joe, but in her mind it wasn't Joe.

It was Brenda.

Loretta stared at the desk chair that Joe had tried to bash over Marvelli's head. She was lost in thought, thinking about Brenda. Brenda Hemingway. Inmate #445619. Twenty-five to life for murdering a rival drug dealer in Jersey City. A male drug dealer. By her own hand. With a razor.

Loretta gritted her teeth and tried to take slow, deep breaths, but the more she tried to change the channel in her mind, the better the reception came in on the Brenda Channel. No matter what she did, no matter how hard she tried, Loretta knew she would never ever forget that face. The broad nose, the malevolent little eyes, the fluttering pink tongue. One hundred and eighty pounds of seething malice just waiting for someone to take it out on. Brenda knew she'd never get out of prison alive, so she didn't care what she did. She had nothing to lose. Unfortunately, the good Lord above had decided to put them together for a while to give Loretta the opportunity to hear Brenda Hemingway's complete philosophy of life in prison—at length.

Twenty-seven hours. Twenty-seven hours *in hell.* Trapped in the prison laundry, alone with Brenda, while the rest of the place rioted. Assistant Warden Loretta Kovacs had been left in charge of the Pinebrook Women's Correctional Facility that night. Wet-behind-the-ears Loretta Kovacs who figured she could cut the troublemakers off at the pass by going straight to the leader of the uprising and listening to her complaints while at the same time making it clear that nothing would be negotiated until the two guards they'd taken hostage were released. She'd been prepared to stare Brenda Hemingway down like a bad dog in order to *make* her obey. But it didn't work out that way because Brenda was no dog. She was a human being full of hate and resentment with absolutely nothing to fear. But stupid Assistant Warden Kovacs had been too cocksure of herself to see that.

The rioters held onto the two guards, and Loretta ended up going one-on-one with Brenda. Twenty-seven hours, naked and trussed up with electrical cord like a calf waiting to become veal. Brenda waving her homemade shiv, a sharpened spoon, using it to poke and prod and terrorize Loretta, using it like a divine da Vinci finger to point out all Loretta's faults: her love handles, her double chin, her jiggly butt, her cottage-cheese thighs, and worst of all, her stupid, arrogant assumptions about prisoners. Twenty-seven hours of Brenda's voice, her cackle, her relentless monologue. Brenda yanking off Loretta's clothes and trying them on, Loretta's blouse on her head like a headdress, her big feet in Loretta's loafers, crushing the backs as she circled the sacrificial calf, prancing like an Ikette, showing the assistant warden that she could have power, too, that she could be the person and Loretta could be the animal.

"Things change, baby," Brenda yelled as she hauled Loretta up by the hair and forced her into the mouth of that giant industrial clothes dryer. "Nobody ever clued you in to that one, did they, honey? Well, I'm telling you now, so pay attention, girl. Even the queen bee can get stung. That's right. Things do change."

The dryer door slammed shut with a pinging bang. Fear and panic choked Loretta like a plastic bag thrown over her head. Suddenly the motor rumbled and groaned, and she started to tumble, gears grinding and stripping with her weight. The burner fired—she could hear the blast beneath her—and the metal started to heat up. She tumbled faster, knocking her head, her knees, her elbows. She could smell the heat rising. On the other side of the round glass window Brenda's cackling face spun round and round. Loretta felt sick to her stomach but was afraid to throw up inside the dryer. The perforated metal walls started to burn her skin. She screamed, but only Brenda could hear her. She screamed again, pleading—

"Something wrong over there?"

"Huh?!" Loretta's chest was heaving as she realized she wasn't in that clothes dryer. She looked all around for the source of the voice, her gaze bouncing around the room like a haywire searchlight. Then her eye found the cinnamon buns on the typing table, and she stared hard at them, finally believing that she was here, now, not back there then, and that Brenda was locked up, in another prison, in another state, far away.

"I said, is there something wrong, young lady? You look like you got the heebie-jeebies over there."

A stout, dark-skinned black man with a pointy goatee was standing in the hallway that Marvelli and Joe the biker had just gone down. He was wearing a pink short-sleeved shirt and a red-and-black-striped tie. A white knit skullcap covered the crown of his round head. Down by his side he was holding a silver flute.

"You Kovacs?" he asked.

Loretta composed herself before she nodded. "Yes. Loretta Kovacs."

"Well, I'm your brand-new pain-in-the-ass." The man opened his mouth wide and laughed out loud. "Come on in and let's be friendly for a while before I get mean again." He turned around and slipped into the hallway, the sound of furious flute music echoing in his wake. It was progressive jazz, the kind with no melody that always gave Loretta a headache. Except this was unlike anything she'd ever heard before. It sounded like a combination of humming and flute playing. Actually, it sounded like the man was trying to eat the instrument, and the instrument was fighting for its life.

Loretta released her white-knuckle grip on the handbag straps and walked across the room toward the hallway. Squeezing the bottom of her leather bag, she felt her gun and sighed with disgust. *Why the hell did she freeze when Joe had that chair up over his head?* she wondered. *What good were all those hours she'd spent on the firing range? She was a pretty good shot now, but so what?* She was still scared shitless. She'd thought she'd gotten over being afraid, but deep down she knew she wasn't even close.

The mantra started up in her head again: *I'm fat; I'm single; my career is in the toilet . . . and I'm still afraid.*

Loretta let out a long, sad sigh. Brenda Hemingway had messed up her life in so many ways. Loretta had become so angry and ashamed after that incident, she couldn't stand herself. She and her live-in boyfriend, Gary, eventually split up, she gained more weight, and now it was almost three years since she'd been with a man. Fat, lonely, and horny—the Triple Crown of single womanhood. Is this what they mean by "having it all"?

"What in the hell are you doing out there, woman?" the man with the flute called out.

Loretta snapped out of it. "I'm coming." She headed into that back hallway and peered into the first office she found.

"Come in, come in. Sit down." Loretta's new boss spoke with the flute up to his mouth. Apparently he wasn't finished assaulting the instrument. His head suddenly jerked back as he made the flute squeal for mercy. His shiny forehead was a venetian blind of horizontal lines from his arched brows all the way up into his disappearing hairline.

Loretta sat down in the chair opposite his desk and made herself comfortable. It looked like this flute attack was going to take a while. Now she wished she had taken a cup of coffee and a cinnamon bun.

The man's office wasn't small, but the stacks of case files all over the floor cut down significantly on the walking space. His file cabinets and desk held still more piles of files. The walls were covered floor-to-ceiling with posters of jazz musicians, all saxophonists as far as she could tell. She even recognized a few: John Coltrane, Charlie Parker, Ornette Coleman. The largest poster was on the back wall overlooking the desk. It was a life-size picture of a black man playing two saxophones at the same time, his inflated cheeks raising the sunglasses off his face. Loretta stared up at it, doubting that anyone could play anything worth listening to with that much in his mouth.

When the man saw what she was looking at, he stopped torturing his flute and grinned at her. "Rahsaan Roland Kirk."

Loretta was confused. She started digging in her bag for her reassignment letter. "I thought I was supposed to report to—"

"Not me," the man said. "Him." He jerked his thumb at the poster. "Rahsaan Roland Kirk. A *true* genius and, like all the *true* geniuses, severely underappreciated. Rahsaan knew what it was all about." The man rolled his eyes toward Loretta and frowned. "I take it you've never heard of him."

Loretta shrugged. "Sorry."

The man tsk-tsked like a cricket. "Like I said. *Severely* underappreciated."

Afraid that she'd already offended him, Loretta kept her mouth shut.

"Julius Monroe," he suddenly said.

"You?"

"Yes, ma'am. Me. In the flesh." He crinkled his eyes and laughed out loud.

She was beginning to feel like Alice with the hookah-smoking caterpillar. She extended her hand to him. "Nice to meet you, Mr. Monroe."

He reached across the desk and shook her hand. "Call me Julius. Call me Monroe. Call me Misterioso. Just don't call me Mister. We don't stand on a whole lot of ceremony down here, Ms. Loretta Kovacs. This is the Jump Squad, after all. You do know about the Jump Squad, don't you?" He dropped his chin and stared up at her from under his brows, waiting for a reply.

"Call me Loretta," she said and left it at that. It was her new policy not to stick her foot in her mouth. Even though the Jump

Squad's reputation was common knowledge to everyone in Corrections, she wasn't going to let on that she knew it was the pits. As part of her new policy, she was going to play the game and stay out of trouble for a change.

Julius Monroe laid the flute down on top of his desk and nodded gravely, stroking his goatee. "Breath control is very, very important to a musician, Ms. Loretta Kovacs." He pointed up at Rahsaan Roland Kirk playing his two saxes. "Please don't make me waste my precious breath with a lot of hellos and how-are-yous because you and I both know that you won't be sticking around here very long."

The blood rose to her scalp. "What makes you say that?"

"This is the Jump Squad, my dear. Deep Space Nine, the end of the line. The people upstairs throw all the problem children down to Uncle Julius, so nobody really *wants* to be here. In the Department of Corrections, this is the 'plank'—as in 'walk the'? The last step before the deep blue sea of good-bye. So unless you really and truly *want* to be here, which I *seriously* doubt, I suggest you do us both a favor and leave now."

"I *asked* to be transferred here."

"Yeah, that's what they tell me." Monroe opened up the top folder on his lowest stack. "I give you 5 out of a possible 10 for that move. Clever, but it's been done before. Ask for the dungeon before they send you there. Makes you seem like a guest. Problem is, the Jump Squad was in your cards, Ruby, My Dear. Three more months and they would've sent you down here anyway. N-forced."

She knew he was right, but she didn't want him to think he was getting a Corrections reject, the typical parole-officer burnout who can't keep it together and ends up taking it out on his cases. "Granted, I've had a few problems, but I'd like you to know that—"

"You're *not* gonna stay here, my dear. Trust me. People like you come in and out of here all the time. It never works."

"No. It's not like that with me. Let me explain—"

"Breath control," he interrupted, putting an index finger to

his lips. "Save your breath. I know your history, Ms. Loretta Kovacs." He tapped on the file. "It's all right here."

"But—"

"Breath control, woman. Let me wail for a while, then you
tell me if I got it right. Once upon a time, way back when, you
started strong—M.S.W. from Columbia University, good field
placements, excellent letters of recommendation from your profs.
After you graduated, you set your sights on Corrections, figuring you could do some real social work in the prisons. Besides,
for a woman it was the right place at the right time. 'Who could
ask for anything more?' they must've said upstairs when your cur-
riculum vitae arrived on their desks. You hit the charts steaming,
my dear. *Hot.* With a bullet. Couple of years in the system and
you made it all the way to assistant warden. And you were just
barely thirty. Then that riot thing happened at Pinebrook and the
incident with that inmate. Bad scene. She messed up your mind.
The hill started going the other way after that—down, down,
down. Assistant warden to staff counselor to regular old PO and
now here. Way down. It's a cryin' shame, but that's how it goes
sometimes. No matter how you bend the notes, some songs are
just natural blues."

"That's not the whole story. What actually happened
was—"

"No, darlin', you don't have to explain it to me. I got the
picture." A sad smile peeked out from under the ends of his mus-
tache. "You're a problem child because you got that big bad
terminal disease that a lot of us have. You've got standards, prin-
ciples, a conscience, call what you will, but you've got it and
you've got it bad. You know right from wrong, and you've got
the guts to say so. But that's what happens to the people afflicted
with this pitiful disease when they start to understand how the
system really works. It's a very bad condition to have if you
wanna work for the state, my dear, but you've got it, and believe
me, there ain't no gettin' rid of it. That's why you're here. That's
why yours truly is here. And that's why I don't want you here."

"But—"

Monroe held up his palm like a traffic cop. "Don't interrupt. It's still my solo. You see, Ms. Loretta Kovacs, I understand your story very well because I made it to assistant warden once myself. Unfortunately, my problem was I got this strange idea somewhere along that line that prisons are for rehabilitation. Then one night a guard got killed in a fight with a con, and somehow it was all my fault. I was too liberal, too lenient; I treated the men too good—that's why this one crazy son of a bitch lost it for half a minute and ended up icing a guard. Makes perfect sense, right? Right. That's when my hill started going the other way. Oh, I bounced through a few different jobs in the system, but then I landed here, no-man's-land. They hoped I'd just quit and go away, but I hung on by my toenails and stuck it out. Now I'm the king of no-man's-land, *bandito numero uno.*" He looked off into the distance, shook his head, and let out a bitter chuckle. "Life can be weird when you're paying attention."

Loretta couldn't agree more. That was pretty much her own story in a nutshell.

"So, Ms. Loretta Kovacs, as you can see, I know your story, and if you want it to have a happy ending, I suggest you delete the Jump Squad episode, walk out that door, and start working on the happily-ever-after part."

But that wasn't the way Loretta had scripted it. She crossed her arms and shook her head. "You can't talk me out of working here, Julius. I *want* this job. I've got a plan for getting to the happily-ever-after part, and it starts right here, with the Jump Squad."

"You better check your health insurance, woman. Make sure you're covered for long-term psychiatric care."

"Look," she said. "First of all, I need the money, and frankly, I'm too much of a bitch to start doing social work with old farts or whiny kids or homeless people or anybody else, for that matter. But more than that, I do *not* want to give the bastards upstairs the satisfaction of knowing that I quit."

"So what are you saying here?"

"I'm saying I want the job."

"Can't have it."

"Why not?"

" 'Cause I say so."

"You can't do that. I was transferred. I'll call Personnel."

"Woman, you don't want this job."

"I'm telling you. I *want* it."

Monroe looked at her from under his brows. "Last woman we had here lasted three days."

Loretta shrugged. "That was her. I'm me."

"We don't bring in female jumpers all that often, Ms. Loretta K. It's 98 percent men, *bad* mothers, worst of the worst. You understand what I'm saying?"

"I understand."

"And you *still* want this job?"

"Yes."

He brought the flute to his mouth and started humming his disapproval into the mouthpiece, his eyebrows snaking up and down. Jitters squeezed through Loretta's stomach like cookie dough through a clenched fist. Julius Monroe did not understand. She really needed this job. If she had to go out and start pounding the pavement, she may as well throw her master plan out the window. She *had* to have this job.

Julius grumbled through the flute and looked her hard in the eye. "Tell you what," he finally said, putting down the instrument. "Since you're so dead set on working here, I'll give you a shot. Can't say Uncle Julius ain't fair with people."

"Thank you."

"No, don't thank me yet. I'm giving you *one* chance. I'll give you a case. You bring the jumper back to me in one week, and the job is yours. But no jumper, no job. You got it?"

"I got it." She nodded, poker-faced, but her stomach was in agony.

"Okay, then." Julius picked the top file off his second-shortest stack and examined it. He closed it and took the next one. He rejected that one and picked up a third. He tugged on his goatee as he pondered the top sheet. Loretta tried to read it upside down, but it was too far away for her to see.

"Here," he finally said. "A female jumper. Bring her back and the job's yours." He tossed the file across the desk.

Loretta opened it and started reading. The jumper's name was Martha Lee Spooner. White female, age thirty-one. Born in Slab Fork, West Virginia. Dropped out of high school. Last address: Margate, New Jersey. Served two and a third for laundering drug money for a biker gang. Unusually sophisticated methods considering the company she kept. She cleaned the money by purchasing residential real estate with the dirty cash, then reselling the properties after a year or so. Martha Lee had a whole Rolodex full of crooked lawyers who played along with her. There was one, though, who crossed her, and he was found in a Dumpster behind his office with a fractured skull and a ruptured spleen. Somehow, Martha Lee beat that charge. But, careful as she was, one of her biker pals got in a jam and gave her up to the cops to save his own butt. She was eventually convicted on a lesser charge but apparently kept her nose clean in prison because she was let out on parole her second time up before the board. Stayed a good girl for almost a whole year after her release, but then stopped reporting to her PO last winter. That was ten months ago. Present whereabouts were unknown.

The mug shots stapled to the folder were the typical head-tilted-back-with-attitude poses. Martha Lee Spooner was pale and slender, with a mess of dark, permed curls and rhinestone blue eyes. Snow White with a record. Pretty—in a hard sort of way.

Loretta knew the type all too well. It was easy to imagine Martha Lee riding on the back of a Harley, hanging onto some hairy creep in a Nazi storm trooper helmet, someone not unlike Joe, the biker who'd just been brought in. Loretta shut the file and started to stand up, determined to get right to work. "Which of those desks out there is mine?"

"Sit down, sit down. The clock ain't ticking yet. First thing you gotta know, Ms. Loretta Kovacs, is that we don't play solos around here. It's strictly ensemble work with an emphasis on duets."

"Huh?"

"In other words, Mama don't 'llow no working by yourself. Jump Squad officers work in pairs at the *very* least. Jumpers tend to be bad dudes. And dudettes." He pointed to the Martha Lee Spooner file. "These people don't run off 'cause the dog ate their homework. You dig?"

"Right." She hadn't thought about having to work with a partner. She'd never had one before, but it did make sense given the job. And with help, she'd probably find Martha Lee Spooner that much faster. Of course, it all depended on who the partner was. Usually she didn't have much patience with coworkers, especially ones who disagreed with her.

Julius cupped his hands around his goatee and shouted at the open doorway, "Marvelli! Stop stuffing your face and get in here."

Loretta looked over her shoulder at the empty doorway. She had a feeling the guy who had brought Joe the biker in was going to be the one—he was the only other PO in the office as far as she could tell. But she was still a little steamed about that comment he'd made about Joe being fat as a kid. On the other hand, Marvelli was kind of cute, and she had to admit, the way he'd handled Joe was very impressive.

But when Marvelli walked into Julius's office and took a seat, the enticing cinnamon aroma came in with him because he'd brought the whole tray of buns, and that riled her because it instantly made her hungry and she knew she really shouldn't be eating sweet cinnamon buns oozing with sugary white icing.

Marvelli smiled at her as he chewed. There was a half-eaten bun in his hand. He held out the tray to her. She shook her head and resisted the temptation.

"What's up, Julius?" he said between bites. Peaks of white icing dotted the corners of his mouth.

"Before I forget, Marvelli," Julius said, "who was that you just brought in?"

"His name is Joe Pickett. You need his file? It's in the car. I'll go get it." Marvelli started to get up.

"Later." Monroe leaned back in his chair and gestured like a preacher. "Frank Marvelli, Loretta Kovacs. Loretta, Frank. You're gonna be partners for the week."

Marvelli smiled and nodded at Loretta, but he didn't stop eating. Instead he stuffed the rest of the bun into his mouth, wiped his fingers on his pants, and offered her his hand. "How ya doin'?" he said with his mouth full.

She changed her mind about him again. He was disgusting. She zeroed in on his slicked-back hair. He must've combed it after he'd secured the biker because there was a little pompadour in front that hadn't been there before. Yes, he was good-looking, but his style was pure Guido—black knit shirt with white rectangular panels down the front, pressed jeans, black leather jacket.

She forced a smile for him—new policy, she kept reminding herself. "Nice to meet you, Frank," she said and shook his hand even though she knew it would be sticky. She was going to make this work. She had to.

"Sure you don't want a bun, Loretta? They're pretty good." He picked out a fresh one for himself, then offered her the tray again.

She scowled down at them as if they were poison. Each one had to be at least 500 calories. "No thanks," she said. They were tempting enough; she didn't need him hawking them.

"Your loss," he said, chomping off half of the new bun.

Her stomach rumbled. She did want one, badly. He smiled at her, his cheeks bulging. He looked like a slaphappy chipmunk. If he were in the middle of the road, she would've run him over. He wasn't *that* good-looking.

Not really.

Julius stood up and moved toward the door. "Stay put, you two. Get acquainted. I have to go see someone upstairs about something. Oh, and remember, Ms. Loretta Kovacs," he said from the doorway, "one week."

Marvelli, still chewing away, was craning his neck, trying to read the Spooner file in her lap. "Fill me in, Loretta. Whatta we got here?"

Just my future, she thought. *That's all.*

She stared at the seven buns left in the tray and sighed.

Martha Lee Spooner stared blankly out the window as she unwrapped another Hershey's Chocolate Kiss and popped it into her mouth. Off in the distance, a shimmering pagan bronze sun was setting over the turquoise waters of the Florida gulf. Martha Lee was in her office on the top floor of "the cube," the three-story mirrored-glass office building that housed the corporate headquarters of Roger Laplante's WeightAway empire, which included WeightAway Food Products, the nationwide franchises of WeightAway Weight-Loss Centers, and Rancho Bonita, Roger's fat farm deluxe. The cube was in the off-limits section of Rancho Bonita's 246 jungle-lush acres.

She swiveled around in her chair and frowned at the fax machine as she crumpled up the tinfoil wrapper and flicked it into the wastepaper basket beside her desk. *Come on, ring, dammit!* she kept thinking. Her hands were shaking she was so nervous. *Come on, ring!*

She chewed the sweet chocolate and swallowed quickly, peering into the basket to make sure the wrapper had gone down to the bottom where it couldn't be seen. Her boss, Roger Laplante, was a goddamn Nazi when it came to his stupid food rules, and she didn't want to piss him off, not now. She was so close to putting this thing together she could taste it.

She looked toward the doorway, then quickly unwrapped another Chocolate Kiss and popped it into her mouth. Eating on the sly like this took all the enjoyment out of it. She hardly tasted anything she was so busy watching out for Roger. She looked back at the doorway, stopped chewing, and listened for a second. It was still quiet. She started chewing again. It should be quiet, she thought. It was after six and everyone was done for the day. But Roger, of course, was liable to be anywhere. She swallowed and started biting the cuticles on her right hand, going from finger to finger, looking for a cuticle she hadn't already destroyed. She scowled at the stubborn fax machine on the side desk, next to her computer.

Come on, dammit! Ring! she thought. *Before friggin' Roger shows up.*

She looked at the framed picture on her desk—Becky, her five-year-old daughter, in pigtails and a hand-me-down pink party dress—and she felt a twinge of panic. What if she got caught doing this? Martha Lee thought. She'd never done anything like this before. Cleaning up dirty drug money was nothing compared to this. She was used to being in control of the assets, hands on. And she was used to having biker muscle backing her up. But this thing was totally different. This was international, and she was doing everything long-distance. In the past she'd never had to rely on anyone else the way she was relying on Luis down in Panama, and that made her even more nervous. She hardly knew him, and they'd never met face-to-face. What if he was a screwup? What if he was just jerking her chain with all his promises? What if he was trying to scam *her?*

She glanced back at the doorway again, then yanked open the bottom drawer of her desk, where she kept the big cellophane bag of Chocolate Kisses. She hesitated, worried about getting caught, but finally she grabbed a whole handful. *To hell with Roger,* she thought. She wasn't on a goddamn diet. She barely weighed a hundred pounds, for chrissake. He could take his god-damn food rules and shove 'em up his ass. That's all he ever worried about, what people were eating. And not eating. Like chocolate. She was sick to death of the healthy crap she had to eat around here—raw carrots and celery, oat-bran muffins and hundred-grain breads, soy milk, and, worst of all, wheat-grass juice. *Jesus, spare me!* she thought as she fumbled with the foil on another Chocolate Kiss.

She checked her watch again and wondered what time it was in Panama. *But that shouldn't make any goddamn difference,* she thought angrily. Luis said he'd be faxing the bill today, and she had to be here when it came. So where the hell was it? She couldn't just leave and have it sitting in the machine overnight where anyone could find it. What if Roger found it and started asking questions?

She swiveled around and gazed out the window at a terraced grove of palm trees about a hundred yards south of the cube. Roger's ultra-modern California-style mansion was hidden be-hind those trees. Roger was a big star because of all the in-fomercials and TV talk shows he did. The fatties loved him—he was their guru—and spa guests were always snooping around, trying to catch a glimpse of him in the flesh. That's why he had to fence off this part of the ranch, to get a little privacy.

Off in the distance toward the gulf, Martha Lee could make out a pack of huffing-and-puffing fatties down on the aerobics court. *Must be sweating like pigs out in that heat,* she thought, shaking her head. *And to think these dumb bunnies pay big bucks just to come here and suffer.* But all the better for her, she figured. The way she saw it, the more money Roger raked in, the more careless he was about spending it. So far he hadn't questioned a single bill she'd paid. Not one. And she hadn't been working there all that long. Whatever she did seemed to be just fine with him. He was more worried about what she ate than what she spent. Going on TV and making personal appearances at the franchises around the country took up most of his time, so he didn't pay a whole lot of attention to day-to-day operations. He said he trusted Martha Lee because she was a former fattie who'd seen the light. He also believed that her name was Martha "Sykes." The man was very trusting.

Her "fat picture" was pinned to the bulletin board on the wall. She'd shown it to Roger back when she'd interviewed for the job, told him how she'd lost all that weight with the Weight-Away program and how it totally changed her life. She'd kissed his ass like crazy that day, and she'd been kissing it ever since to keep him from suspecting anything. Martha Lee knew from experience that the secret to handling people like Roger was to always make them feel smart, even when they're dumb as shit. They'll believe anything you say as long as they think they're on top. That picture was a good example. She treated him like the Lord Jesus of fatness, and so he took her word for it that the picture was her. It wasn't her at all. She'd been skinny her whole life. It was actually her fat-ass sister-in-law, all bloated and sloppy at somebody's birthday party, wearing a pointy party hat and so much makeup she looked like a floozy raccoon. Just thinking about her crazy in-laws made Martha Lee shiver. She was sure glad to be rid of them. They were too much like her own family.

But thinking about her own family got her to fretting about her daughter, Becky, again and how her mom was bringing Becky up back in Slab Fork. Kids shouldn't be raised by their grandparents, and they shouldn't have to put up with places like Slab Fork, West Virginia, where your life is all written out for you before you're even off the tit. Becky's father, Tom Junior, had never taken much interest in her, and Martha Lee didn't see any point in finding a substitute father figure because she intended to provide for all of Becky's wants and needs all by herself. Just as soon as Luis got the goddamn money, and she and Becky were safe and sound down in Costa Rica.

She made a face at the fax machine and popped another Chocolate Kiss into her mouth. "Come on, Luis," she moaned. "Where the hell are you? You said today."

"Martha!"

She sat up straight and froze. It was Roger, standing in the doorway, and he had that look of horror and disappointment on his face, the one he used on his infomercials whenever he listened to the cooked-up testimonials by the supposedly former fatties who were actually over-the-hill fashion models. She squeezed the Chocolate Kisses in her fist, but there was a mess of foil wrappers with their telltale paper tabs scattered all over her desk. Shit!

"Martha!" Roger cried. "Why? Why are you doing this to yourself?" He stepped into the room and took her hand, gently opening her fist to reveal her dirty little secret. He acted as if he'd just found track marks on her arms. "This is dietary assassination, Martha. Don't you know that?"

She looked at the floor and swallowed what was in her mouth. She was trying hard to look ashamed, but she really wanted to kick him. What the hell was he doing here *now?*

She picked up her head and shook out her dark curls, showing him eyes of contrition. As usual, he looked terribly hurt but ever willing to forgive. Just like in his infomercials.

Roger was a big guy, over six feet, and despite the tan, the expensive haircut, and the Hollywood wardrobe, his French-Canadian lumberjack roots still showed if you looked hard enough. He was a strawberry-blond with the squarest jaw she'd ever seen—squarer than Jay Leno's. He also had earnest little eyes that would've looked perfect on a moose. She could just imagine what he looked like as a kid, all bundled up and chubby, trudging through the snow with an ax over his shoulder, chopping down trees with his father and brothers way up in that freezing ass-end of New Hampshire where he was from.

Except that despite the melodramatic way he acted sometimes, Roger was no dummy. He'd wised up somewhere along the line. No one makes as much money as he has by accident. She hadn't worked for him very long before she recognized that Roger Laplante sure had what it takes to make it: he was greedy, he had nerve to spare, and deep down inside he was a real prick.

Roger took the last two Chocolate Kisses from her hand and held them up by their paper tabs as if they were mice. "You're not supposed to have these here, Martha. Fat, sugar, sodium, and cholesterol are forbidden on the grounds of the spa. You know that."

"But, Roger, *I'm* not on a diet."

He nodded at the photo of her sister-in-law on the bulletin board. "Overweight people are like alcoholics, Martha—we're never really cured. You don't want to go back to being like *that* again, do you?"

"No, but a couple of Chocolate Kisses couldn't hurt—"

"Wrong! A *couple* of Chocolate Kisses can only lead to a *few more* Chocolate Kisses and that leads to *chocolate ice cream* and chocolate ice cream leads to chocolate cake and eclairs and pudding and milk shakes and cookies and candy bars and chocolate mousse and fudge and brownies. And it doesn't stop there. It just goes on and on and on until you're right back where you started from."

Martha Lee hung her head in shame. "I know, Roger, I know. You're right."

Prick.

She noticed him glaring at the photo of Becky on her desk. He made no bones about the fact that he hated kids, especially his own three. He bitched like hell whenever his ex-wife shipped them down here from New York for school vacations. Couldn't wait to ship 'em back.

"You're not thinking about bringing your daughter down here, are you, Martha?" he asked.

"No. I—"

"Well, just so you know, if you did bring your daughter down—permanently, I mean—you'd have to move out of your bungalow. Kids aren't allowed in staff quarters. It's in your contract."

"Yes. I know, Roger."

Prick!

"I just wanted to make sure you understood."

Martha nodded and looked down at the carpeting. She was boiling inside. She wished she were stealing more from him.

But that reminded her about the fax. She glanced sideways at the fax machine, and suddenly her heart started to pound. *Sweet Jesus, not now, Luis. If Roger sees a bill for ninety tons of cocoa, he'll go ape-shit.*

"Martha," Roger said, "what if one of the guests wandered in here and found these?" He was still holding the chocolate vermin by their tails.

"Guests never come in here, Roger. This building is off-limits. I mean, has a guest ever gotten into this part of the ranch?"

"Overweight people get desperate when they're deprived, and they can be amazingly resourceful. I can very well imagine someone sneaking in here looking for forbidden treats." He shook the Kisses like jingle bells. "Can you imagine what would happen if one of our guests found chocolates here at the spa and that got out to the press? God forbid. It could ruin me!"

"Roger, I think you're exaggerating."

"I'm *not* exaggerating. I know how these people are. *Fat is my life!*"

She had to hang her head to hide her pissed-off expression. "I'm sorry, Roger. I really didn't mean to upset you."

At least not yet, she thought. She glanced at the fax machine and wished to hell he'd get lost.

He closed his eyes for a moment and took a deep cleansing breath. "I'm sorry, too, Martha. I didn't mean to yell at you. It's just that I'm very stressed out. I can't stop thinking about that IRS guy."

"What IRS guy?" She didn't know what he was talking about.

"Didn't you get my memo? I sent it to you this morning."

"Ah . . . no." In fact, she had gotten it, but she hadn't read it yet. She was too busy getting things ready for Luis. They'd been working on this scam for months, and today was the big day, the day they finally got the ball rolling. "What IRS guy?"

"His name is Lawrence Temple. He's from their Office of Criminal Investigations, and he wants to see the books. You didn't get my memo?" Roger looked a little panicky.

"Why does he want to see the books?"

"To get more money out of us. Why the hell else? We're okay, though, aren't we? The books are presentable now, right?"

"What do you mean by 'presentable'?" Her heart was banging dangerously, like her daddy's old Ford pickup chugging down the interstate, the one with the faulty engine mounts.

"Christ, Martha, this is why I hired you, to straighten out the company books. They were such a mess, remember? You said you could fix them up for me just in case we ever got audited." A squiggly blue vein had popped up on his temple. This wasn't the smooth infomercial Roger. "I'm getting very stressed, Martha. Tell me you straightened out the books. Please!"

Sweat was dripping down her armpits. "Yes, of course, I straightened out the books. What do you think I've been doing here the past five months?" She'd hardly done a thing to those books. She'd spent most of her time trying to figure out some kind of scam that would earn her enough money to take Becky to Costa Rica, where it was warm and sunny and there were no extradition laws.

It had taken her five months to locate Luis, a Panamanian lawyer, and set this whole thing up. She'd given Luis the last of the money she'd swiped from Tom Junior and his drug buddies to set up the Alvarez Cocoa Company, S.A., in Panama City. Since WeightAway used real chocolate in some of their frozen foods, Martha Lee had worked out a scheme whereby the Alvarez Cocoa Company would bill WeightAway International for ninety tons of raw cocoa. Martha, as one of the bookkeepers for the company, would pay the bill, same as she paid all the others, except Luis wouldn't be delivering any cocoa to WeightAway, not a single Chocolate Kiss's worth, because there was no cocoa. Luis was just going to deposit the money she wired to him into two numbered accounts at a bank in the Cayman Islands: one for him, one for her. Half the money in one account, the rest in the other. As soon as she got confirmation from the bank that there was somewhere in the neighborhood of $210,000 in her account, she'd sit tight till Friday, then fly up to Slab Fork, pick up Becky, and high-tail it down to Costa Rica as fast as she could. Home free with her baby, safe at last.

Martha Lee was so close to pulling it off, she was getting light-headed. All she needed was the goddamn bill from Luis so that she could pay it. Plus, she needed Roger to get lost. But he was in a weird mood now, worried sick about the IRS. What if the fax suddenly came through and he looked at it? He'd definitely get suspicious. They didn't use *that* much real chocolate in their foods, not even in the Double Dutch Chocolate Shake-a-Meal. Her back was soaked with sweat. She had to get him out of there fast before this whole thing blew up in her face.

She took the Kisses from his fingers and tossed them in the trash. "Why don't we go downstairs and have a wheat-grass juice? You look like you could use one, Roger."

"But, Martha, don't you understand? I have to know that the books are all in shape. I want to see—"

The high-pitched electronic ring of the fax machine made Martha jump.

Shit!

"What's that?"

"Oh, it's just the fax machine. Don't be so jumpy." She was trying to stay cool. She stood up and took his elbow. "Come on. Let's go sit outside, get some air."

"Wait." He nodded at the machine. "What if it's important? Maybe it's from that bastard Temple."

"I doubt it. This time of day all you get is junk faxes. People selling office supplies and stuff."

It stopped ringing and automatically picked up. The LCD readout on the face of the machine said: "RECEIVING." Roger was peering down at it, waiting for it to start printing.

"Come on, Rog. You're stressed out. Let's go—"

"One minute." The fax machine clunked, then started printing.

Shit! He was gonna screw up everything. Her supervisor was on vacation this week; that's why she had waited till now, so that no one would be there to question the bill. But if Roger saw it, he'd start asking questions that she didn't have answers for, and the foods division up in Illinois wouldn't vouch for this purchase. She'd be up shit's creek then.

The paper started to scroll up over the roller. She could see the letterhead starting to take shape, the tall oversize "A" in "Alvarez" sprouting up first. In a few seconds the word "Cocoa" would be plain as day, and that would be the end of it. Roger would go nuts, and she could forget about the whole thing.

But she wasn't going to forget about it, goddammit.

"Roger!" She grabbed his sleeve. "I need you, Roger! I need your help!" She stooped down and yanked open her bottom desk drawer, pulling out the jumbo two-pound bag of Kisses. "I'm backsliding, Rog. You're absolutely right. Inside I'm still fat. I need help. I'm afraid of what I'll do to myself. Help me, Roger. Please!" She locked eyes with him, forcing herself to keep from looking at the fax machine, but she could hear it working away, and it was making her heart thump like crazy.

He tried to pull away from her, but she thrust the bag of Kisses in his face. "Help me, Roger. Please!" she pleaded, pointing to the photo of her good-for-nothing husband's sister on the bulletin board. "I don't want to look like that ever again. Please, Roger!" She started to hyperventilate.

He sniffed the chocolates in the bag and made a face. Roger thought all sweets were evil, that they could jump right up and bite you on the ass if you weren't careful. Well, chocolate was sure gonna bite *him* on the ass. If she could just get him the hell out of there.

The fax was printing.

She shook the cellophane bag frantically until it broke and Chocolate Kisses rained down on his suede Ferragamo loafers. "Please, Roger!" she screamed. "Please!"

"All right, Martha, all right. Calm down. I'll help you. Now listen to me. Do you have any spring water in here?"

She shook her head.

"Okay, then let's go get that wheat-grass juice," he said. "And some water. A lot of water. That'll dilute some of the choco-

late and get it out of your system faster." He took her by the
elbow and led her out into the hallway, kicking the Hershey's
Kisses out of his way as if they were cockroaches.

"I don't want to be fat again, Roger," she moaned. "I don't."

"It's all right, Martha. Don't worry. I'm here for you." He
put his arm around her.

"I'm sorry, Roger. I let you down. I'm so sorry." She buried
her face in his shoulder, but inside she was relieved to be out of
her office. As they walked toward the elevators together, she
could faintly hear the fax machine grinding away. The bill was
finally here. She'd come back and get it later, as soon as she got
rid of Roger.

"Take it easy, Martha," Roger said. "Just breathe in through
your nose and out your mouth, nice and easy. You'll be fine."
They came up to the chrome elevator doors, and he pressed the
down button. "We'll fix you right up. Nothing a good coffee
enema won't cure."

Her body went stiff. "A what?"

"Think you can take a high-colonic?"

Marvelli crossed his leg over his knee and started shaking his foot, getting more impatient by the minute. He was sitting on the end of a lumpy couch on a screened-in porch in the farm country of northwest Jersey. Loretta was on the other end of the couch, her head still buried in the Spooner file as if something new would materialize if she kept staring at it. A Confederate flag hung on the wall behind their heads, and the coffee table was littered with hot-rod and motorcycle magazines as well as an empty Bud can that had been used as an ashtray. A sewing machine was set up on a vinyl-top card table facing the road. He kept shaking his foot. He didn't like being here, even though it had been his idea to come here in the first place.

He glanced at his watch and made a face. It was almost three. It would take him at least an hour and a half to get home, but he was going to have to swing through Newark first to drop Loretta off so she could pick up her car, and that would take another forty-five minutes, at least. He'd promised Renée he'd be home early tonight, and he knew he shouldn't be breaking promises to her. The doctor said he shouldn't let her get upset about anything anymore.

He looked at his watch again. The doctor didn't say anything about *him* not getting upset. But that didn't matter. Renée was the one who had the problem, not him.

He crossed his arms and pinched his nose. He didn't like the smell of this place either. Outside it was warm and sunny, but inside it smelled like a tomb—cold and clammy, musty and stale. In fact, just about everything about Olivette Macrae's ramshackle house bothered Marvelli because it was so depressing. The roof sagged over the porch, and he was willing to bet the exterior hadn't been painted in over thirty years. Most of the window shutters were either missing or hanging by a thread. The grass was overgrown, and weeds grew high around an old refrigerator lying on its back in the front yard. A couple of sad-looking junkers sat in the dirt driveway, like two tired old dogs. There was also a "muscle car" back there, a late-sixties Chevy Malibu that was up on blocks.

The Chevy was flat black with yellow and red flames painted over the hood and front fenders. On the driver's door "Miss Behavior" was written in flaming, charbroiled lettering right under a naked female red devil with horns, tail, a pitchfork, and a wicked pair of 38 D cups. Marvelli assumed this was Olivette Macrae's son's car. He could just imagine the kind of asshole who'd have a car like that.

Marvelli tilted his head back and started wondering if this was what *he* had to look forward to. Would *his* house end up looking like this? He didn't know how to fix things; he didn't even know how to clean. Renée had always taken care of all that.

He gazed down at the mess on the coffee table. *And what about Nina?* he thought. Would his daughter end up with some punk who used his beer can as an ashtray? Nina would be a bona fide teenager pretty soon. How the hell was he going to bring up a teenage daughter all by himself? *How?* He started rubbing his arms, suddenly chilly.

He looked over at Loretta. It felt weird for him to be hanging out with a woman who wasn't his wife, even though this was just work. He wasn't used to it. He and Renée used to go out all the time, just get in the car and cruise around for the hell of it, no particular place to go. But they hadn't done that in God knows how long. Renée didn't leave the house much anymore.

Loretta finally closed the file on her lap. "Why are we here, Marvelli? I don't know why you decided to start with the mother-in-law. There's nothing in Martha Spooner's file that indicates that she was particularly close to her mother-in-law."

"Was there someplace else you wanted to start?" he asked.

She shrugged. "You're supposed to know this job better than I do."

"No, please. If you have any ideas, just let me know. I'm open to anything."

Like getting the hell out of here, he thought.

"No, no, you're the senior man here," she said.

"Well . . . yes and no."

"What do you mean?"

"Well, I guess I'm senior in terms of working on the Jump Squad, but you've been with Corrections longer than I have. Right?"

"I don't know, have I?" She sounded a little peeved.

"Well, let's see. I started with Corrections when I was twenty-three, and I'm thirty-two now. And you started when you were twenty-four, and now you're thirty-four. So you've got a year on me. Right?"

"How do you know I'm thirty-four?"

She was mad. He could tell. He knew he should've kept his mouth shut. Renée's doctor was right. It's never a good idea to get *any* woman upset.

"So how do you know how old I am, Marvelli?" Her voice was getting up in the bird-of-prey range. "How do you know?"

"Well . . . I read your personnel file."

"Oh, really?" She snapped her head and threw her hair over her shoulder in a huff. She had great hair. The kind you'd like to walk through barefoot, like those women in the shampoo commercials. Too bad she's so heavy. "And how did you happen to see my file, Marvelli?" Her nostrils were doing that mad-bull thing.

"Well, I didn't go looking for it or anything. It just happened to be on Julius's desk with all the case files when I was in there looking for something else. I happened to spot this nice thin file sitting there, so automatically I thought to myself, Whoa, here's an easy one for a change, some jumper who doesn't have a rap sheet like Jack the Ripper. I figured I'd just take this little piece of cake for myself before someone else grabbed it. So I took a look at the file and found out it was yours. That's how it happened."

"And you read enough to find out how old I am."

"Actually, I read the whole thing."

"You've got a lot of goddamn nerve, Marvelli. What's in my file is none of your business."

He pursed his lips and stared straight ahead through the porch screens at the field across the road. She was definitely pissed. He waited a minute, then tried to sneak a quick glance at her to see if she was still mad, and suddenly he realized that her eyes were gray-green. For some reason he'd thought they were blue. "You're absolutely right, Loretta," he said. "I'm sorry. It's none of my business. I apologize. . . . Except—"

"Except what?" She was glaring at him.

"Except when you think about it, it kind of *is* my business."

"The hell it is."

"Well, think about it, Loretta. We're partners. If I'm gonna trust you, I should know something about you. Right?"

"And what about *me?*" she said. "Don't I deserve to know something about *you?*"

"Sure, you do. I don't have any secrets. Whatever you want to know, just ask. But I'll tell you right now, my personnel file must be about a half-page long. This is all I've ever done really: track down jumpers and bring 'em back alive. It's the only real job I've ever had."

And Renée is the only wife I've ever had, he thought.

"So the way you see it, you're the pro, and I'm the old washed-up rookie. Is that it?"

"That's not what I said, Loretta. Don't put words in my mouth."

She was still glaring at him. If looks could kill . . .

Kovacs, he thought. *What's that, Hungarian? Wild gypsy blood? Maybe.* She certainly wasn't shy about picking fights. He remembered when he and Renée used to fight. Renée always looked incredibly sexy when she was mad—so sexy that he always ended up with a big hard-on for her, which made it impossible for him to keep up any kind of argument. But they didn't fight at all now. She didn't have the strength, and he didn't have the heart.

Marvelli started to zone out, staring at the cornfield across the road, thinking about Renée. But *why*? he asked for the bazillionth time. Why her? Why *him*? What the hell was he going to do when she—

"Sorry about that." Olivette Macrae, Martha Lee Spooner's mother-in-law, came out onto the porch from inside. "That was my mom on the phone," she said. "Hard to get rid of her when she gets started."

Marvelli nodded. "I know the problem." His own mother-in-law was the same way.

Olivette pulled out a Marlboro from the pack on the sewing table and lit it with a tangerine-colored disposable lighter. She sucked in a deep drag, her cheeks sinking into her face, which made her look more like a witch than she already did. She had a long, haggard face and stringy limbs, but under her pink sweatshirt she had a basketball-sized belly. Her dull gray-brown hair was dry as straw and hung down long and limp to the middle of her back. Even though she looked like a moderately old hag, Marvelli had a feeling she wasn't even fifty yet.

"Just give me a minute here, folks, so I don't forget where I was with this." The woman sat back down at the sewing machine and continued what she'd been doing before the phone had rung. The sewing machine clacked away as she ran up some curtains, guiding the seams under the needle. "So what was it you two wanted?" she shouted over the noise, the cigarette bobbing between her lips.

Loretta made a face at the drifting smoke. "We'd like to ask you a few questions about your daughter-in-law. Martha Lee Spooner?"

Olivette stopped sewing. "Did you say Martha Lee?"

"Yes. Martha Lee Spooner."

"Phew." Olivette shut off the sewing machine and turned sideways in her seat to face them. "When you said you were from the Department of Corrections, I thought you were here about Ricky."

"Who's Ricky?" Marvelli asked.

"My kid with Bobby. Bobby Macrae was my second husband, bless his soul. Tom Spooner was my first."

"Has Ricky ever been in prison?"

"Not yet. Just a matter of time, though, if you ask me." Olivette knocked the ash off her cigarette into a plaid beanbag ashtray set next to the sewing machine.

Marvelli gazed up at the Rebel flag. He knew it. Young Ricky would probably end up a parole jumper, too. Marvelli leaned forward on his knees and studied Loretta's face while she wasn't looking. She actually had very pretty eyes. Soul eyes, they used to call them in high school. He'd never seen a color quite like that, a deep gray-green. Very unusual. He tried to imagine what she'd look like about twenty pounds lighter.

Or maybe thirty.

"Has Ricky ever been convicted of a crime, Mrs. Macrae?" Loretta asked.

"No, ma'am."

"So why would you think we were here about Ricky?"

"Well, I saw something on TV a while back that they were arresting troublemakers and lockin' 'em up *before* they did anything wrong. This was out in Oregon or Seattle, one of those places out there. I figured maybe they'd started up something like that here in Jersey. My Ricky'd be the first to go if they did. Sure as shit."

The woman didn't seem very upset about the idea of her kid going to prison. She was probably wishing for it, hoping to get the punk out of her hair for a while. Marvelli was actually surprised to see that the lady didn't have a totally negative attitude toward corrections. The mothers of convicts usually did.

"So what is it you want to know about that no-good chippy Martha Lee? I told Tom Junior when he married her that she'd be nothing but heartache and misery." Olivette took another cheek-sucking drag off her cigarette and emphasized her point with a sharp nod.

Marvelli couldn't hold back his grin. This was why he always liked to begin with the in-laws when he started looking for a jumper. They always had plenty to say. Just like his mother-in-law.

Loretta closed Martha Spooner's file and set it aside on the couch. "When did you last see your daughter-in-law, Mrs. Macrae?"

"Why? She forget to call in to her parole officer? I'm not surprised. She's living it up, from what I hear. Don't mix with the hoi polloi no more. Thinks her shit don't smell."

"Have you seen her recently?" Loretta pressed.

Olivette shook her head as she sucked in more smoke. "Hope I never do neither. The little bitch."

Loretta nodded, and Marvelli watched her face to see if she was losing her patience with Mrs. Macrae. Loretta seemed like the type who expected fast answers. He had a feeling that *shmoozing* wasn't her thing. Too bad. *Shmoozing* went a long way in this job. Renée used to be a great *shmoozer, shmooze* your pants right off. But these days she didn't talk very much. Too much talk tired her out.

"Do you know where Martha Lee Spooner is, Mrs. Macrae?" Loretta asked.

"Florida, from what I hear."

"Florida!" Loretta said, furrowing her brows. "The last address we have for her is Washington Avenue in Margate, down near Atlantic City."

Marvelli winced. He didn't want to go to goddamn Florida. He couldn't leave Renée for that long.

Olivette Macrae stubbed out her cigarette and lit up a fresh one. "Well, I can't say for sure whether she is or she isn't down Florida, but that's what Tom Junior told me. He's doing time down in Trenton for selling drugs, which by the way I don't believe he ever did himself. He was just in the wrong place at the wrong time with the wrong crowd if you ask me. It was his dear wife Martha Lee who snitched on him and his buddies, by the way. What I want to know is, how come she got out in two years and the rest of 'em are all doing fifteen in, minimum? You tell me that. How come?"

"I'm afraid we don't know anything about that, Mrs. Macrae," Marvelli said.

"Well, it's a damn shame if you ask me. You only have to meet Martha Lee once to know what she's all about. Better yet, play cards with her sometime."

"What do you mean, play cards with her?" Marvelli asked.

"The girl's a natural-born cheat. Counts cards in her head like it's nothing. Barely got out of high school, but she's something else when it comes to numbers. Specially numbers that got dollar signs up front. She's the one who handled the money for those dope fiends my boy Tom Junior got involved with. She was the brains of that operation if you ask me."

Marvelli caught Loretta's eye. They were thinking the same thing. Martha Spooner was a card counter, which explained why she had been living down by the casinos in Atlantic City. If she was discreet and didn't get greedy, she could've made a nice living for herself bilking the tables. So why did she relocate to Florida? Florida didn't have legalized gambling. Of course, Florida did have the drug trade. South Florida supplied the whole East Coast. Drugs were bigger than orange juice down there.

Maybe Martha Lee was up to her old tricks, laundering drug money.

"Do you have any idea where your daughter-in-law is in Florida?" Loretta asked. "An address, even a phone number would help."

Marvelli winced again. *Don't even ask,* he thought. *We're not going down there.*

Olivette shook her head as she twirled the end of her cigarette in the beanbag ashtray. "I woulda thrown that little so-and-so's address in the garbage if I'd had it. Maybe Tom Junior's got it. I don't know. Ask him."

Loretta made a face. She looked very disgruntled, and Marvelli was suddenly disappointed in her. What'd she think, this was gonna be easy? That you just ask a question and get the answer you want, easy as pie? Well, go to the library if you want to look stuff up. When you're tracking down a jumper, you have to finesse your information. Loretta would have to learn that if she intended to stay with the Jump Squad, which she probably didn't. He could teach her, though, if she wanted to learn.

Loretta collected her things and stood up. She looked at Marvelli. "Well, I guess we're going down to Trenton to see Tom Junior."

Marvelli gave her a dirty look. Yes, of course, they were going to go see Tom Junior in prison, but she'd better not get any big ideas because they weren't going to Florida. They'd investigate it up here, then pass along whatever they found out to the locals wherever Martha Lee Spooner was. Let them deal with her.

He stood up and extended his hand to Olivette. "Thanks for your help, Mrs. Macrae. Sorry to take up your time."

"No problem at all. If I knew it'd put Martha Lee's snippy little butt back in prison, I'd let you stay all day."

Loretta offered her hand to the woman. "Thank you for talking to us, Mrs. Macrae."

Olivette was reaching over to shake Loretta's hand when she

was suddenly distracted by an eighteen-wheeler that came out of
nowhere and pulled to a screeching stop in front of her house.
The cab of the truck was shiny black, the trailer dull silver. The
door on the passenger side opened and out hopped a hefty young
woman in a black leather vest, skin-tight black jeans, and black
suede, fringe-top cowboy boots. As the young woman crossed the
lawn and mounted the porch steps, Marvelli could see dark roots
under a rat's nest of badly permed henna-red hair. Her upper arms
were huge, and she was spilling out of the vest. The porch door
banged behind her when she came in, and Marvelli noticed that
she had a tattoo on her fleshy bicep, a red she-devil just like the
one painted on the Chevy in the driveway.

Olivette Macrae crossed her arms and smirked. "Well, look
who's home? You run out of money again? Or did'ja just miss
me?"

The young woman glowered at her, ignoring Loretta and
Marvelli.

"This is my darlin' daughter Ricky," Olivette said with a
smirk.

"Hi, how ya doing?" Marvelli said.

Ricky Macrae ignored him, taking a cigarette from her
mother's pack without asking. She lit it with her own lighter and
spewed out a cloud of smoke. "What the hell do they want?"
Ricky said to her mother.

"They're from the state. They're looking for Martha Lee."

"Oh, yeah?" She gave Marvelli the once-over and was totally unimpressed. Ricky had attitude to spare.

She sent another cloud of smoke up to the ceiling, then let
her gaze settle on Loretta. Suddenly Loretta went pale, brows
slanted back, jaw clenched. The look passed quickly, but it was
there, Marvelli had seen it. It was fear, he was certain. But why?
Ricky was a bruiser, but she wasn't that scary.

Ricky curled her upper lip Elvis-style and blew smoke out
of the side of her mouth. "So whattaya want with Martha Lee?"

Loretta's face hardened. "I don't think that's any of your
business really."

"Oh, no? How about if I slap you across your big fat face? Think it would be any of my business then?"

Loretta didn't flinch. "Go ahead. Try it."

Ricky dropped her cigarette and tried to get off a slap, but before she could even get her hand above her shoulder, she froze, mouth open, plucked eyebrows arched high.

The barrel of a snub-nosed .38 was poking into Ricky's gut, Loretta's hand around the grip.

Marvelli was speechless. Son of a bitch, he thought. Where'd that come from? Her purse? He hadn't noticed Loretta going for it. Neither had Ricky obviously. Pretty damn slick. *He* sure as hell couldn't do that. He was always dropping his gun. That's why he almost never used it. But this Loretta Kovacs, she was all right.

"What're you looking at, Marvelli?" she grumbled. "You never saw a gun before?"

"I didn't say anything."

Ricky backed away from the .38 and bumped into the coffee table. She looked a little pale under the rouge.

"That's what you get for sassing people," her mother scolded. "I keep telling you, little girl. One of these days you're gonna be sorry."

"Oh, shut up, will ya? No one asked you." Ricky recovered her attitude. She stomped on the cigarette smoldering on the painted wood floor, then locked eyes with Loretta again. They stared each other down for almost a full minute. Finally Ricky looked away and mumbled, "Bitch. . . ."

Loretta ignored her. "Thank you for your time, Mrs. Macrae," she said again, then let herself out and walked down the rickety porch steps to the white Department of Corrections Dodge Aries parked at the end of the drive. The .38 was still in her hand, though, as if she expected trouble.

As he watched Loretta get into the car, Marvelli felt for his own gun in the belt-clip holster under his jacket, just to make sure it was still there. He was still trying to figure out why Loretta had been so spooked by Ricky . . . and how she had gotten her gun out so smooth and quiet. Damn, he wished he could do that.

He looked at Ricky and her mother and nodded toward Loretta. "A very dangerous person, my partner."

"Dangerous, my ass," Ricky snorted. She turned and went into the house.

He said good-bye to Olivette Macrae again and went out to the car. Through the windshield, he could see Loretta in the driver's seat, drumming her fingers on the steering wheel, waiting for him. Her green eyes were glowing in the direct sunlight.

A very dangerous person, he thought.

She growled when he got in: "What're you smiling at, Marvelli?"

"Nothing." He felt for his gun again, wondering what it would be like to go out on a prolonged search with her.

But it was a moot point, he told himself. He wasn't gonna be doing any overnights, not with her or anyone else. And he wasn't going to Florida.

No way.

The visiting room at Trenton State Prison was painted stark
white, and, except for a couple of Formica-top tables and a bunch
of blue plastic stacking chairs, it was bare. Loretta was sitting at
one of the tables with Marvelli and Olivette Macrae's son, Tom
Spooner, Jr. They were the only ones in the room. A guard was
posted outside the door.

Martha Lee Spooner's file was open on the table, and Tom
Junior couldn't keep his eyes off the mug shot stapled to the
jacket. He rubbed his Cro-Magnon forehead and drifted off into
his own world again. Loretta wanted to bop him over the head
to snap him out of it. She wanted to know where in Florida his
wife was because she only had a week—six days actually—to find
her. No Martha Lee, no job. No job, no master plan. No master
plan, no law degree. No law degree . . . no career, no life, no hap-
piness. No pleasing Dad.

Please, God, she thought, *the only other thing I ever asked
you for was to lose twenty pounds for the senior prom and you
didn't help me then, so make it up to me now. Make Tom Junior
tell us where his wife is. Please, God.*

But Tom Junior wasn't saying much. The former biker was squat and brawny, with a misshapen splat for a nose and a fright wig of dark brown hair. But despite his looks, he wasn't very scary. Sad was more like it. Loretta studied his face, looking for any resemblance to his half sister, Ricky Macrae. He didn't look anything like Ricky, but it aggravated her that she was still obsessing about Ricky.

For some reason, when Loretta had first seen Ricky getting out of that truck with her big bruiser arms and her go-to-hell expression, she immediately thought of Brenda Hemingway, and she freaked. What was worse, she'd overreacted and pulled her gun. *But why?* she kept asking herself. Ricky was just a wiseass kid. She wasn't Brenda. Why the hell was Loretta still letting her fears run her life? *This had to stop*, she told herself. It had to, or else she was going to drive herself crazy.

Loretta looked at her watch. No one was saying anything—again—but Loretta was dying to because it was her clock that was ticking. Unfortunately, she'd agreed to let Marvelli do the talking this time—he'd insisted, actually. But all they were doing now was staring at Tom Junior, who was staring at the photos of his estranged wife, tears brimming in his bloodshot eyes. Loretta couldn't believe what a dope this guy was, pining away from the woman who'd stabbed him in the back. She looked at Marvelli, hoping he'd take the hint and put it in gear, but he was ignoring her, keeping his focus on Tom Junior instead.

Loretta frowned at both of them. She was itching to grab a fistful of Tom Junior's hair and shake his big stupid head. *What the hell're you doing crying over this skinny little bitch?* she wanted to shout. *She's the one who ratted on you and your biker buddies. She's the one who turned state's witness to get a reduced sentence for herself while you're doing fifteen years in, mandatory. Skinny women like that cannot be trusted, you freakin' bozo! Don't you know anything?*

But then she thought about Brenda Hemingway and Ricky Macrae. The hefty ones weren't always trustworthy either.

Tom Junior let out a shuddering sigh then. Marvelli furrowed his brows deeper, patiently waiting for Tom to go on with the story he'd started ten minutes ago. But Loretta still wanted to shake Tom Junior and tell him to wake up. He was doing hard time at a maximum-security state prison, for chrissake. He was supposed to be pissed off, angry, mad as hell! He was supposed to be cursing and pounding his fists on the table, turning on his dear wife Martha Lee the same way she'd turned on him. Except he wasn't doing that. He was *crying* for her, the stupid jerk.

High on the bicep where the sleeve of his blue work shirt had been cut off, Loretta noticed that there was a tattoo of an anatomically correct heart dripping blood with a banner spiraling around it. Printed on the banner was: MARTHA LEE & ME—FOREVER. He really loved her, the dumb sap. He wasn't gonna give her up. Damn!

Marvelli leaned over the table. "Listen to me, Tom. I'm gonna ask you again. Do you know where Martha Lee is? That's all we want to know."

Tom Junior swallowed hard. "I'm still thinking." His eyes never left the mug shots.

Loretta bounced her knee. The map of Florida was burned into her brain. *A city, a county, anything that'll point us in the right direction,* she thought. "Come on, Tom. We're waiting."

Marvelli gave her a dirty look.

She crossed her arms and gave it back to him. So what if Marvelli was the senior officer here? He didn't know everything. And it wasn't as if he were on the verge of a big breakthrough with this mook.

Marvelli turned back to Tom Junior. "What's the problem, Tom? Just tell me. Your mother already told us that Martha Lee is in Florida. If you know where in Florida, just tell us. No one has to know it was you who gave us the information. I give you my word."

"That's not it." Tom Junior wiped his eyes with the back of his stubby index finger, squeezing out a tear. "What I'm worried about is Martha Lee. What happens to her if you pick her up? She's got a kid, a little girl. It's mine, I think. What'll happen to *her*?"

"Martha Lee will go back before the parole board, and they'll decide if she has to go back to prison to serve out the rest of her original sentence. Social Services will take care of the kid. Or maybe your mother can take her."

Tom Junior just shook his head as if it were hopeless. He touched one of the photos of Martha Lee and looked like he was going to start blubbering.

Loretta started bouncing her knee again. *Come on, Tom! Today!*

Tom Junior let out a long sigh. "I don't expect you to do me any favors," he finally said. "But just promise me one thing, okay?"

"What's that?" Marvelli said.

"When you catch up with her, don't tell her I told you anything, okay? I don't want her to hate me."

Loretta threw up her hands. "Why?! She didn't have any trouble giving it to you up the yin-yang—"

Marvelli glowered at her. "You mind, Loretta?"

She shut up, but her knee kept bouncing. "Sorry." She stared down at the tabletop and focused on Marvelli's clasped hands. There was a gold wedding band on his left ring finger. She'd noticed it before, back at the office. She wondered what his wife was like. A big-hair bimbo, probably. An Italian-American princess who worried more about her nails than her marriage. But Loretta had a feeling Marvelli wasn't exactly the faithful type. He seemed too casual about things, too off-the-cuff, and he was a real slave to his appetites. He'd finished off that whole tray of cinnamon buns this morning, didn't he? What kind of self-control is that?

"Where is she, Tom?" Marvelli asked. "Come on, you *want* to tell us. I can see that you do. Just say it."

Tom Junior exhaled his turmoil. "She's . . . well, she's supposed to be in a place called—" He shook his head. "I can't."

"Yes, you can," Marvelli urged. "Just say it. She'll never know it was you."

Tom Junior looked up at the ceiling, blinking back tears. "All right, all right . . . Bonita Springs. It's down by Fort Myers."

Loretta's face fell. Bonita Springs? She knew Bonita Springs.

"How do you know she's there?" Marvelli asked. "Did she write to you?"

Tom Junior shook his head. "My sister found out."

"Your sister Ricky? Ricky Macrae?" Marvelli looked at Loretta. "How does *she* know where Martha is?"

Tom Junior hesitated.

"You've come this far, Tom. You may as well spill the rest."

Tom Junior looked from Marvelli to Loretta, then looked down at the mug shots again. "Ricky hired a private investigator to find out where Martha Lee was. Now she's got a contract out on Martha Lee's head."

"Mob?" Marvelli asked.

Tom Junior shook his head. "Worse. Biker."

"Who?"

Tom Junior looked back at the doorway and chewed on his thumbnail for a while before he leaned forward and whispered, "Torpedo Joe Pickett."

Loretta's bouncing knee stopped dead. She looked at Marvelli. Joe Pickett? Wasn't that the monster he'd brought in that morning? She looked at Marvelli, wanting answers, but he kept his eyes on Tom Junior, not letting on that he recognized the name.

"You probably never heard of Torpedo Joe," Tom Junior said, "but a lot of bikers know who he is. He don't ride with no gang or nothing. Strictly solo. But if you got something nasty needs doing and you can't do it yourself, just call Torpedo Joe. The man is good."

Loretta felt a little queasy. Back at the Jump Squad office, she'd thought Joe was just your run-of-the-mill creep, but a vision of him coming at her with that chair up over his head freeze-framed in her mind. Her hands were clenched tight under the table.

"So what's the deal with this Torpedo Joe?" Marvelli asked. "Did he do her yet?"

Tom Junior's chin crumpled. "I hope not." He swallowed hard. "I don't think he did. He ain't had enough time yet."

"What do you mean?"

"It was about a week ago that Ricky told me she had the contract out on Martha Lee. Said she'd lined up Joe Pickett to do the job. See, Ricky is just trying to piss me off, knowing how I feel about Martha Lee. The little bitch is hurtful like that. She told me Torpedo Joe was coming out from Ohio to pick up the down payment, then he was gonna head south to do the job."

"What's Ricky got against Martha Lee?"

Tom Junior rubbed his forehead. "Well . . . Do I have to tell you?"

"You want us to find Martha Lee before this Torpedo Joe does?" Marvelli said.

"All right, okay. Martha Lee was holding thirty grand that belonged to us—the gang, I mean. She took off with it when she got out of prison."

"You saying that Ricky was dealing drugs with you and your buddies?" Marvelli asked. "And Martha took off with the gang's money?"

Tom Junior didn't answer. He didn't have to. "Look, I been worried sick about Martha Lee. Just do me a favor, will ya? Go down there and get her before Torpedo Joe finds her. That's the only reason I'm telling you all this. I don't want her to die. That kid . . . *my* kid deserves at least one parent who gives a shit. I've had my problems with Martha Lee, but I don't hate her. Not like that I don't."

There was a lump in Loretta's throat. As much as she hated to admit it, Tom Junior's devotion to his wife was genuinely moving. Particularly because she was such a scrawny little thing. Must be hard to love something that unsubstantial.

"Can you be any more specific about where Martha Lee is?" Marvelli asked.

"Well, she's supposed to be working for some outfit called

WeightAway. The guy who runs it is supposed to be famous or something, but I never heard of him."

Loretta's jaw clenched. She'd sure as hell heard of him. His name was Roger Laplante, the founder and chairman of the WeightAway weight-loss scam. "Diet control plus positive motivation to help you lose weight and keep from gaining it back once you've lost it." The biggest crock of smooth-talking, pseudoscientific horseshit she'd ever heard. Picking people's pockets for a living was more honest than this WeightAway racket. Twenty-eight hundred dollars! That's what Loretta had lost thanks to goddamn WeightAway. Twenty-eight hundred bucks and she didn't lose a single pound!

Loretta saw red just thinking about it. WeightAway was just like all the other bullcrap diets on the market—lo-cal milk shakes that tasted like chalk, overpriced frozen meals that tasted worse than the boxes they came in, and imitation chocolate desserts that didn't even come close—but what made WeightAway different was that it had its own spa, Rancho Bonita, where results were guaranteed or your money back.

What a load!

Twenty-eight hundred bucks! Gone! Good-bye! Poof!

She'd gone to Rancho Bonita while she was on leave after the Brenda Hemingway incident, when she had decided that she was going to revamp her life and change everything, soup to nuts. But she didn't lose an ounce down there, nothing, nada, and the bastards refused to give her money back. "Unwillingness to comply with spa guidelines and extreme bad attitude" were the reasons they cited. Extreme bad attitude?! All things considered, she'd been pretty goddamn cordial. It's kind of hard to be Tipper Gore when a bunch of fanatic body Nazis are making you run around in the hot sun all day, doing stupid aerobics, and then all they feed you is roots and berries in nonfat yogurt. Try being Miss Congeniality on that routine.

When she stopped seeing double, Loretta suddenly realized that both Marvelli and Tom Junior were staring at her.

"Something wrong, lady?" Tom asked.

"You were mumbling to yourself," Marvelli said.

"So." Loretta looked away. Her face was flushed.

"You looked pretty mad about something, lady," Tom Junior said.

She gave them both dirty looks. "Never mind about me. What about your wife, Spooner? What's she doing for Weight-Away down in Florida?"

Tom Junior shrugged. "I dunno."

"Take a guess."

Tom Junior looked down at the floor. "She ain't waiting tables, that's for sure. If I know her, she's probably doing what she does best. Pulling some kind of money scam."

Loretta caught Marvelli's eye. She had to talk to him in private. WeightAway was a huge company with franchises all over the country and a line of products sold in supermarkets from sea to shining sea. If everyone in America on that diet had put up even a fraction of what she had, Roger Laplante was sitting on a shitload of money. Someone like Martha Lee Spooner could have a field day with that much cash. The opportunities for financial hanky-panky were almost unlimited for someone with her expertise. Loretta had to tell Marvelli about this. Law enforcement in Florida had to be notified, so they could pick up Martha Lee right away. Those sons of bitches had to be stopped before any more innocent fat people were rooked.

But then something occurred to her. If they called the locals in Florida, they wouldn't be able to bring back Martha Lee, and Julius Monroe wouldn't let her have the job. She couldn't let that happen. They had to go down and pick up Martha Lee themselves. And if they went down there and broke up whatever little scam Martha Lee had going with WeightAway, it just might give Loretta a leg up in her master plan. Two POs from Jersey just doing their jobs make a major fraud case against the biggest player in the American bullshit diet industry. Christ, they'd be heroes. They'd get their fifteen minutes of fame, be all over the news, and with some luck she just might get a few decent job offers, nine-to-five jobs that paid well enough for her to start going to law school at night right away. That would be great.

Her gaze shifted to the wedding ring on Marvelli's hand, and all of a sudden a wicked idea slid into her brain.

There were some nice secluded beaches down near Bonita Springs. Despite the greaseball haircut, there was something very attractive about Marvelli, the way he handled people, the way he'd subdued Torpedo Joe Pickett that morning as if it were nothing. God, how she wished she could've handled Brenda Hemingway that way. Loretta hadn't been with a man since she'd moved out on Gary the computer scientist whose idea of sex was more virtual than reality, and that had to have been . . . Oh, my God! Was it almost three years now? If she weren't so horny, she'd be depressed.

But she wasn't looking for a hot and heavy affair with Marvelli, not Deborah Kerr and Burt Lancaster rolling around in the surf in *From Here to Eternity*. No. It would just be nice to be with a man for a change—a man without a record. If they grabbed Martha Lee Spooner as soon as they got down there and parked her in a local jail, maybe there'd be some time for an afternoon at the beach. Nothing serious or anything. Just a little R and R in the sun.

Unless of course something developed. . . .

She looked down at Martha Lee Spooner's mug shots, and a naughty grin crossed her face. *Martha Lee*, she thought, *your skinny little ass is mine.*

Loretta stood up, went over to the heavy metal door, and started pounding on it. "Guard! We're through in here."

Marvelli bunched his fingertips and shook them at her, giving her one of his Italian gestures. "Whoa! What're you talking about, we're through? Sit down."

"We've got more than we need, Marvelli. Trust me."

A tall, craggy-faced guard unlocked the door and poked his head in. "You through with the prisoner?"

"Yeah, take him back up." She turned to Tom Junior. "Thanks for your cooperation, Tom. You can go now."

"Loretta!" Marvelli said.

"Chill, Marvelli."

The guard motioned for Tom Junior to get out of his seat. "Let's go, Tom."

But Tom Junior didn't move. "Lady," he said to Loretta, "will you find my wife before—" He glanced up at the guard. "Will you go down there and find her? Promise me that. Please." His beady caveman eyes were heartbreaking.

Loretta couldn't help feeling for him, the poor shmuck. "We'll do our best, Tom. I promise."

"Loretta!" Marvelli snapped. "What the hell're you talking about? We're not going down to Florida."

She waved Marvelli off. "Don't listen to him, Tom. We'll find her. Don't worry. She'll be all right."

"You promise?"

"Cross my heart."

The guard took Tom Junior by the arm and led him out of the room.

After he was gone, Marvelli exploded. "Hey, Kovacs! What're we, friggin' marriage counselors now? Is that what you think?"

"Trust me, Marvelli. I know what I'm doing."

"No, you don't. You think we're going to Florida. Well, let me clue you in on something: we're not."

"Yes, we are."

"Then you're going by yourself."

Loretta's heart sank. "Marvelli, listen to me—"

"I don't even want to discuss it, Loretta. I am not going to Florida. Period!"

"Come on, Marvelli."

He closed his eyes and stuck his fingers in his ears.

"Marvelli!"

"I can't hear you."

"Marvelli!"

"I don't want to hear it."

"*Marvelli!*"

Torpedo Joe Pickett wasn't happy. He was riding down a country road, passing cow farm after cow farm, smelling nothing but cow shit and cow farts. His head itched, he hated this Jap bike he'd stolen, and he was horny as hell. And it was all that guy Marvelli's fault.

He veered the blood red Kawasaki Katana to the left, staying with the main road, passing a cluster of mobile homes, hoping this was still Thornberry Road. There weren't many signs out this way. The Kawasaki was a piece of shit as far as he was concerned—one of those stupid Jap speed bikes the young punks liked, the ones you had to lean forward on with your face on the handlebars. He didn't like it at all. A decent bike should be comfortable. You lean back on it, like an easy chair. Joe would've preferred to have stolen a Harley, of course, but he didn't have time to be picky. He had to get moving.

The road was shady for a mile or so, woods on both sides; then it opened up again with farmland stretching for acres. Corn and cows. *They must eat a lot of corn chowder around here,* he thought.

He crested a rise in the road, and suddenly he spotted a wreck of a house with a screened-in porch up ahead on the right. *That could be it,* he thought. He downshifted the Kawasaki as he got closer, squinting to see the number on the dented mailbox at the end of the front walk. #1570. *Yup, that's it,* he thought, and pulled the bike into the dirt driveway, going all the way in and parking the stupid thing in the backyard so it couldn't be seen from the street.

Country cops like to be heroes, he thought to himself as he cut the engine, *'cause they're so bored.* He didn't want to give them an excuse.

He got off the bike and stretched. That bent-over position was for the birds, he thought. Lying on your dick with the motor revving underneath you—no wonder he was so horny.

He pulled off the dark-tinted Darth Vader helmet he'd stolen with the bike and wandered over to the Chevy up on blocks in the driveway. He grinned when he saw the she-devil with the big hooters painted on the door. Miss Behavior. Topedo Joe smiled. Little Ricky Macrae, Tom Spooner's half sister. She sure was sweet the last time he saw her.

But then he got a look at himself in the Chevy's driver's side window, and he frowned. He wasn't too keen on the new do. Just looking at himself made his head itch. He was completely bald now, shaved clean, face and head. He'd done it himself in the bathroom of a Burger King on a highway somewhere outside of Newark. Used a whole pack of disposable razors and half a can of Gilette Foamy. The only thing he left was the soul patch right under his bottom lip. Those hairs were long enough to braid, so that's just what he did. It was holding together with a paper clip he'd found on the floor of the bathroom. He wasn't sure if he liked it or not, though. He'd have to live with it for a few days.

He'd gotten that shitty Jap bike at the Burger King, too. He was just coming out of the bathroom when he spotted this doo-fus college kid sitting on the Kawasaki at the drive-up window. The kid got himself a jumbo Coke, then pulled over at the end of the driveway and took off his Darth Vadar helmet to drink it. The little twerp didn't know what hit him. Joe took him from behind and threw him down on the pavement. The little doofus was still seeing stars when Joe put on his helmet and pulled out onto the highway. It felt weird wearing that helmet over his fresh-shaved scalp, though. His head kept squeaking against the foam-rubber padding.

Joe ran his hand over the top of his head and studied his reflection in the glass. He wasn't sure if he liked the Kojak look either. It made him look like a mean mother, but it was the wrong kind of mother. He was a biker, plain and simple, a man of the road, not some Nazi-loving skinhead freak.

"Hey! What the hell you want here?"

Joe turned around and saw Ricky Macrae standing at the back door of the house, scowling at him like he was worse than dirt. She didn't recognize him.

But truth be told, he probably wouldn't have recognized her either if he wasn't looking at her right here at her own house. She'd put on a few more pounds since the last time he'd seen her. Changed her hair, too. But she didn't look bad, he thought as he took a gander at those melons she was carrying out front. He always did kind of go for big girls, and Ricky sure looked juicy and sweet to him. *Corn-fed,* he thought with a grin.

"What the hell're you smiling at, asshole?"

She always did have a smart mouth, he thought. *It was cuter when she was a kid.*

Then he noticed what she had in her hand. A little old derringer aimed right at his chest.

"Honey pie, in all honesty I don't believe that peashooter of yours can carry that far. Why don't you come a little closer?"

"Why don't you just shut your mouth and get the hell outta here?"

He stared at her for a second, waiting to see if she'd recognize him.

"You waiting for me to shoot you or what?"

He crossed his arms and shook his head. "You don't know who I am, do you, Ricky?"

"I don't know and I don't care, asshole." She cocked the hammer on her little derringer.

Torpedo Joe just laughed and thrust out his arms, flipping his palms up to show the twin torpedoes tattooed to the insides of his forearms, each one stretching from the wrist to the crease of the elbow. One was blue, the other red.

"Jesus Christ," she said. She pointed at his shaved head with her little gun. "What the hell did you do to yourself, Joe? You look like a dick."

"I'm in-cog-nee-to," he said, laughing at the word. It sounded funny coming out of his mouth.

She uncocked the derringer and stuck it between her boobs. It looked like a tight fit, and Joe worried that the poor little thing might go off by accident in there. "So is this, like, a disguise or something?" she asked.

"Yeah, you could say that. Probably won't hurt when I get down to Florida either. Martha Lee won't be expecting a clean-cut guy like me coming after her."

Ricky's pouty lips drooped.

"What's the matter?" he asked, already getting mad. "You send someone else to do the job?"

"Shit no. Why would I do that when I already hired you?"

"Then what's the problem? You want her dead, I'll make her dead. That was the deal, right?"

"*Was* the deal. Ain't worth bothering with now." She stuck a Marlboro between her lips and flicked her lighter. "Sorry if you went to any trouble."

His eyes crossed, he was so mad. He felt as if his head were going to burst open. "You're damn straight I went to some trouble. I didn't come all the way back to Jersey for my health, god-dammit. I'm wanted in this state, for chrissake. I got picked up yesterday, but I broke out. Now they must be really looking for me. We had a deal, Ricky. I came east for my down payment, and if you changed your mind, well, that's too goddamn bad. The deal was fifteen grand for doing Martha Lee, half up front. So you still owe me."

She blew smoke out of the side of her mouth, staring at him dead-eyed as if *he'd* done something wrong. "I didn't change my mind. But by the time you get down there, there won't be no Martha Lee to do."

"What're you talking about?"

"Couple of parole officers from the state came by this morning. They're looking for her. Gonna throw her ass back in jail."

"You're lying." He saw right through this one. She was just saying this to get out of paying him.

"I am not lying. You ask my mother if you don't believe me."

"And they just happened to come by this morning. What a friggin' coincidence that is."

"They did. Two of 'em. A fat-assed bitch whose face I'd like to slap and some guy named Marvelli."

"Marvelli?" Joe saw red.

"Yeah. Marvelli. You know him?"

"Oh, yeah. I know him." He'd like to rip Marvelli's grease-ball head off and use it for a bowling ball.

She stuck her hands in the back pockets of her jeans, cigarette clenched between her teeth. "I wanted that little bitch Martha Lee dead so bad, but they're gonna get to her first. Shit!" She kicked the dirt.

"Hold on there. We're not talking about Federal Express, Ricky, we're talking about the state. You think they're gonna hustle their butts down to Florida just to grab Martha Lee on a parole violation? I don't think so. Too many doughnut shops between here and there."

"I don't know about that. The woman seemed pretty anxious to get her."

"Bullshit. I'll get down there and have Martha Lee talking to the angels before Marvelli and his pal finish putting through the paperwork for their plane tickets."

Ricky pouted. "Yeah, I doubt it."

"You don't think so? You're talking to the best, woman. The best."

"You may be good, Joe, but I still don't think you can do it."

He stared at her nipples pressing through that black leotard top she was wearing. "You don't believe me, you can come with me. I'll show you how good I am."

She took one last drag and flicked the cigarette into the grass. "I know what you want to show me, and I don't want to see it. You can just forget about that."

He shrugged and stepped closer. "You sure about that, Ricky?" He stepped right up to her and looked down into her cleavage. There was no sign of the derringer anywhere in there.

"Yeah, I'm sure." Her eyes were narrow. She looked suspicious.

He reached around her and gently pulled her hands out of her pockets, examining the rings on her fingers. There were a lot of them, but he didn't see anything that looked like a wedding ring. "Not married?" he asked.

She whipped her hands out of his and sneered at him. "None of your goddamn business."

"Are you single and lonely, Ricky? Is that your problem?"

She stuck her face in his. "No, it is not. I *have* a boyfriend . . . if it's any of your business."

"You two aren't serious, though."

"Serious enough. He drives a rig, and he'll kick *your* ass if he catches you here."

Joe grinned. "Will he now? Go call him up. We'll see who kicks whose ass."

"Can't. He's on the road."

"When's he coming back?"

"Couple of weeks. He's gone to Montana."

"Oh, really. Hell, we can make it down to Florida and back in half that. I can do up Martha Lee, and we'll still have time for a little fun." He reached around her and grabbed his own wrist

behind her back. *Big woman,* he thought. *Firm, too. No jiggle.*
He liked that.

"Forget it," she said.

"We can use the down payment. Rent us a nice room. It'll
be fun."

"Forget it." But she was grinning like she wanted to.

He bent his head down and pressed his tongue against his
bottom lip so that his little braid stuck out. He slowly outlined
her eyebrows with it, then brushed down the slope of her nose
and started tickling her upper lip, moving real slow, making sure
she felt just the very end of it.

She grabbed the little braid between her thumb and forefinger. "You're bad, Joe," she said. She was grinning like the she-
devil on her arm.

"Tell you what," he said. "You come down with me, I'll
show you how I work. Maybe even set it up so that you pull the
trigger. How would you like that?"

She was tugging on his braid. "I don't know, Joe. I don't
think I should." She wasn't letting go, though.

"Well, it's up to you, honey pie. I'm not gonna force you.
But I'll tell you right now. I'm not doing Martha Lee unless you
come with me. So you make up your mind."

She didn't answer. Instead she pouted her lipstick lips and
shrugged, looking up at him from under her eyebrows. She leaned
in, and he thought she was fixing for a kiss, but he was surprised
when she pulled out his paper clip with her teeth instead. She spit
it out on the ground and grinned at him.

"Do I take that as a 'yes'?" he asked.

What do you mean, 'he got away'? How?" Marvelli was up on
his feet, having a bird.

Loretta watched him from the dark brown couch in Julius
Monroe's office back at the Jump Squad. Julius was behind his
desk, cradling his flute like a baby. Loretta wasn't saying anything, but she was getting antsy because they weren't sticking to

the subject at hand. They were all worked up about Torpedo Joe Pickett, but Loretta had to get them back on track with the Martha Lee Spooner problem, which was going to be her problem if they didn't bring her in.

"How could this have happened, Julius?" Marvelli was rapping his knuckles on the file cabinet. "I don't get it. It's not like Joe Pickett is easy to lose. You know what I mean?"

"Someone screwed up on the paperwork, O marvelous one," Julius said with a frown. "*Someone* who was supposed to get Pickett's file out of his car and bring it to me but forgot to do that. Guards came down before lunch to bring the jumpers we had here up to the county lockup. I wasn't here, and they didn't find any paperwork on old Joe, so . . ." Julius dangled Torpedo Joe's black leather vest by one finger. "I guess old Joe's a pretty good *thespian*. He told the guards he was a DEA undercover trying to work one of the other guys we were holding. The guards bought it and let him go." Julius held the vest by the shoulders, showing the patch on the back—crossed torpedoes, one red, the other blue. "No paperwork, O marvelous one."

"That's no excuse," Marvelli snapped. "They should've left him here if they couldn't find his paperwork."

"Coulda, woulda, shoulda," Julius said. "That's the purgatory cha-cha."

Loretta was ready to jump out of her skin. Marvelli hadn't told Julius what Tom Spooner, Jr., had told them, that Torpedo Joe had been hired to kill Martha Lee. And Loretta knew why Marvelli wasn't telling him, because he was dead set against going down to Florida. But, Christ almighty, they couldn't keep this to themselves. Even if Martha Lee was a perfect size 6, they couldn't just let her die. Besides, what was so important here in Jersey that Marvelli couldn't spare a few days to prevent a murder? And salvage Loretta's job.

No, this was too important, she decided. Too bad if Marvelli was a homebody. A sleepover would be good for him. Good for her, too, maybe. She cupped her chin to cover the grin.

She looked up at Marvelli. "So you gonna tell him?"

He gave her a dirty look. "Tell him what?"

She rolled her eyes. "That the sky is blue," she said. "Or how about that Joe Pickett is on his way to Florida to ice Martha Lee Spooner? Julius, you think you'd want to know about something like that?"

He cocked an eyebrow at her. "Tell me more."

"Not much else to tell—"

"Loretta," Marvelli snapped, but she ignored him.

"The Torpedo is on his way," she said. "But we could stop him if we hurry."

"Oh, no, we can't." Marvelli was shaking his head, arms crossed over his chest.

"Marvelli, we're talking about a homicide here—"

"I don't care—"

"Silence!" Julius shouted. He pinched his nose and laid the end of his flute against his forehead. He was thinking. He looked like a snake charmer conferring with his snake. "Not good," he finally proclaimed. "Not good. Two jumpers from Jersey down in Florida spilling blood. Not good."

"We know where he's going," Marvelli said. "Just call the sheriff's department down there and let them pick up Joe."

Julius tugged on his beard and nodded. "Yes, we can do it that way," he said. "But the 'but' is a big one here."

"What do you mean?" Loretta asked, about to be offended.

"We can have the cops in Florida do our dirty work for us, sure, *but* . . . the paperwork will eventually lead back here to Joe Pickett's file, which you left in your car, O marvelous one, which will mean your J-O-B if Torpedo Joe hits his target before he can be stopped. And it will mean my J-O-B, too, for embarrassing the department across state lines."

And it'll mean my J-O-B for not bringing Martha Lee in on time, Loretta wanted to add, but she kept her mouth shut.

Marvelli was adamant. "I cannot go down to Florida, Julius. I can't be away that long."

Julius brought the flute to his lips and tooted a short note. "What about the benies, O marvelous one? No job, no benefits. Will you be able to deal with that?"

That shut Marvelli up, but Loretta was confused. What was so important about Marvelli's benefits? Was he sick?

"Look, I'll make this easy for everybody," Julius said. "You two go down to Florida and grab Martha Lee Spooner before she gets dead. Call me as soon as you've got her, and then I'll call the boys in blue down there, tell them all about Torpedo Joe. Let Joe get used to that cracker hospitality down there."

"But, Julius, I cannot leave for that long—"

"If you hustle like good little worker bees, you can do it in a day, one-night stay-over at the most."

"But, Julius—"

"Please don't make me act like a boss, Marvelli. It is such a drag."

"Come on, Marvelli," Loretta urged.

He stared at the floor, looking grumpy. "I can't," he grumbled.

Julius suddenly turned serious. "Benefits like you're used to from the state will cost you big time. *If* you can find a company to cover you. They don't dig preexisting conditions."

Loretta screwed up her face. What was he talking about, preexisting conditions? Was there something wrong with Marvelli? She hadn't even had a decent fantasy about him, and now she finds out he's damaged goods.

"Can't you send someone else?" Marvelli pleaded.

Julius pointed out his door. "You see anyone out there when you came in? We're shorthanded as it is, and your old partner just went out on sick leave. There is no one else. *You* are the someone else."

"Come on, Marvelli," Loretta said. "We'll catch a plane tonight, grab her in the morning, and be back before dinner tomorrow. What do you say?"

Marvelli still looked grumpy. "I don't know. I can't think," he said.

"Why not?" she asked.

"I can't."

"*Why not?*"

"Because I'm hungry."

Julius looked at his wristwatch. "If I were you, I'd boogie, children."

Marvelli jerked his thumb toward the front room. "Are there any buns left?"

Loretta rolled her eyes. *God, help me.*

It was just getting dark as Marvelli pulled into his driveway. The neighborhood was ur–Jersey shore, Loretta thought. Split-levels and ranch-style houses, nearly all of them aluminum-sided. Every third house, including Marvelli's, had beige pebbles raked across the lawn instead of grass. Marvelli was growing some serious weeds on his.

A maroon Buick Regal was already parked in the driveway. Loretta was surprised. She'd expected the Marvellis to have a Trans Am.

Marvelli shut off the engine and put the transmission in park. "Okay, I'm just telling you," he said. "If we don't get Martha Lee Spooner by noon tomorrow, I'm coming home. You can stay down there and arrest her by yourself, but I'm coming back."

Loretta nodded. "Yes, you told me." She restrained the sarcasm for a change because she was thinking about tonight, about sitting next to him on a plane down to Fort Myers, then going to a motel with him. Who knew what could happen?

"Loretta? You coming?"

"Hmmm?"

Marvelli was already at the front door, waiting for her. The door was open, light from inside spilling out onto the porch. "Come on in," he called to her, then stepped inside.

She followed the concrete walk and went to the door, expecting Marvelli to be there to show her in, but he wasn't. He was in the living room, screaming at a busty redhead in her late sixties.

"Annette, I don't have any choice," Marvelli was yelling. "I *have* to go."

The woman bunched up the fingers of one hand and shook them at Marvelli, doing that Italian gesture. "What do you mean, you *have* to go? Who do you think you're kidding? You *want* to go."

"Dad! Grandma! Don't yell!" a little girl yelled from the back of the room. She was about ten or eleven years old, Loretta guessed, that in-between age between kid and preteen. Her hair was long and red, but a natural red—unlike her grandmother's hair—and she had Marvelli's sloped-back eyes. She was sitting on the end of a couch, watching TV. Loretta didn't notice right away that there was someone lying on the couch with the girl, someone covered in a blanket. Loretta couldn't see the person's face, though, because the arm of the couch was in the way. "We can't hear the TV with you two yelling," the little girl yelled.

"Be quiet, Nina," the grandmother shouted. "We're discussing something important over here."

"Don't yell at her," Marvelli shouted. "She didn't do anything."

The woman's eyes bugged out of her head. She shook a threatening finger in Marvelli's face. "Don't you tell me not to yell. I'm not yelling. *You're* the one who's yelling. And you're yelling because you feel *guilty.*"

"Guilty about what?"

"Going to Florida?"

"I have to go. I told you. It's for work."

"Yeah, sure." The woman crossed her arms under her heavy bosom.

Marvelli balled his fists. "Annette, I love you for all that you do for us, but sometimes I could kill you. You know what I'm saying?"

"Don't try to butter me up, mister. I know what you're up to. My Leonard—God bless his soul—used to try to pull the same kind of crap on me. I know what you're up to."

"You know nothing! That's what you know!"

"Dad! Grandma!"

"Don't tell me I don't know nothing, mister. I've been around. I know plenty."

"Oh, yeah? What do you know? Tell me what you know."

"I don't have to tell *you,*" the woman yelled in a huff, flipping her hand in his face.

As this dragged on, Loretta realized that they weren't really fighting about anything. They were just yelling for the sake of yelling. And in a way, Marvelli and this woman named Annette seemed to be enjoying it because every so often Loretta would catch crafty grins flashing over their faces. There was no real anger here. It was more like some kind of family blood sport.

"You don't know what the hell you're talking about, Annette," Marvelli shouted with a sly smile.

"Oh, yeah? We'll see, Mr. Know-It-All."

"Dad! Grandma!"

"Be quiet, Nina! We're talk—"

Suddenly a dinner plate flew across the room from the couch and hit the wall next to the television. The plate was plastic, so it didn't break, but from the scarred condition of the wall, Loretta assumed this wasn't an isolated incident. Maybe it was part of the family sport. But all of a sudden everyone shut up, and only a sitcom laugh track could be heard. Marvelli, Annette, and the little girl exchanged silent glances.

"Enough," a feeble voice rasped from the couch.

"Sorry, Mom," Nina said.

Marvelli and Annette rushed to the couch.

"You okay, baby?" Marvelli asked, sitting down on the edge, suddenly hushed and concerned.

"What is it, sweetheart? What is it?" Annette fretted. "What can I get you?"

Loretta could see that she wasn't going to get an introduction, so she walked into the living room and inched toward the couch, waiting to be noticed. She was shocked, though, when she saw the person on the couch. Loretta suddenly felt like an intruder.

The woman lying on the couch was wearing a New York Giants sweatshirt, a wool blanket pulled up to the middle of her chest. Loretta thought she might be in her thirties, but it was hard to tell because she looked so awful. Her skin was gray, and there were heavy bags under her dark eyes. Her below-the-shoulder-length hair was tangled and very dry, almost black, with a lot of silver sprouting from the temples. She had a Roman nose, and her lips were full but pale. She had probably been considered petite once, but now she looked emaciated. But despite her condition, her face was still beautiful.

The woman noticed Loretta standing there. "Hello," she croaked.

"Hi . . ." Loretta tried to be friendly, but she felt very out of place.

Marvelli banged his forehead with the heel of his hand. "Oh, jeez! I forget all about you, Loretta. I'm sorry. This is my family. My daughter Nina. My mother-in-law Annette. And my wife Renée." He was holding Renée's hand, his thick fingers interlaced with her frail, bony ones. His other hand was carressing her hollow cheek. They were all smiling at Loretta.

Loretta coughed. "Nice to meet you all. Marvelli, maybe I should wait in the car while you . . . get ready."

"No, don't be silly. Sit down. Make yourself comfortable." Marvelli turned to his family. "Loretta's my partner this week. We're working a special case together." He pressed his lips together and looked down on his wife. "I gotta go down to Florida tonight. But I'll be back by tomorrow. I promise." He tilted her chin up with his finger and kissed her on the lips. Not a French kiss, but not a honey-I'm-home kiss either. When he pulled away, he gazed into her eyes for a long time as if no one else were in the room.

Loretta wished she were somewhere else.

"Can I fix you a cup of coffee, honey?" Annette asked Loretta. "How about some macaronis? I got some baked ziti all made. I'll just heat it up."

"Oh, no, please," Loretta said. "I'm fine."

"Oh, just a taste," Annette insisted. "I make 'em really good. I mix it up with ricott'. They come out beautiful. You'll see."

"Thank you, but I'm really not hungry—"

But Annette was already on her way to the kitchen.

Loretta didn't want to stay any longer than she had to. "I'm really not hungry," Loretta pleaded to Marvelli.

"You gotta let her make you something," Marvelli said. "Or else she'll drive you batty."

"All right, just coffee then," Loretta said.

Marvelli turned to his daughter. "Nina, go tell Grandma to forget the ziti. Tell her to just put on some coffee."

"Okay." Nina rolled her eyes as if she knew there was no stopping her grandmother, but she went anyway.

Renée Marvelli winced and groaned as she propped herself up on her elbows. "If you want a cup of coffee, doll, go make it yourself. My mother can't make coffee for shit."

Loretta pressed her lips together and nodded. She didn't know what to say to this.

"It's not that bad," Marvelli said.

"It's *real* bad," Renée said to Loretta.

Marvelli glanced at his watch. "Shit, I better get moving if we're gonna catch that nine-thirty flight." He stood up and headed for the short staircase that led to the upper level. "I just have to grab a few things. I'll be right back."

Loretta wanted to go with him. More precisely, she didn't

want to be left alone with Renée. Not after what she'd been thinking about doing with her husband.

"Sit down," Renée said, pointing toward the end of the couch. She struggled to sit up straight. She seemed to be in a lot of pain. "Go 'head. Sit. I know I look pretty bad, but I won't bite."

"Oh, no, that wasn't what I was thinking."

"Yes, it was," Renée said.

If you only knew, Loretta thought as she took a seat.

"So you're Frankie's new partner," Renée said with a smile of pity. "You'll hate it. They all do."

It was hard for Loretta to think of Marvelli as Frankie, but he was obviously Renée's Frankie.

"He seems pretty easy to get along with," Loretta lied.

"How long have you known him?"

"Since this morning."

"You're a very kind person, Lorinda."

"Loretta," she corrected.

"Loretta. Sorry. I think it's spread to my brain sometimes."

"What?" Loretta asked.

"He didn't tell you? I have cancer. In both breasts. Can't do anything about it. It's too far gone." She shrugged and smiled.

Loretta tried to hold a sympathetic expression, but she felt like an idiot. What was she supposed to say to this? She'd just met the woman. A showy outpouring of heartfelt emotion would look pretty phony—even if she were capable of that kind of thing, which she wasn't.

"Anybody do a laundry today?" Marvelli yelled down from upstairs. "I can't find any underwear."

"Helpless," Renée said, shaking her head. "Tell him to look in the laundry basket," she said to Loretta. "I can't yell anymore. My voice is shot."

Loretta felt funny about telling Marvelli where his underwear was, but Renée had asked. "Look in the laundry basket," she called up to him.

"Where's that?" he called back.

Renée rolled her eyes. "On the bureau, in our bedroom."

"On the bureau," Loretta repeated, "in . . . your bedroom."

"Oh, I see it," he said. "Thanks."

"Right in front of his face," Renée said in a hoarse whisper. "Totally helpless."

Loretta nodded. "Guess so." She didn't know what else to say. She wished someone would come back in here.

Renée didn't say anything. She just sat there, her eyes a little out of focus. It was as if she'd suddenly shut down to conserve energy. Loretta tried not to stare. She also tried not to think about Marvelli's underwear. It wasn't easy.

Marvelli came bounding down the stairs then. He was holding a wrinkled brown-paper grocery bag. "Okay," he said. "I've got what I need."

Renée snapped out of her trance and glared at the paper bag. "Use your gym bag. You look like a *jooch* with that thing."

"It's all right. We're only going one night."

"Use your gym bag," she repeated.

He cradled the grocery bag as if he'd grown attached to it. "It's okay. This is fine."

"If you get on a plane with your clothes in a paper bag, I swear to God I will drop dead on you."

Marvelli's face fell. "That's not funny, Renée."

"I'm serious, Frankie."

He didn't argue. Instead he went straight to the hall closet, dug out a navy blue old-fashioned, hard-bottomed gym bag, and dumped the contents of the grocery bag into it. "Okay. You satisfied?" he said, zipping up the gym bag.

"Maybe," she said.

He dropped the bag and grinned at her. Then he looked at Loretta and shrugged. "Some women are very hard to satisfy," he said as he went to the couch and sat on the edge next to his wife. "Do not die until I get back. You hear me?"

"But what if I can't help it?"

"I'm warning you. You are not allowed to die when I'm not here."

"But—"

He smothered her objection with a long tender kiss.

Loretta sat there, staring at the TV, embarrassed to death.

Marvelli was trembling inside as he held that kiss. He was joking with Renée to keep her spirits up, but it wasn't a joke anymore. The doctors had said she was getting weaker. She could hang on for another year, or she could go tomorrow.

He didn't know what the hell he was going to do when that happened. He tried not to think about it, but he couldn't avoid it any longer. He had to face reality. But the thought of losing Renée was hard to hold onto. She had always been a brick. He couldn't imagine her not being there. But he knew he'd better start.

But what was making him feel worse was this trip to Florida with Loretta. He'd been looking at Loretta all day, and she didn't look that bad. As a matter of fact, she looked pretty nice to him. He knew he was thinking with his dick, but he couldn't help it. He and Renée hadn't made love since she'd started chemo, almost a year ago. She just didn't have the energy, and what was he going to do, force her? That's why he was nervous about this trip. Alone, away from home, in a motel, with Loretta—it was a bad situation.

And it wasn't like he really wanted Loretta for Loretta. It was just a matter of opportunity . . . and extreme horniness. It wouldn't be fair to Loretta if he did anything with her.

And anyway, he couldn't do that to Renée. He was a jerk, but he wasn't that bad.

But he couldn't stop thinking about doing it.

This was bad, he thought. Very bad.

Renée finally turned her head to the side, pulling away from his lips and coughing into her fist. "You better go," she whispered with difficulty. "You'll miss your flight."

"Yeah . . . you're right." He squeezed her hand, then stood

up. "We better get going, Loretta." He had a hard time looking Loretta in the eye.

"It was nice meeting you, Renée," Loretta said as she moved toward the front door.

Renée started coughing again, nodding her reply.

Marvelli picked up his gym bag and went to the kitchen door. "Nina, I'm going now."

The girl came running out, throwing her arms around her father's waist. "Bye, Daddy. I love you."

"I love you, too, sweetie," he said. He felt like lead. *I shouldn't be leaving,* he kept thinking. *Something bad is going to happen if I go.*

Annette came out of the kitchen, a condemning look on her face. "Where you going? I just put the coffee on. And the zitis are in the microwave."

"I'm sorry," Loretta said. "We have a nine-thirty flight, and I didn't realize it was so late. Maybe next time."

Marvelli was grateful that Loretta had bailed him out of that one. Annette would've just screamed if *he* had said they couldn't stay.

"I'll be back by dinner tomorrow," he said to his family as he backed toward the door.

Annette looked put out. Nina put on a mock frown. Renée was still coughing, waving with her skinny fingers.

He didn't want to go.

"Come on, Marvelli," Loretta said. "Let's go."

He looked at Loretta, then he looked at Renée. Something bad was going to happen. He could feel it.

It was after 1:00 A.M. when Loretta and Marvelli arrived at the motel Julius had booked for them. The Seminolian Motor Lodge was on a flat-out stretch of two-lane highway just outside Bonita Springs, across the road from a gas station/convenience store. Except for the blinking yellow traffic light at the crossroads up the road, there was nothing else within sight, just acres and acres of tropical scrub.

Loretta was too tired to have an opinion about the place as Marvelli pulled their rented Ford Crown Victoria into the lot. They'd lucked out at Hertz. There were no small cars available, which was what Julius had booked for them, and the Tauruses were all spoken for, so they ended up with a big Ford for no extra charge. Loretta took this as a good omen. She hated compact cars. Her car back home was a rusting '84 Chevrolet station wagon with imitation wood paneling painted on the sides, a living room on wheels, the kind of vehicle whose mere presence proudly proclaimed that it could inflict more damage than it would take, so just get out of the way.

The rental car was so comfortable Loretta had started dozing off on the ride in from the Fort Myers airport, but all she wanted now was a bed. The flight down from Newark had been pretty uneventful, except for the fact that Marvelli must've set an airline record for conning a stewardess out of the most number of little bags of peanuts on a single flight. They hadn't talked much on the plane. He'd rented a set of headphones and listened to music; she'd picked up a mystery at the airport and gotten through most of it. But as she read, she couldn't stop sneaking glances at him, especially his hands as he ripped open those little foil bags of peanuts. He had beautiful hands. He also had a sick wife, so she forced herself to concentrate on the book.

Marvelli parked the car and shut off the ignition. "You stay here. I'll get our rooms."

Loretta just nodded, her eyes half-closed, as Marvelli got out and went to the motel office, where a neon Indian head stood guard in the picture window. A neon cartoon bubble sprouted from his lips. He was saying: "No Vacancy."

Very tasteful, Loretta thought, closing her eyes.

She was roused when Marvelli opened the back door and took out his gym bag and her garment bag. "You're not going to like this," he said.

"What?"

"Somebody screwed up the reservation. They've only got one room for us."

"Oh. . . ." She picked her head up and stretched. "So what do you want to do?"

"The clerk says the nearest decent motel is about twenty-five miles from here, back toward Fort Myers."

She yawned and checked her watch. "It's late. Maybe we should check out this room first. Maybe it's big enough for both of us."

"Maybe." He shut the door.

She got out and locked her door. "I don't mind sharing a room," she said over the roof of the car. "If it's big enough. It's no big deal."

He shrugged. "I don't care. I thought *you* might not like it. You know, sharing the bathroom and all."

"No. I don't care. It's only one night."

"Okay," he said. "Let's go see what it looks like."

She followed him as he walked along the concrete walkway, passing all the motel rooms in descending order. Theirs was the last one in line, Room #1. He set down his gym bag and unlocked the door, but he didn't go in. He just looked in from outside, waiting for her to take a look.

She peered in over his shoulder. The room was a typical budget motel room—small. Twin beds with barely enough room between them to walk, TV set on a long bureau, big mirror facing the beds, bathroom all the way in the back.

He let out a sigh. "So what do you think? Too small?"

"It's fine. I'm too tired to go back and get another room. It's just one night."

Just one shot, she thought, glancing at the beds. She hated herself for thinking what she was thinking, but she couldn't help it.

They went in, and Marvelli laid her garment bag on the bed near the door. "You want this one?" he asked. "Or would you rather have the one near the bathroom? Renée always takes the bed closest. . . . Whatever you want."

"I don't care," she said. "That one's fine."

He'd left the door open, so she went over to close it.

"You want me to rig up a blanket or something?" he asked.

"What? Between the beds?"

"Yeah."

"You sleep with your eyes closed?"

"Yeah."

"So do I. We don't need a curtain."

"All right." He looked awkward, just standing there not doing anything.

"You want the bathroom first?" she asked.

"All right. If you don't mind."

"Go ahead."

"Thanks." He picked up his gym bag and went into the bathroom. He kept his sport jacket on.

A moment later she heard water running. He was brushing his teeth, she could hear. She unzipped her bag and took out her robe and a man's white V-neck T-shirt, which was what she usually slept in. She quickly stripped, pulled on the T-shirt, and put on the robe. She wondered if she should've brought a nightgown, something a little more Victoria's Secret. Maybe she shouldn't wear anything at all. Which would he prefer?

Then she frowned at herself for being so stupid. Nothing was going to happen.

The toilet flushed, and Marvelli came out of the bathroom. "Your turn," he said.

She slipped past him and went into the bathroom, closing the door behind her. She squeezed out some toothpaste on her toothbrush, but before she started to brush, she stared at herself in the brightly lit mirror.

Stop thinking about it, she told herself. *Even if it did happen, you'd feel like a bag of shit afterward. The guy's got a solid relationship with his wife. He doesn't want to fool around. Besides, the woman's dying. He's not going to cheat on her now. What kind of bastard would do that?* Loretta would throw him the hell out of bed if he tried something with her.

Of course, if she went over to *his* bed, and one thing led to another . . .

Loretta glared at herself in the mirror. *Stop it!*

She started brushing her teeth, hard.

When she went back out into the room, Marvelli was already in bed, the covers pulled up to his chin. She wondered if he was naked under there. When she went over to her bed, he turned over and faced away from her. The toilet was still running. She waited by her bed, leaving her robe on in case she had to go back and jiggle the handle. It stopped running after a second.

She took off her robe and draped it over the end of the bed, then pulled back the covers and got in. "Good night," she said, reaching over to turn off the lamp on the bed table between them.

"Good night," he said, muffled by the covers.

She lay on her back and closed her eyes, but her thoughts were racing now. She was thinking about Marvelli and his wife and her cancer and his daughter and his mother-in-law and his underwear in the paper bag and the terrible coffee his mother-in-law made and the baked ziti in the microwave. She opened her eyes and stared at the ceiling in the dark. The pole lamp out in the parking lot threw a sliver of light through a chink in the curtain, crossing the foot of her bed. She was wide awake. She couldn't stop thinking about it.

"You still awake?" she said softly.

"Yeah. What's the matter?"

She was tempted to get out of bed, but she had no idea how to start something. She felt stupid. She'd never done anything like this. *Forget it,* she said to herself. *This is stupid.*

"What's the matter?" he repeated. "Something wrong."

"No."

"Then what is it?"

"Well . . . I was wondering about something."

"What?"

"When you said good-bye to your wife before we left? Why did you tell her not to die before you got back? That sounded pretty heartless."

Loretta heard him turning over. "It wasn't meant that way."

"That's how it sounded."

"Gallows humor. That's what they call it in group."

"You go to group therapy?"

"Yeah. We both do. Us and five other couples. The women all have breast cancer. The therapist says it's good to joke about it. It helps to laugh."

"I've heard that."

"You ought to hear some of the stuff Renée says. She'll make you piss your pants. I mean it's not really funny, but when she says it, it is."

"Ummm," Loretta grunted. She really didn't want to hear about Renée.

"Renée actually has names for her—you know—for her boobs. She calls them Fred and Ethel. And she talks to them. Sometimes in this Ricky Ricardo accent. Cracks me up. She calls the cancer Lucy."

Loretta frowned. "Why?"

"Because Lucy's always getting Fred and Ethel into trouble. Get it?"

"Ummm."

"I come home from work, and she tells me everything that happened to Fred and Ethel that day. I mean, some of the weird stories she makes up are really hilarious. Fred and Ethel go to Vegas and get radiated. Fred and Ethel deal with the insurance people. Fred and Ethel go on chemo. Fred and Ethel kill Lucy and chop her body up into little pieces, then go fishing with her. . . . That's my favorite story."

"Why's that?"

"They live happily ever after in that one. No more Lucy making trouble."

Loretta heard him sigh. She wondered if he was crying. She closed her eyes, wishing she could fall asleep so she wouldn't have to deal with this.

"No more Lucy . . . ," he said. "That would really be wonderful. Life was great without Lucy. I wish I had realized it back then. We always had fun, though, so I shouldn't say that. We met in high school, Renée and I, and we've been acting like teenagers ever since. At one point I actually bought an old '57 Chevy and had it restored. Black and red, real sharp. Renée and I used to go out cruising in it. No particular place to go. Even after Nina was born, the three of us would go out riding around. . . . But after Lucy showed up, I sold it. Renée didn't want me to, but I said we were going to need the money. That wasn't the real reason, though. I thought it was time to grow up and face reality. Cancer was serious stuff. *I* had to be serious. . . . But I was wrong about that. Being serious doesn't do anything. Makes things worse, I think. . . . Now that I think about it, I should've kept that car. It would've been good for Renée."

Loretta felt hollow listening to him ramble in the dark. She didn't want to hear this. She'd wanted him to be her fling, to have some fun with him; she didn't want to hear his confession, and she definitely didn't want to be his pal. Being a guy's pal was death.

But what was she worrying about? She wasn't going to be his pal *or* his lover, so what was the point? Even sick, Renée was beautiful. And petite. Marvelli didn't want a big-boned girl. Obviously, she wasn't his type. Just the thought of them together as a couple embarrassed her. She couldn't see it. And she could just imagine taking him to meet her father. Oh, that would be a laugh and a half. Dad would just love Marvelli. A parole officer! And an Italian! Strike one and strike two. She could just hear that caustic tongue of his cutting into Marvelli like razor wire. Nothing less than a Philadelphia lawyer would please Dad. And even then, Dad would have to scrutinize his courtroom record to see if he was truly worthy. As if anyone ever was in Dad's book.

"Loretta?" Marvelli's voice came out of the dark. "You still awake?"

"Unfortunately."

"Me, too. I think I'm too wound up to sleep."

Thinking about your wife, she thought.

"Tell me something," she asked. "Are we gonna touch base with the local cops before we go out looking for Martha Lee?"

"What're you, crazy? Cops never go out of their way to help POs, especially out-of-state POs. Out in the field you're pretty much on your own."

"That's what I figured."

"Unless we do something wrong," he added. "Then everybody'll be on our case. That's why I want to do this thing quick and dirty, in and out."

So you can get home to Renée, she thought.

"So I can get home to Renée," he said. "And Nina."

"What about your mother-in-law?"

"Yeah, her, too."

Loretta turned over and stared at the sliver of light on her covers. The guy was a saint—still in love with his wife and absolutely devoted to his family, even his mother-in-law. Loretta didn't stand a chance with him. Guys like Marvelli didn't cheat. Not that she really wanted him to. Not really. . . . Sort of.

She turned her head and listened to see if he was still awake. "Marvelli?" she whispered.

Nothing but quiet.

"Marvelli?"

He stirred and let out a deep sigh. She listened closely for his breathing to go back to a normal pattern, but pretty soon she couldn't hear anything at all.

Jesus, she thought. *He doesn't even snore.*

Loretta turned over and made a face in the dark. She closed her eyes, but she knew it was going to be a long time before she fell asleep. Her head was too full.

Loretta was in a crappy mood the next morning as she and Marvelli drove out to Rancho Bonita. She'd slept badly, and at the diner they'd found on the highway, Marvelli had eaten French toast, six sausage links, a corn muffin, an English muffin, two big glasses of orange juice, three cups of coffee, and a side of grits because he'd never had them before. He'd consumed more butter in one meal than she did in a year. On top of that, she was wearing an orange short-sleeve camp shirt with the tails out over a pair of pleated jeans, and she felt fat. When she'd packed these clothes, she'd figured that she should dress comfortably for the arrest, just in case Martha Lee gave them any trouble, but now she didn't like the way she looked, and the only other clothes she had was the nice dress she'd brought thinking she and Marvelli might go out to dinner some night, a pair of khaki shorts, two oversize T-shirts, and the rumpled skirt and blouse she'd worn down on the plane.

With one hand on the steering wheel, she pushed her sunglasses up her nose and glanced at Marvelli, who was trying to read the map, making a crumpled mess of it. The road ahead was monotonous—flat and straight for as far as she could see, scrub forest on both sides. She hadn't said a thing to him since they'd left the diner because he was aggravating her. She'd been up most of the night—wanting him, not wanting him—and now his mere presence annoyed her. She didn't even want to look at him. She was tempted to tell him to get in the backseat.

Marvelli narrowed her eyes, staring through the windshield. "Did you pass Sea Conch Road?"

"No."

"Then it should be up here someplace. When you find it, take a left."

"Mmmm." She resented him telling her where to go.

"There it is." Marvelli pointed to a street sign up ahead. "Turn left here."

"I see it," Loretta grumbled.

She flipped on her directional and made the turn. Sea Conch Road was narrower but just as flat and deserted as the road they'd just been on. Every so often she'd see a cheap ranch house set back in the scrub all by itself. *Hermit quarters*, she thought. *Maybe she should look into buying one of those places.* That's what she was turning into—a lonely hermit.

After a couple of miles, they didn't seem to be getting any closer to civilization. "Is this the only way to get to Rancho Bonita?" she asked.

"No, it's a shortcut."

"Some shortcut."

"You don't like back roads? I do. I mean, why take the highway when you can see something different?"

She nodded at the scrub. "You call this different?"

He shrugged. "Sorry. I just thought you might want to see a little of Florida while we're here. We're not gonna be here that long."

Go ahead, rub it in, she thought.

They drove for a few more miles in silence, then the road ended in a T. The property straight ahead was bounded by a seven-foot cyclone fence. "Which way?" she asked.

"Take a right."

It wasn't long before the scrub behind the fence gave way to evenly spaced palms reaching up to the cloudless sky. Then the cyclone fencing abruptly stopped and was replaced by a black wrought-iron fence with pikes and curlicues along the top. High on a hill just beyond the edge of the property, a modern three-story office building covered with mirrored glass reflected the blue sky. It had its own entrance with a toll-taker barrier manned by a uniformed guard in an air-conditioned guardhouse.

"This must be the place," Marvelli said, wrapping the map into a ball and tossing it in the backseat.

"Why don't you fold it?" Loretta asked.

"Later." He was leaning over on her side of the front seat, trying to get a closer look at the grounds of Rancho Bonita. "Just follow this road," he said. "It should get us to the front entrance."

Loretta wanted to smack his face. Just the sound of his voice, that take-charge tone all men have, made her want to smack him one.

After another quarter-mile or so they came up to the front gates of Rancho Bonita. There was a guardhouse at this entrance, too, but no toll-taker barrier.

"May I help you?" a smiling female guard asked when Loretta rolled down her window. The guard was pretty, with dark Hispanic features. Loretta guessed she was somewhere in her midtwenties.

"We're here to see—"

"The spa," Marvelli interrupted, leaning over the seat to see the guard.

Loretta watched his eyes. He was checking her out, the son of a bitch.

"We're considering a stay here," Marvelli explained. "We were hoping we could see the place."

"Of course, sir." The girl smiled wider. "Drive in and park in any of the visitor spots. Someone at the front desk will help you."

"Thanks," Marvelli said. He was flirting with her, the bastard.

"Thank you," Loretta said as she pressed the window button. So that was it, she thought. Marvelli liked the young ones, the *skinny* young ones. Well, frig him.

The place looked familiar as soon as she drove in. The road bisected a manicured jungle setting with several winding pebble paths running through it. The road turned from blacktop to cobblestones and led to a circular drive in front of the thatched-roof main bungalow. Elephant-ear palms were planted everywhere. Staff people—all of them young and beautiful, it seemed—rushed in and out of the building. They all wore black shorts or slacks and white polo shirts with RANCHO BONITA embroidered over their hearts. Even the maintenance people were good-looking in their khakis and pith helmets. If Disney designed a fat farm, this would be it.

Loretta parked the Ford and took off her sunglasses, a feeling of dread sitting in her stomach like a mean little troll. It was being here again that made her feel this way. She had despised this place the time she'd stayed here, and those wonderful memories were all coming back now. The fairy-tale jungle setting, the false friendliness of the staff, the beautifully prepared starvation rations, the hearty but cruel encouragement from the body Nazis urging her to try a little harder, do a few more reps, go a little longer—it all came back to her in a distasteful rush.

Suddenly, Loretta's door swung open. She assumed it was Marvelli trying to be polite, and she was ready to slug him in the gut, the bastard. But when she saw who it was, her stomach bottomed out.

"Hi!" a wiry little man in an aqua-blue jogging suit said. "Welcome to Rancho Bonita. My name is Lance. How can I help you?"

Loretta was afraid to say a word. He didn't seem to recognize her, but she sure as hell recognized him. Lance Talbot, chief aerobics instructor, commandant of the body Nazis, and fat-free cheerleader number one. The week she'd stayed here, Lance had made her his personal mission. When she left, he saw her off and glumly told her she was his first failure. He'd actually shed a few tears when he told her, the little wuss. He begged her to stay a little longer, promised to get her a reduced rate if she'd give him another week to help her lose weight. She'd told him that if she had to stay in this hellhole another day, she'd eat *him*.

"So are you just here to visit or are you checking in?" Lance asked. He was still as peppy as a Broadway chorus boy and just as swishy.

Loretta didn't know what to do. If he recognized her, he'd surely remember that she worked for the New Jersey Department of Corrections—he'd called her "Warden Loretta" the whole time she was here—and if that got back to Martha Lee, she'd head for the hills, sure as shit.

Lance hunkered down next to the car and tried to make eye contact. He bounced as he hunkered. She remembered that about him. He never sat still. He always had to be exercising something. "What's the matter, honey?" he asked with a pout. "Bashful?"

Marvelli came around the back of the car. "No, no, no, not bashful," he said. "Well, maybe a little. You know how it is?"

"Do I ever," Lance said, patting Loretta's hand on the steering wheel. "I know it's hard," he said softly, just to her. "Admitting your problem is the hardest part *and* the biggest step. But once you take that first big step, then it's easy. Believe me, I know about these things." He gave her a wink. "And I can see a bikini in *your* future."

Loretta arched her back so that her breasts stood out. She could string him up from a palm tree with a bikini top that would fit her. And it would be a fitting death. The bottoms she could use on Marvelli.

Lance tried to peel Loretta's hand off the steering wheel, but she wasn't letting go. He sighed with a patented note of sympathy. "Denial is your worst enemy, honey." Then he flashed a devilish grin. "So let's kill him."

Loretta closed her eyes, ready to sock the little pest. He'd said the exact same thing, word-for-word, to a crowd of people at an aerobics class the last time she was here.

Marvelli reached in and took her wrist. "Come on, sweetheart, let's not start out with a bad attitude."

She whipped her hand away and glared at him. Sweetheart! Who the hell did he think he was talking to? She got out of the car, wishing an alligator would drag Lance into the bushes, so that she could really lace into Marvelli.

"You see," Marvelli said to Lance, "we're thinking about signing her up for a couple of weeks, but my wife is still a little unsure about all this. She doesn't think it works."

Loretta pressed her lips together. She could feel her face getting hot. Wife? What the hell was he talking about, wife? She was gonna kill him when she got him alone. Did he think this wife shit was funny, or was he playing Mission Impossible without telling her about it? Well, she had some news for him: parole officers don't do undercover work.

"Would you excuse us for a minute?" she said to Lance. "I want to talk to *my husband.*" She gave Marvelli the eye as she went to the front of the car and waited for him.

Through the palm fronds she could see a group of fatties on the aerobics court, huffing and puffing in the heat, trying to keep up with some little twenty-year-old with great legs and an off-center ponytail sprouting out of the top of her head. These people were in misery, and the sight of them made Loretta angry. With clothes on, they were probably competent, professional people who functioned just fine, except for this one hang-up about their weight. But in shorts and T-shirts, all tired and sweaty and out of breath, they were just pathetic grade-B cattle, following along with the program, thinking that being this miserable would eventually make them happy. It made Loretta want to break something.

Marvelli came up behind her. "What's the matter?" he whispered.

She glared at him. "What the hell do you think you're doing? Is this supposed to be funny?"

"You got a better idea for getting on the grounds so we can take Martha Lee? Or should we just ask for her at the front desk? You think she'll surrender voluntarily?"

"I don't need the sarcasm, Marvelli."

"She'll scram if she finds out we're here. We gotta take her by surprise. You know that."

"Of course, I know that," she snapped. "But you could've told me what you were going to do. Jesus!"

"Loretta, it's not like I had a plan or anything. It just sort of came to me when that guy came to the car. I figured this was the easiest way to get in."

"Well, next time let's discuss it first because we may have already blown it, thanks to you."

Marvelli frowned. "What do you mean?"

She rolled her eyes toward Lance. "If that guy remembers me, we're sunk. I stayed here a couple of years ago."

"You stayed here?"

"Sssshhh! Keep it down."

"You really stayed here before?"

She gritted her teeth. "Yes."

"Why the hell didn't you tell me? Now who's withholding crucial information? Jeez!"

"Just because we're partners, you don't have to know everything about me."

"In this case that's no excuse." He was mad, but she didn't care.

"How about if we just get on with it since we're here?" she said. "We can always argue later."

"Count on it."

She looked him in the eye. "I will."

Marvelli put on a smile for Lance, who was in the next parking space doing back bends to keep busy. "You think he recognized you?"

"No," Loretta said. "If he did, he'd be gushing all over the place."

"So what's the problem?"

"What if it comes back to him? Then what?"

"Don't worry about it. We won't be here that long."

Loretta was dubious. "I don't know. . . ."

"Look, how many people come in and out of here every week? At least a hundred? You were here a couple of years ago. He sees five thousand people a year. What are the chances that he'll remember you?"

Loretta shook her head. "I still don't like it."

"So what if he does remember you? You don't have to tell him why we're here."

Loretta just grumbled. Her real fear was that Lance would harangue her about her weight, about her being his one and only failure, about his wanting to succeed with her. She didn't want to deal with that.

"Listen," Marvelli said. "Let's just go take the tour. Let the guy show us around. Maybe we'll get lucky, spot Martha Lee on the grounds, take her by surprise, and just get the hell out of here. We can be on a plane by noon."

Loretta glowered at the fat people killing themselves on the aerobics court. *So much for reckless abandon on the beach with Marvelli,* she thought. *It was a dumb idea anyway.*

"Okay," she finally said. "Let's take the tour."

But Marvelli's attention had wandered off. He was staring at a silver-gray sedan that had just pulled into one of the visitor spaces. A tall black man in a gray business suit and gold-frame glasses stepped out and walked across the cobblestones toward the main bungalow. He was carrying a black leather attaché case.

"Holy shit," Marvelli said under his breath. He had this funny grin on his face.

"You know him?" Loretta asked.

"Oh, yeah."

"Ex-con?"

"Worse. He's an IRS agent."

"Is he a friend of yours?"

"IRS people don't have friends." But Marvelli was still grinning, staring at the black guy's back. "You go take the tour," he said to her. "I'll catch up with you in a few minutes."

"Marvelli!"

But he was already trotting off to catch up with the man.

Lance was pulling his elbow behind his head, stretching his shoulder, but he was also staring at her, his eyes as eager and pathetic as a puppy dog's.

She flashed a nervous smile and put her sunglasses back on.

Marvelli, she thought, glaring at his back, *I am going to kill you.*

"Shall we take a look around?" Lance asked.

Marvelli caught up with the tall black man at the front entrance to the main bungalow. He came up from behind and whispered over the man's shoulder, "So whose balls are you busting today, Lawrence?"

Lawrence Temple turned around, and, as soon as he recognized Marvelli, he cocked an unamused eyebrow. He was a lean, good-looking guy, even with the straight-arrow, gold-rimmed glasses on, but he was pure fed. Stiffer than a white man with that ramrod-up-the-ass posture all feds seemed to have.

"Still with Criminal Investigations, Lawrence?"

Temple scrutinized him for a minute before he answered. "Mr. Marvelli," he declared in his superiority-complex baritone, "what an un-nice surprise."

"Come on, Lawrence. Don't tell me you're still pissed off about that Paul Gaines thing."

"Why shouldn't I be pissed off about Paul Gaines? My boss cited that in my year-end review. Delayed my promotion by six months."

Marvelli chuckled to himself. *Spoken like a true fed,* he thought.

"Listen to me, Lawrence. Gaines had been in prison on a second-degree murder conviction. They let him out early, but he didn't report to his PO for almost five months. The guy was a cunning mother—not to mention ruthless—and we all knew that. We also knew that before his conviction he had ordered a shit-load of killings that couldn't be pinned on him. So what am I supposed to do? Let you take him in for tax evasion where he gets vacation time at Club Fed? Or do I take him back to Trenton where he can serve out the last seven and half years on his term? You tell me, Lawrence. What would you do if you were me?"

Temple was shaking his head. "You do not play by the rules, Marvelli, and you never have. That's what pisses me off."

"Those rules being: I should take a backseat because you're a fed and I'm just a mutt from the state."

"Cooperation, Marvelli. The way I learned it, law enforcement agencies are supposed to cooperate with each other."

Marvelli had to laugh. "This is funny, Lawrence. I have yet to meet a fed who could bring himself to share information, *any* information. You ever hear of 'anal retentive'? It's in the dictionary under 'Fed.' You guys couldn't cough up the truth, the whole truth, and nothing but the truth if your promotions depended on it."

Temple smiled to show that he was big enough to overlook an insult. "So what brings you down to Rancho Bonita, Marvelli? Working on that eating disorder of yours?"

"Business, my friend, business."

"Really?" Temple nodded, waiting for Marvelli to make the next move.

"Okay, Lawrence, you show me yours, and I'll show you mine. I'll even go first to show how much I trust you." Marvelli nodded at Loretta and Lance, who were still standing over by the car. "The woman's my partner. We're here to pick up a jumper who works for this place."

Temple stared at Loretta for a minute, then flashed a big grin. "And I thought we brothers were the only ones who liked 'back'?"

Marvelli's smile disappeared. "She's my *partner,* not my squeeze. And don't give me this 'brother' shit. Nothing more pathetic than a fed trying to be black."

Temple gave him the hairy eyeball, but Marvelli didn't give a shit. That crack about Loretta was out of line.

"So what're you doing here, Lawrence? I showed you mine."

Temple let his glare smolder. "Tax fraud. What else?"

"Who?"

"I didn't hear *you* mentioning any names, Marvelli."

"A woman named Spooner."

"Never heard of her."

"Good. We won't have another Paul Gaines situation then."

"I'm delighted."

They stood there, eyeballing each other. Marvelli didn't trust the guy as far as he could spit, and he was pretty sure that the feeling was mutual. He also knew how IRS Criminal Investigations people worked. They'd round up as many WeightAway office workers as they could, separate them, then see who they could get to rat on who. If Martha Lee Spooner was working in the administrative offices, Temple would probably take her in with his sweep, and once she got under the fed's wing, he and Loretta would have to move mountains to get her back.

"Excuse me. Mr. Temple?" A cute blonde in the Rancho Bonita long-pants uniform came up to them, looking from Marvelli to Temple.

"That's me," Temple said.

"Oh." She laid her hand on her chest and looked overly relieved. "Mr. Laplante asked me to find you. He's waiting for you in the conference room. If you'll just follow me."

"Have a nice life, Marvelli," Temple said, glancing back at Loretta.

Marvelli didn't like the dismissive look on his face. Of course, feds weren't totally useless, he thought. Temple had led him to Paul Gaines that time. It just might work again. Marvelli followed Temple and the cute blonde into the main bungalow, keeping a safe distance as they passed through the busy lobby to a doorway off a wide hallway.

"In here," the blonde said, opening the door for Temple.

Marvelli picked up his pace and slipped in right behind him. "We're together," he whispered to the blonde.

Inside, a tall white guy with weird-looking hair stood up from the head of the conference table and extended his hand to Temple. "Mr. Temple," he said with a smile. He was wearing a cream-colored linen suit and tan huaraches. "Roger Laplante," he said. "And this is Martha Sykes, from our accounting department."

A petite brunette nodded to Temple from her seat. Marvelli recognized her from the mug shots in her file.

Martha Sykes, huh? he thought, half-amused by her alias.

Martha Lee stayed in her seat as she shook Temple's hand. Her hair was longer than it was in the mug shots, but it was definitely her.

"And you are?" The big weird-looking guy flashed a feeble smile at Marvelli.

Temple just noticed that he was there.

"Special Agent Paul Gaines," Marvelli said quickly. He pointed back and forth from Temple to himself. "We're partners."

Temple's eyes were bugging out of his head.

Marvelli ignored him and took a seat. A large bowl of fresh fruit was sitting in the middle of the conference table. He grabbed a banana and started to peel it. "So, Lawrence, shall we get right down to business?" He bit off the top of the banana as he nodded at Temple's briefcase. There were some interesting-looking fruits in the bowl, things he'd never seen before. He'd let Temple talk for a while, so he could try a few before he gave Martha Lee the good news about her free one-way trip back to New Jersey.

Temple took a seat and opened his briefcase, scowling the whole time. He pulled out a legal pad and a pen, leaned back in his chair, and propped the pad on his knee. Marvelli watched him write in big block letters: "Obstructing a federal investigation is a <u>FELONY!</u>" He underlined "FELONY" a few times to make his point.

Marvelli finished off the banana and reached for something that looked like a small, round apple. He bit into it. He had no idea what it was, but it wasn't bad.

"Mr. Laplante," Temple began, "you have resisted all our efforts to resolve this problem. For the past sixty days, we've had to fine you $500 a day for noncompliance. You have already been notified that as of tomorrow the fine increases to $2,500 a day until such time as you turn over your books to our auditors. You already owe us some $30,000 in penalties. How much longer do you intend to continue with this nonsense, sir?"

Laplante smiled and wagged his finger. "I take offense at your characterizing this situation as 'nonsense,' Mr. Temple. I certainly don't consider it nonsense—no, I don't."

Marvelli watched Laplante as he finished off the little apple. He was thinking, *Snake oil.*

"Then I take it you're ready to make your books available to us?" Temple said.

"Yes. Soon."

"How soon, Mr. Laplante?"

"Very soon."

"Could you be more specific?"

"Well . . . I'd like to be." Laplante glanced at Martha Lee, who'd been smiling pleasantly through all of this, but Marvelli could see that she was getting a little green around the gills. This Laplante guy was smooth, but Marvelli could tell from Martha Lee's strained smile that they were both in deep shit, and the walls were closing in.

Temple rolled his gold Cross pen between his palms. "A date would be helpful, Mr. Laplante. Can you give me a date?"

"I will."

"When will that be?"

"Well, what would be convenient for you?"

"Right now."

Laplante frowned and exchanged glances with Martha Lee. "I'm afraid that wouldn't be good for us."

Temple leveled his stare at him.

Another fruit caught Marvelli's eye. He thought it might be a tangelo, but he wasn't sure. He picked it out of the bowl and started to peel it, but as he watched Martha Lee watching Temple, it struck him that this was a bad situation.

It was obvious that Laplante had a lot to hide. If he was willing to pay 2,500 bucks a day in penalties, he had a lot to cover up for. But Marvelli couldn't care less about him. It was Martha Lee he was worried about. Fear was seeping out of her pores—he could smell it. Unfortunately, so could Temple. He was going to try to flip her and use her against her boss. He was going to make her queen for a day, promise her the world with a ribbon tied around it if she ratted on her boss. That wasn't good.

If Temple got to her first, he and Loretta would lose her. And if they lost Martha Lee, Loretta would lose this wonderful job she wanted so badly. He didn't like the fact that she'd finagled this Florida trip, but he did care about what happened to her. She seemed like someone who hadn't had a break in a long while.

Marvelli popped a section of tangelo into his mouth and glanced down at Temple's warning on the legal pad. Obviously he couldn't grab Martha Lee right here. But he couldn't wait too long either. Not with Temple around. He examined the fruit that was left in the bowl, looking for a knife so he could cut into that mango. He had to think of something pretty fast. He couldn't hang around here. He had to get back to Renée.

Temple tapped the pad with his Cross pen, still giving Laplante the deadeye stare. "So when exactly can I expect to see your books, Mr. Laplante?"

Laplante looked greener than the mango, Marvelli thought.

Mr. Laplante? Mr. Laplante, are you with me?" Temple, the IRS guy, was eyeing Roger like a water moccasin eyeing a juicy little frog.

Roger nodded and smiled at him, but Martha Lee knew he wasn't listening. He was scared stiff, frozen to his lily pad.

The other guy—Martha Lee didn't catch his name—was shooting grapes into his mouth. He was making her nervous with all his eating. *Christ, don't they feed this guy?* she wondered.

But even without the second guy, Martha Lee was ready to jump out a window, she was so nervous. This Temple was out for blood, and he wasn't going to be satisfied until he got to see the books.

Her face ached from smiling, trying to act as if there were nothing wrong. But there was plenty wrong. To begin with, Roger was all wrong. He was acting like a big dope, talking out of both sides of his mouth. He was *acting* guilty. Shit, with all his money, Roger should just try to bribe these two characters. Make it worth their while. It would be worth it. Roger owed the government an awful lot of money in back taxes. If Temple saw those books the way they were now, Uncle Sam would end up owning WeightAway. If she were Roger, she'd try the bribe.

But she really didn't give a damn about what happened to Roger or WeightAway. All she cared about was wiring that money to Luis for the bogus cocoa, so she could get the hell out of there before the shit hit the fan, which was definitely going to happen as soon as Temple and his pencil pushers got a hold of those books. Over the past few months she'd slipped in entries of fictitious payments to the Alvarez Cocoa Company all over the ledgers to cover her ass just in case she was caught wiring the money to Panama. She wanted to be able to say she didn't know any better because according to the books, WeightAway had dealt with Alvarez in the past, so she had no reason to question their bills.

But that didn't ease her mind any. These government bastards were out for blood. Roger was the big prize, but they weren't gonna stop with him. They were gonna want a whole passel of people to take the rap for this. And she couldn't depend on good old Rog to protect her. Christ, he'd point the finger at his own grandmother if it could get him off the hook. That's what these big guys do, blame the bookkeepers. *I didn't know this was going on, Your Honor. I swear. They were doing it behind my back.* She could just hear Roger saying this, sounding so hurt and sincere.

These bloodsuckers, though, they might buy his story, but they'd never buy hers. If Roger got off, a lot of other people were gonna have to take the rap, and she was a pretty likely candidate. Once they found out she wasn't really Martha Sykes and that she had a record, that would be it. She'd be the one.

Sweat was dripping down her armpits. She watched Temple's mouth moving, and Roger's mouth moving, their heads bobbing up and down, but she couldn't concentrate on anything they said. And this character with the fruit was driving her batty. Now he was working on an orange, spitting seeds into his hand and dumping them into the ashtray. Eat 'em up alive. That's what these people do. They're like monsters. That's what they were gonna do to her. Throw her ass back in prison so that she'd never see her little girl ever again.

"I said, isn't that right, Martha? Martha?" Roger was looking at her. So was Temple. But she had no idea what Roger was asking her.

"Why, yes," she said quickly. "Of course." She cranked up her pleasant smile another notch.

Roger flipped his hands over, palms up, as if to say it were obvious. "So you see, Mr. Temple, it's not that we're *trying* to be difficult. It's simply impossible to accommodate you at this time. . . ."

Blah, blah, blah. Roger was digging his own grave, and he didn't even know it. Throw them a bone, for chrissake. Give 'em something, Rog. Get off the defensive.

But then something occurred to her. What if these sons of bitches had a spy in place somewhere at the spa? It wouldn't be hard, what with all the fatties that came in and out of here. What if they were already on to Roger? What if their spy got into the cube and had a look around? What if that person found something? That would be just like the feds. Use Temple and this food-processor partner of his as decoys, making a big show about wanting to come in the front door when they've already got someone coming in the back way. Jesus, they were insidious. She had to get it in gear, fast. They could have a whole army of feds in their IRS-FBI-ATF-whatever-the-hell-else windbreakers waiting outside the gates to break in and arrest everyone in sight. She had to get that damn money wired to Luis and get the hell out of there before it was too late. Shit!

She reached down for her purse and put it in her lap, then started rummaging through it. The three men were watching her. Good. When she found what she was looking for, she brought it up to the top of her purse just long enough for them to catch a glimpse of the white paper-wrapped tampon.

"Would you excuse me for a moment?" she said, standing up.

No one questioned her. She'd done this once before with a state trooper in Pennsylvania. It worked then. She hoped it would work again.

She walked around the table and went out into the hallway, closing the door softly behind her, passing through the lobby and out a side door. She was sweating buckets, but she was glad to be out of there. On the pebbled path she picked up her pace a little, then forced herself to slow down and act normal. She didn't want to look obvious. Their spy could be watching.

Martha Lee passed the cafeteria building and the indoor pool and headed for the staff compound, a cluster of stucco bungalows where the resident staff lived. She figured going back to her apartment wouldn't look as suspicious as going directly to the cube. She'd grab some clean underwear, her contact lens kit, a few other things, stick them in her bag, and head for the cube. She'd wire the money to Luis while Roger was still with the feds, then take off. Maybe send Roger a message that she had a real bad headache, so they wouldn't miss her till tonight, maybe even till tomorrow.

Cutting through the palms that bordered the tennis courts, she came out into a parking lot where the staff kept their cars.

Her red Chrysler Le Baron convertible was parked near her bungalow, a cute little cramped pink one, just like all the others. She pulled out her keys as she walked and went right in. When she closed the door behind her, she locked the dead bolt, just in case. She was proud of herself that she wasn't panicking. She was nervous, but she wasn't panicking. She'd been in bad situations before, she kept telling herself, so she could handle this one. Just stay cool and it would all be over in forty-five minutes. She'd be on her way to the Fort Myers airport by then. Take the first plane going north, then figure out the rest from there. One way or another she'd get to Slab Fork by tomorrow. Then Costa Rica. Roger and the feds could kiss her sweet little ass because they wouldn't be able to touch her then.

She went to the bureau on the other side of the double bed, pulled out the top drawer, and reached in for the envelope taped to the underside. Opening it, she did a quick count—twenty hundred-dollar bills, emergency traveling money. She tucked it into the inside compartment of her purse, then headed for the bathroom to get her contact lens kit and some makeup.

Co-*sta* Ree-*ca,* she thought, singing a bossa nova in her head.

In the beige-tiled bathroom she hit the lights, turning on the ceiling fan, too, by mistake. She didn't bother to turn it off, just went to the medicine cabinet to get her stuff, unzipping a small gray pouch and filling it with rewetting solution, saline solution, lens cleaner, enzymatic cleaning pellets—

Suddenly the shower curtain whipped open. She yelped, staring into the mirror, her heart thumping, thinking, *Spy!*

Oh, God! Oh, God! Oh, God! she thought. *Don't panic!*

The humongous character standing in the tub smiled at her in the mirror. He was huge. A little braid hung from his bottom lip.

Oh, God! she thought.

"How's it going?" the monster with the braid said.

She turned around but didn't say a word, thinking hard, telling herself there was a way out of this, there was a way.

But then she saw his arms, and her eyes shot open as if she'd seen a ghost. He flipped them over so she could get a better look. Twin torpedoes on the insides of the forearms, one blue, one red. Her stomach suddenly ached like hell. *Jesus, Mary, and Joseph,* she thought. *Oh, God!*

"Guess you know who I am, don't you, Martha Lee?" He scratched his shaved head and laughed through his nose.

There's a way out of this, she kept telling herself. She thought about the money in her purse. *Bribe him,* she thought. But she didn't want to give up that money. That was her escape money. *Then give him something,* she told herself. *Give him* something.

"Torpedo Joe Pickett," he said, extending his paw as if he were inviting her in to take a shower with him.

Her legs were shaking like crazy. *Do something!* she screamed at herself. *Do* something!

"Can't say hi?" he asked, tugging on his braid.

Without thinking it through, she pulled her blouse over her head and undid her bra, letting everything drop. "Hi," she said. She wished she were bigger on top.

Torpedo Joe stared at her boobs and laughed through his nose. "Hi."

11

Sitting in a booth at the Sunset Diner, a few miles down the road from Rancho Bonita, Loretta inched over toward the window to get as far away from Marvelli as possible. Marvelli was sitting next to her; Lawrence Temple, the IRS guy, was by himself on the other side of the red vinyl booth. She was pissed at both of them, but more at Marvelli for pulling that wife stunt back at the spa and then leaving her alone with Lance.

She held her coffee cup to her mouth, frowning behind it. These two jerks were screwing up this whole thing.

"You don't get it, Marvelli. Do you?" Temple was leaning over the table, getting frustrated with Marvelli. "You think this is a game, playing cops and robbers. But I'm telling you, Laplante is big-time. He must owe the government at least 20, 30 million in back taxes."

"So arrest him," Marvelli said, taking the last dinner roll in the basket and unwraping another pat of butter. "You're the government."

But Temple was shaking his head. "It's not that easy. We suspect he's been hiding income, but we don't have any real proof.

It's all conjecture based on estimates. We have to see his books to prove it."

Marvelli bunched up his fingers and did that Italian gesture. "You don't think this guy has a second set of books? Get real, Lawrence."

"I'm sure he does, but that's okay. All we have to find is a discrepancy between his books and our estimates, and we've got probable cause to put his ass in the meat grinder."

Loretta glared at him. Two years ago she'd been audited by the IRS. Some dweeb who smelled of BO had tied her up for six hours going over all her receipts and giving her an ulcer. The smelly geek ended up charging her $159 in taxes owed, most of which was the late penalty. Talk about a profitable use of government resources.

"We suspect that a substantial part of Laplante's franchise business is unreported cash income," Temple said. "The local WeightAway places have this thing they call Pound for Pound. Members have to weigh in every week, and for every pound that they don't lose on schedule, they have to contribute five dollars, which they're told goes to a local food bank or homeless shelter. Based on the skimpy contributions WeightAway has made in the past, we think Roger Laplante is pocketing this unreported cash."

Loretta's eyes were crossing. Did Temple have to bring that up? She'd almost forgotten about Pound for Pound. With all the money she'd paid in, WeightAway could've fed India.

"Then there's the frozen foods. WeightAway Food Products claims enormous business expenses on the quality ingredients they supposedly use. But we had some of the frozen dinners analyzed by an independent lab. Considering what's in them, the markup is astronomical."

I could've told you that, Loretta thought with a frown. The memory of WeightAway's pressed-sawdust veal Parmesan patty haunted her whenever she passed the frozen-food section at the supermarket.

Marvelli bit into his buttered roll, chewing as he talked.

"Sounds like you've got more than enough on Laplante to make his life miserable."

Temple shook his head. "The frozen foods are a rip-off, but they're not illegal. That's the whole problem. On the surface WeightAway is on the up-and-up, but there's a lot of room for hanky-panky in an operation that big and that diverse. And given Roger Laplante's lifestyle and his public image, malfeasance seems very likely. The only thing is, he's clever. He doesn't use a big accounting firm. Everything is done in-house, which is all part of his evangelical I'm-only-doing-this-for-the-health-and-happiness-of-America bullshit. He has the spa, a house in Palm Springs, a co-op in Manhattan, a vacation condo on the Baja, and twenty-eight hundred acres of investment property outside Montreal, and he's not in it for the money."

Loretta's stomach growled just thinking about her hard-earned money going to Roger Laplante's fat-scam empire.

"And that's not all," Temple continued. "He's got a—"

He abruptly stopped talking when the waitress came with their orders. She was a white-haired, lacquered-hairdo granny type with no personality at all. She set down the platters without a word: grilled cheese and bacon for Temple, shrimp salad on rye for Loretta, meat loaf and gravy with mashed potatoes, creamed corn, and a side of coleslaw for Marvelli.

"I'll be right back with more coffee," the waitress said as she hurried off.

"And another Coke," Marvelli called after her.

That would be his third, Loretta noted as she pulled out one of the toothpicks from her sandwich. They had crinkly cellophane ruffles on top—one blue, the other green. She took off the top slices of bread and sprinkled salt on the lettuce and tomato.

"I'll tell you what I really need," Temple said after the waitress left. "Someone to go undercover at Rancho Bonita. Someone who could get into the WeightAway headquarters and find something I can use against Laplante. Something on paper." He sucked the straw in his iced tea. "Yeah, that's what I need. Someone who could get into the spa and get the goods on Laplante. Not a plant who'd go to work for them. That could take months, maybe years. I need someone who could do a quickie black-bag job. In and out. Just find something, anything that I could use to start building a case. But it would have to be someone who could blend right in over there."

Loretta was biting into her sandwich when she realized that Temple and Marvelli were both staring at her. A glob of shrimp salad tumbled out the side of the sandwich and plopped into her plate. She glared at their stupid, eager faces. "Don't even think about it," she said with her mouth full. "Forget it."

Temple played it cool, biting into his grilled cheese and chewing deliberately as he stared at Marvelli. "You owe me, Marvelli. For Paul Gaines."

"Yeah, well, *I* don't owe you," Loretta said. "So just forget it."

"You'd be passing up a rare opportunity, Ms. Kovacs."

"Opportunity for what?"

"Interagency cooperation. If, down the line, you ever need a recommendation, or perhaps you might want to transfer to a federal agency, I could be very helpful."

Marvelli was remashing his mashed potatoes, mixing in the pool of gravy that had been sitting on top of the mound. "That's the name of the game, Loretta. You scratch his back, he'll scratch yours."

Loretta glared at him. The only scratching she felt like doing was scratching his eyes out. "Are you telling me I should do it?"

Marvelli shrugged, noncommittal. "I'm not saying you should or you shouldn't. That's up to you. I'm just pointing out that it could be beneficial to you down the line. I mean, you told me you want to go to law school, didn't you? A good recommendation from Lawrence wouldn't hurt. Lawrence, you must have better connections than the people in Corrections. Don't you?"

The IRS agent sucked on his straw before he answered. "I know some people, sure. And one of the good things about working for Internal Revenue is that people tend to pay attention when you ask for favors." He raised his eyebrows at Loretta and shrugged.

Loretta didn't like being ganged up on. "I am not going back there to act like an idiot, posing as some pathetic housewife who hates the way she looks. I could never pull it off."

"Sure you could," Marvelli said, shoveling meat loaf into his mouth. "We've already laid the foundation."

"What the hell are you talking about?" Loretta could feel her blood pressure rising. She was going to kill him.

"Don't you remember?" He paused for a drippy forkful of creamed corn. "We told that aerobics guy that we were checking the place out because you were considering a stay there. Don't you remember?"

"I don't know what you're talking about." She sipped her coffee, refusing to look at him.

"You know what I'm talking about," he insisted. "What the hell's his name? Vance, Lance, Prance—you know."

If they had to stay over another night, she'd kill Marvelli in his sleep, she swore to God.

Lawrence Temple stayed poker-faced through all of this, calmly eating his grilled cheese. After he finished half of his sandwich, he propped his elbows on the table, linked his long fingers, and leveled his gaze on her. "You want Martha Spooner, right?"

"I'm not going undercover—"

"Yes or no—do you want Martha Spooner?"

"Of course, I want her. What the hell do you think we're doing here?" She glanced at Marvelli feeding his face. She'd already given up on the other thing she had wanted, the *From Here to Eternity* night.

"Okay, here's the deal," Temple said. "You help me get Laplante, and you can have Martha. Very simple."

"And who the hell are you to make deals like that?" Loretta said, her voice rising. "These are people we're talking about, not trading cards."

"You and Marvelli are from a state agency, and you're out

of your jurisdiction. I'm federal; the whole country is my jurisdiction. That's number one." Temple bent back the thumb of one
hand with the forefinger of the other. "Two. You and Marvelli
can try to snatch Martha Spooner, but I can detain her first,
along with anyone else I can find in the WeightAway offices,
which is precisely what I will do if you choose not to cooperate."

"What! You can't do that."

Marvelli forked up some coleslaw. "This is what they call
'playing hardball,' Loretta."

She made a face at him. "Thanks for the insight, Einstein."
Then she pointed at Temple. "You're full of it, you know that?
Do you think I'm stupid or what? You can't just barge into the
spa and start rounding up people."

Temple was grinning, nodding his head up and down. "Oh,
yes, I can. The IRS is not bound by the same restrictions that all
other law enforcement agencies must comply with. If Uncle Sam
thinks you are withholding monies due to the government, the
IRS is empowered to do whatever it deems necessary to recover
those funds. In other words, we can act first and worry about the
details later."

"So if you can do that, why do you need me?"

"Because, Ms. Kovacs, my primary goal is to recover money,
not put people in prison. The government does not want to put
Roger Laplante away. We want all Americans to thrive and pros-
per and continue to make profits, so that they can continue to
pay taxes. Which is why I want you to help us. If I can get some
indication of how much income he's hiding, I will have a basis
for recovering his back taxes. If we simply arrest him, the money
will stay hidden and we may never get our share. That's not what
we want."

"So what you're telling me here is that you want the money,
not the man."

Temple nodded. "Essentially, yes."

"But if I say no to you, you're gonna pick up Martha Lee
and keep us from getting to her."

He nodded again. "Essentially, yes."

Marvelli sopped up gravy from his plate with the rest of his dinner roll. "He's playing hardball."

Temple pulled out a folding cellular phone from his inside pocket and laid it on the table. "We have an arrest team in the area. All I have to do is call them, and Martha Spooner is ours." He picked up the other half of his sandwich. "But you take your time and think about it, Ms. Kovacs. Just give me an answer by the end of lunch." He took a bite. The rest of his sandwich wasn't that big, and she had a feeling he wasn't going to have dessert.

Of course, Marvelli's plate was already clean, and he was looking at her with those sad puppy-dog eyes. He wanted her to do it. She picked up half of her shrimp salad sandwich, then put it right down. She'd lost her appetite. For him, too, the son of a bitch. Why was he siding with Temple? Why wasn't he taking for her? She'd thought he was a nice guy. Why did he want her to make a fool of herself posing as a "fat lady"?

"Excuse me," she suddenly said, sliding out of the booth toward Marvelli. "I said, excuse me," she repeated, plowing her hip into his.

"All right, all right, take it easy." Marvelli got out of the booth.

She slid out and headed straight for the ladies' room without looking at either of them. She wasn't going to cry, she told herself. She was just going to pee.

"Ladies' room is right back there." The granny waitress pointed with her hairdo as Loretta whizzed past.

Loretta paid her no mind. She found it herself and went right into a stall, undoing her jeans, pulling down her panties, and sitting down. The room reeked of disinfectant. She ripped off a piece of toilet paper from the roll and blew her nose. She wasn't going to cry, she told herself. Kill maybe, but not cry.

But just as she started to pee, she heard the door opening.

"Loretta?"

She clenched and stopped peeing. It was goddamn Marvelli. "Get the hell out of here, Marvelli."

"I know you're mad, but—"

"Get out!"

"Don't yell. People are eating out there. You'll get them upset."

"I said, get out. Whatever you have to say, I don't want to hear it." She could see his black loafers under the stall door.

"What about your master plan, Loretta? Did you forget about that?"

Her face turned red. She'd forgotten that she'd told him about that on the plane. She was astounded that he'd remembered.

"What about all that stuff you told me about?" he said. "Going to night school, passing the bar, going into practice with your sister? Did you forget about that?"

"Shut up, Marvelli. I'm still mad at you."

"Yeah, yeah, I know. But what about you? What about your plan?"

"You think Temple's right? You think I should go back to the spa and play the fat lady?"

"I think we should play ball with him, get Spooner before he changes his mind, and get the hell out of here. That's what I think."

"You're only saying that because you want to get home to your wife."

"You're right. I do want to get home to Renée. But I want you to get what you want, too."

"You're just saying that."

"Loretta, you're making a big deal out of this. It's not."

How do you know? she thought. She ripped off more toilet paper and wiped her eyes. *Shit,* she thought with a sniff. She'd promised herself she wasn't going to cry.

"Loretta? What do you say? Should I go tell Temple you'll do it?"

"Can I have a little privacy here, Marvelli? I'll let you know when I get out. Okay?" She stared at the back of the gray stall door. She hated it when people turned nice on her just when she was ready to hate their guts. Goddamn Marvelli. Why was he worrying about her plan? What did he care? Why was he being so nice? Was he trying to make her like him or what?

She wiped her eyes again and tried to pee, but now she couldn't.

"Loretta?" His voice echoed into the stall.

"Are you still here?"

"I was just wondering about something."

"What?"

"Are you gonna finish your sandwich?"

Marvelli was behind the wheel of the rented Ford, peering under the edge of the visor, driving into the sun on a four-lane highway. Loretta was in the passenger seat, her overnight bag on the floor by her feet. They'd just come from the motel, and now they were heading back to Rancho Bonita.

"Why are you so quiet?" Loretta asked.

"Hmmm?" Marvelli was distracted.

"You've been quiet all afternoon. Something wrong?"

"No."

He glanced in the rearview mirror. Lawrence Temple's gray Cutlass was two cars back, following them. The SOB didn't trust Marvelli. But that was okay, he thought. He didn't trust Temple either.

He pushed his sunglasses up his nose and changed lanes, wishing Temple would disappear. This whole thing was a bad idea, he thought. Maybe they should reconsider it. Loretta didn't have any undercover experience. She had no business doing this. What if she got into a jam in there? Would she know how to handle herself? What if she got hurt? He glanced over at her. She'd been right on the money when she'd said that he was only going along with this caper because he wanted to get back to Jersey as soon as possible. He *was* worried about Renée.

But part of him was having a good time here, and that was making him feel guilty. He sort of liked being with Loretta, even when she got nasty with him. She was proving to him that it wasn't so bad being with a woman other than Renée. Not that he had anything in mind. It wasn't like that at all. He just liked hanging out with Loretta. Nothing serious. Even though it had taken him a long time to fall asleep last night. He'd been thinking about her in the next bed, wondering if something could possibly happen in a situation like this—if he weren't married, of course.

He frowned at himself for even thinking about it. He wasn't supposed to be thinking like this. It wasn't exactly positive thinking, and that was bad for Renée. She needed positive thoughts, lots of them. But still, horny is horny. And he couldn't deny that Loretta was having an effect on him.

Sort of. A little bit.

He glanced over at her. She was staring out the window. He wondered if she was nervous about going undercover. She looked like she could be nervous.

"If you want to back out of this, Loretta, that's okay. I understand."

"No," she said, turning to face him. "I said I'd do it."

"I'll just tell Temple the deal's off."

"I said I'll do it."

"You're not worried? What if something happens?"

"I can take care of myself. I'm not completely inept."

"I never said you were. It's just that, you know, when people feel cornered, they get desperate, they do crazy things."

"Marvelli, we're talking about embezzlers, not killers. Martha Lee has no history of violence. And Roger Laplante? Come on. Have you ever seen a bigger wuss?"

"Don't underestimate them, Loretta? Never underestimate *anyone*. You're going in there to take Martha Lee's life away from her. You realize that, don't you? Same thing with her boss. You'd fight for *your* freedom, wouldn't you? No reason to think they won't do the same."

"Stop worrying, Marvelli. I don't take unnecessary risks."

He looked at her. "You asked to work for the Jump Squad, didn't you?"

She didn't answer him.

"Here." He pulled out his wallet and dug out a business card. "See my beeper number on the bottom? Use it if you have to."

"Marvelli—"

"For *my* peace of mind, okay? If you get in any trouble and you need me, call my beeper and just leave any number that ends in 1111. That way I'll know it's you."

Marvelli put on his directional and turned left off the highway. The front entrance to Rancho Bonita was down this road about a mile or so. He drove for a while without saying a word. All signs of civilization soon disappeared as the brush along the road grew thicker and took over the shoulders. He looked sideways at Loretta. His card was still in her hand as if she didn't want to keep it.

"Take it, Loretta. Just in case."

She responded with a testy sigh.

"Any number with four ones on the end and I'll be there in a flash."

"Will you bring doughnuts?" she asked sarcastically.

"Just take it," he said as he pulled up to the guardhouse at the front gates.

A perky little blonde poked her head out of the guard booth. "Welcome to Rancho Bonita," she said.

"Hi," Marvelli said, forcing himself to look pleasant because he knew Loretta was scowling at the girl.

"Do you have a reservation, sir?"

"Yes. For my wife." He could hear her shifting in her seat.

The blonde pulled out a clipboard. "And the name, sir?"

"Mrs. Frank Marvelli."

She ran her finger down the clipboard, then looked up and smiled. "Okay," she said. "Drive right in and go to the front desk.

I'll call ahead and let them know you're here." She bent down so she could see Loretta. "Enjoy your stay, Mrs. Marvelli."

Marvelli pressed the accelerator and drove through the gates before Loretta gave her the finger.

"Mrs. Marvelli, huh? When did we get married?" Loretta was doing a slow boil.

He shrugged helplessly. "I had to make the reservation in my name. We told that guy Lance that we were a couple."

"*You* told him. I didn't."

He pulled into a parking space and shut off the engine. "Is this gonna be a problem?" he asked.

Loretta was still fuming when she got to her suite, which was on the first floor of a small two-story town house. The entrance to the suite upstairs was on the other side of the building, assuring privacy for both guests. There were dozens of these little town houses in this section of Rancho Bonita, but they were positioned at all angles, buried in palms and ferns, so that despite their proximity, every suite seemed to be all by itself buried in the jungle. She'd stayed in one of these town houses the last time she was here, and she hated the design.

Why isolate people? she wondered. Or was it that fat people shouldn't be able to look at each other? You put too many of them together, they might start thinking they're normal. God forbid.

The room was nice, but a little too Laura Ashley for Loretta's tastes. She noticed that there wasn't a little courtesy refrigerator anywhere in sight, which didn't surprise her. That had pissed her off the last time she was here. Roger Laplante didn't trust his guests to control themselves, which she had absolutely no intention of doing anyway.

The Hispanic bellboy—who was dressed in black shorts and a white polo shirt like everyone else who worked here—set her overnight bag down on the luggage caddy. He was smiling like an idiot, thinking he was going to get a big tip, but she glowered at him the whole time, so he didn't even bother to hang around. He wasn't going to get squat from her because she didn't want to be here.

But after he left, she felt bad. It occurred to her that maybe a lot of fat people were angry that they'd come here, so they didn't tip. She thought about calling him back to give him a couple of bucks just so she wouldn't be like the rest of them, but by the time she poked her head out the door he was already gone. Nothing but gently swaying ferns in his wake.

Crap, she thought as she started to close the door. She'd catch him later.

"Hel-lo-o!"

Loretta cringed when she heard the voice.

The last person in the world she wanted to see came bounding down the path like a raptor in Reeboks. Lance the aerobics instructor stood at her door, smiling like a dope, running in place. "I just wanted to welcome you to Rancho Bonita and tell you how glad I am that you decided to stay with us . . . again."

Loretta's heart stopped. "Excuse me."

He rubbed his index fingers together, shame-shame. "You were here before, weren't you? I thought you looked familiar this morning. I'm terrible with names, but I never forget a shape."

Her vision blurred as an overwhelming urge to punch his lights out came over her. She clenched her fists until it passed.

"Come on, admit it," he said. "You stayed with us a few years ago, right? And it didn't work for you, right?"

"Well . . . yeah. . . ." She wanted to kill him, hide his body in the bushes.

"Well, I just want you to know that when people come here and they don't get the results they want, I take it as a personal failure. I just didn't work hard enough with you last time, and I apologize. But this time I'm going to make it up to you. Cross my heart and hope to die."

That can be arranged, she thought.

But she suddenly realized that this wasn't funny. How much did this little creep remember about her? She'd checked in as

"Mrs. Frank Marvelli," and Marvelli had suggested she use her own first name, so she wouldn't get caught not answering to a fake name. But Lance could be a big problem. He knew her as Loretta Kovacs the last time she was here. She also seemed to remember some sort of touchy-feely get-together that Lance had run the last time where the fatties were supposed to tell the group something about themselves and bare their souls. Problem was, she didn't remember how much of her soul she'd bared. It had been right after the Brenda Hemingway incident, so she'd been pretty shaky at the time. She wished she could remember how much she'd said about herself. What if this little twerp blew her cover? He could ruin everything.

But how much could *Lance remember?* she reasoned, trying to calm herself down. That had been three years ago. As Marvelli said, thousands of guests must have passed through here since then. *You'd have to be pretty outstandingly plump for anyone on staff to remember you,* she told herself. And that, she wasn't.

Lance's eyes were squeezed shut, his hand on his forehead, like a mind reader. "It's an *L* name, right?"

"What?" Her heart was suddenly pounding.

"Don't tell me now. I'll think of it." He pressed his lips together, thinking hard. "Is it Lori? Laurel? Something like that?"

The blood drained out of her face.

"Lorinda maybe?"

"Rumpelstiltskin," she said.

His eyes popped open. "O-ho! You *are* funny." He tilted his head to the side and looked up at her with an impish twinkle in his eye. "So are you going to tell me your name? Or are you going to keep me in suspense?"

She gritted her teeth and forced a smile. "I'm going to hang you up by your toes and tickle you to death."

And then eat you, she thought.

He stopped jogging and clutched his belly, laughing like a real bozo. But suddenly he switched gears and pouted like a mime. "You're not going to tell me your name, are you?"

She grinned at him, wishing he would have a stroke. "No. I want you to guess."

He brushed away an imaginary tear, still pouting.

"And I bet you won't remember by the end of the week," she said.

"Okay, you're on." He started to jog in place again. "This'll be fun."

"Absolutely."

"So how about we go over to the gym and get you started on some toning exercises? Then we can get you into the sauna and maybe fit you in for a Scotch hose before dinner."

Loretta shuddered. She remembered the Scotch hose. Some sadistic matron taking target practice on your naked body with a fire hose fitted with a pinprick nozzle. It was amazing the Geneva Conference hadn't outlawed it.

"Gee, that sounds great," she said, "but I promised to meet an old friend at"—she glanced at her wristwatch—"three-fifteen. She works here."

"Well, all right," he said, jogging along, bouncing up and down, going nowhere. "But I'm going to make you my personal mission while you're here. I guarantee I'll get you down to a size twelve in no time."

"I *am* a size twelve." You fucking little shit!

"Really?"

"Yes."

Most of the time, she thought.

He shrugged and started to jog off. "I'll see you later then."

"Oh, before you go," she called after him. "My friend told me to meet her at her apartment, but she didn't tell me where the staff lives around here."

Lance pointed down another path. "Follow this past the building where the restaurant is. Then go past the tennis courts and turn left. Staff housing is on the other side of the parking lot. Do you want me to take you there?"

"No, that's all right."

Just get lost, dweeb!

"Okay, bye-ee," he said as he jogged backward down the path.

"Later," she said, heading back into her room.

But then she heard him yelling from twenty yards away. "I've got it! It's Loretta, right? Loretta. And you do something in law enforcement? Am I right?"

Loretta's stomach bottomed out. *Oh, shit!*

Martha Lee kept thinking about the Browning automatic in the night table drawer, buried all the way in the back behind the nail polish bottles, nail polish remover, emery boards, scissors, barrettes, the earrings that didn't have a match anymore, all that stuff. Naked, lying on her back in bed and staring at the ceiling, Martha was thinking about getting the gun out. But there was a problem. Torpedo Joe had his big leg draped over her legs and his big paw on her tit. She could barely move. The gun was stuck in her mind, though. She couldn't think of any other way to get rid of him.

She glanced at his face. He seemed to be sleeping, but she couldn't tell for sure. He ought to be sleeping, goddammit, she thought. After one go-round, most men just conk right out, and she and Joe had already done it twice. He wasn't half-bad, all things considered. Pretty gentle for a guy his size. And he had waited for her to come first both times. It wasn't exactly her idea of romance, but she didn't realize how much she'd missed sex until Joe had shown up.

Of course, the fact that having sex with him had saved her life for the time being probably had a lot to do with the way she felt. He hadn't actually threatened her yet, or even said what he was here for, but she knew. When Torpedo Joe Pickett showed up at your door, you didn't have to ask why.

Something suddenly occurred to her. Maybe this was something new for him. Instead of coming to shoot her, he was planning on fucking her to death. He had a dick like a Louisville Slugger, and she swore to God she'd never come so many times in a row in her life. Maybe his plan was to keep doing it until she had a heart attack and died.

She thought about the .22 again and frowned. Even if she could get to it, it wouldn't do her any good. She didn't know how to use it really, and Joe probably got into fights every day. He'd take it away from her in no time flat. Or else she'd get a shot off and then find out that a little .22 couldn't pierce his thick rhino hide.

She wiggled her toes and tried to bend her knees, but his leg was a deadweight on top of her, cutting off the circulation. Maybe *that's* how he planned to kill her. Fuck her a few more times, then just lie down on top of her. Death by weight.

But even if she could get away from Joe, the goddamn IRS guys were gonna screw everything up. Once they got into the books, they'd figure out that the Alvarez Cocoa Company was a scam. They probably already knew that if, as she suspected, they had a spy here at the spa. That's how they operated, those bastards. Undercover agents snooping around, getting in your underwear, finding out everything. Low-down sons of bitches, that's all they were.

She glanced at Joe's closed eyes. At least he was out in the open about it, she thought. He didn't sneak around pretending to be somebody else. He was what he was. Ding-dong! Hit man! Here to kill you.

Ding-dong, she thought glumly.

Hmmm . . . maybe.

"Joe," she said. "You awake, Joe?"

"Yup," he said right away. He didn't open his eyes, but he'd apparently been awake the whole time.

"I got a proposition for you, Joe. You wanna hear it?"

He scratched that little braid under his lip but didn't open his eyes. "I'm listening."

"I know you didn't come here to see me because I look like Cindy Crawford or anything. You're here to kill me, right?"

"Yup." He rubbed his nose with the back of his finger.

"How much they paying you to do me?"

"Can't tell you that, Martha Lee."

"Why not?"

"It's unethical."

"Whatever it is, I'll double it."

"For just going away?"

"Nope. I got somebody you have to do for *me*."

He opened one eye a slit. "You couldn't afford it."

"Oh, no? Name your price."

"I'm getting fifteen to do you, honey bun."

"Then I'll give you thirty. Fifteen for the hit, fifteen to leave me be."

Joe grinned at her. "You're full of it, sweetness. You ain't got that kind of money."

"You don't think so? What do you think I'm doing here then? Working on my tan? Moving money around is my specialty, in case they didn't tell you that up north. I move it places where no one else can get to it but me." She didn't have squat on hand, but that didn't bother her. If she knew anything, she knew that she could be damn convincing when it came to bullshitting people about money.

Joe opened his eyes all the way and stared into her face as he circled her nipple with his index finger. It was as big and blunt as a Havana cigar but very gentle to the touch. "Who is this person you want done?"

"We talking hypothetical, or we talking deal?"

"Tell me who it is and I'll let you know."

"I've got a bad feeling the government's got an undercover agent here snooping on me. You find out who that person is and get rid of him, and you got yourself thirty grand."

Joe laughed his husky laugh. "You mean to tell me you don't even know who this person is? You want me to play detective *and* do the deed? Get real, darling."

"Thirty grand. Cash. No bullshit." She looked him right in the eye and didn't flinch. It was her bear-trap face. If she could get him to buy the hard sincerity of the bear-trap face, she had him caught.

"I'm talking cash, Joe. I got it in a safety-deposit box not too far from here. Find the rat and eliminate my problem. That's all you have to do."

Joe grunted. His eyes were slits.

"What do you think, Joe?"

Joe tugged on his braid and seriously considered it. Thirty grand was hard to turn down. It would get him another Harley, a nice one. It would also bankroll him for a while, give him a nice little break from all the bullshit. He was getting tired of all this killing shit.

"Hello, Joe? I want you to go up to Maine and do this guy who screwed me."

"Hello, Joe? You got time to go down to Oklahoma and show my old lady she fucked with me for the last time?"

"Hello, Joe? I gotta little job for you if you wanna go out to Vegas."

All those miles were wearing him down. He wouldn't mind sitting tight for a couple of months. Maybe renting a room and getting himself a coffeemaker. Get up every morning and make himself a good cup of coffee. Just stare out the window and take his time drinking it, enjoying every drop. He thought about that a lot. It was one of those simple pleasures he never got to have because he was always on the road, at the mercy of every stinking greasy spoon between here and there, always having to rush off to kill somebody new. Yeah, thirty grand would be real nice.

But then he remembered Ricky Macrae waiting for him back at the ratty motel where they were staying a few miles down the road. Ricky was obsessed with getting back at Martha Lee. That's all she'd talked about since they'd left Jersey—Martha Lee this and Martha Lee that. He had promised her that he'd do it, and he'd taken a down payment from her, so it wouldn't exactly be ethical to back out now. And if anything, Joe Pickett was true to his word. Besides, Ricky came from a biker family, and bikers don't fuck bikers. He sincerely believed in that.

But he could sure use the extra cash. A Harley Softtail would be nice. So would a clean room with a view of the water, any kind of water—salt, fresh, a stream, anything. And a Mr. Coffee all to himself. He could grind his own beans and try all those coffees he'd just heard about but had never tasted. Like Kona and Sumatra. Jamaican Mountain Blue. Tanzanian Peaberry. He'd even drink it with half-and-half instead of plain old milk. It would be awful nice.

"So what do you think, Joe?" Martha Lee was looking him in the eye. She was serious.

So was he.

Ricky was a good kid, but thirty grand ain't fifteen. He'd make it up to her somehow.

"Okay," he finally said. "You got a deal, honey bun. Now where do you suggest I start looking for this government rat?"

Loretta nearly peed her pants when she heard this. She was on her hands and knees in the bushes under Martha Lee Spooner's open bedroom window. After she'd found Martha Lee's bungalow and heard voices through the door, she'd decided to investigate by crawling through the peat moss in the beds around back to eavesdrop. But she couldn't believe this. She'd been an undercover agent for less than two hours, and already she was a failure. Martha Lee and her boyfriend—whoever the hell he was—knew she was here, and they were plotting to *kill* her. Loretta peered through the bushes, her pulse racing.

She had to get to a phone and call Marvelli. Any number that ended in four ones.

She crawled backward through the stinky peat moss and got away from the window. They wanted to *kill* her, she kept thinking. It was incomprehensible. You need a pretty good reason to kill someone, don't you? Well, that meant Martha Lee had something pretty big to hide, Loretta reasoned. Martha Lee didn't even *know* her and she wanted to kill her. Not even Brenda Hemingway had wanted to kill her. At least Loretta didn't think so.

Loretta stopped and listened, then when the coast was clear, she stood up and hopped out of the bushes. She glanced back at the open window as she brushed off her hands and knees and started walking toward the parking lot. She had to get to a phone, she kept thinking. She had to call Marvelli. *Anything that ends in four ones,* she kept telling herself as she rounded the corner of the bungalow. *One-one-one—*

"New Jersey!"

Loretta looked up. Lance was standing at the edge of the parking lot, bouncing a volleyball on the blacktop. He was smiling like a little dog who'd just done his duty and was proud of it.

"Lance," she said, trying to keep her voice down without whispering. She smiled, not knowing what else to say to him. Her pulse was beating jungle drums in her ears.

Lance stopped bouncing the ball and waved his hand over it as if it were a crystal ball. "New Jersey," he said in a fake spooky voice. "You are from New Jersey. The Amazing Lance knows all."

"You certainly are amazing, Lance." The smile was petrified on her face as she edged toward the parking lot.

"And that is not all," he said, continuing with the Bela Lugosi routine. "I seem to remember that you were living with a man who was a computer nerd. Is that Mr. Marvelli by any chance? Is the amazing Lance not correct, *Loretta?*"

Her stomach tightened when she heard him say her name. She tried to be cool, but she felt like throwing up.

"So," he said, going back to bouncing the ball, "you're name is Loretta, you're from New Jersey, and you're a cop. Right?"

She shook her head, wanting to strangle him. She glanced back at the front door to Martha Lee's apartment. If Martha Lee and her boyfriend heard this, they'd come out with guns blazing. And chances weren't very good that they'd hit the skinny little asshole by mistake. She was definitely the easier target.

"Close, Lance, but no cigar." She did a fast walk toward the parking lot, grabbing him by the arm and taking him with her. Unfortunately, he was wiry, and he squirmed out of her grip.

"Are you arresting me, Officer Loretta?" he shouted in the middle of the parking lot. "This feels like police brutality to me." He was laughing. He thought this was a riot.

Loretta turned and started across the lot. A phone, she needed to find a phone.

"Hey, what's the rush?" Lance zipped around her and got in her way. His bouncing ball was making a racket in the otherwise quiet lot. He was too damn loud.

"Look, Lance, I've had about enough—"

But then she heard them coming out of the bungalow. They were about twenty feet behind her, but she didn't dare turn around and look for fear that Martha Lee knew what she looked like.

"That was sure nice, honey bun," Loretta heard the boyfriend saying. "We gotta do that again soon."

"Sure," Martha Lee said. "But let's take care of that other thing first. Okay?"

"You got it, my dear. Consider it done."

Lance tilted his head to the side like a parrot. "What were you saying, Loretta? You've had about enough of what?"

"I—" Loretta couldn't get the words out.

They were coming this way, Martha Lee and her boyfriend the assassin. Loretta could hear their footsteps.

"I—I—"

They were right behind her.

"What, Loretta?"

"I—I've had just about enough of being overweight, Lance. I'm ready to get serious about losing weight." She took his arm again and led him across the parking lot.

"Fantastic!" he gushed. "I'm so glad to hear that, Loretta."

"That's right. I'm ready to do it. And it won't be like the last time." She was practically dragging him. Martha Lee and her boyfriend were crossing the parking lot. Loretta could hear them.

"So, Officer Loretta," Lance said, "how about starting off with a Scotch hose? I highly recommend it."

Loretta cringed. "How about something else?"

"Gotta clean out those toxins from your pores, honey. I am going to hound you to death until you do it." He was getting loud again.

"Okay, okay." She picked up the pace to get away from Martha Lee and her friend.

"Loretta, you'll be glad you did it when it's over."

"I wish it were over now," she said, walking faster.

Four ones, she kept thinking. *Four ones and Marvelli will come running.* As soon as she could ditch Lance, she'd call him.

Marvelli was at a pay phone outside a pizza parlor in a strip mall on the highway. Lawrence Temple was sitting in his gray Cutlass with the air-conditioning on, waiting for him. Marvelli turned his back on Temple. His hands were shaking.

"What do you mean Mommy isn't doing well?" He was talking to his daughter, Nina. She was on the verge of being hysterical.

"She was really bad this morning, Daddy. She couldn't breathe. Grandma called an ambulance, and they took her to the hospital. I'm scared, Daddy."

So am I, he thought.

"It's all right," he said. "Just calm down, Nina. I'm coming home. First flight I can get."

"What if she dies, Daddy?" Nina was sobbing. He could hear the panic in her voice.

"I'll be home tonight, Nina. I promise."

"Her face was all gray, and she couldn't talk. I didn't know what to do, Daddy." She was crying her eyes out. "She's going to die, isn't she?"

"Don't think that way, Nina. I keep telling you—positive thoughts, think positive thoughts. It helps Mommy."

"I'm afraid."

"Is Grandma home?" he asked.

"No, she's at the hospital. Mrs. Donahue from across the street is here. So's my friend Margaret."

"All right, tell them to stay with you until I get there. I'm on my way. I love you, sweetheart. Don't worry, it'll be all right. It will."

"Okay." But Nina didn't sound convinced. "I love you, Daddy. Come home as soon as you can."

Marvelli hung up the phone, feeling as if there were ropes pulled tight around his chest. His head was light, and he was breathing hard, trying to get enough oxygen out of the thick, humid air. Renée couldn't breathe either, he thought. Renée was having a hard time. She needed him.

He went back to Temple's car, the cold blowing air inside making him shiver. "Take me to the airport," he said to Temple. "Hurry up."

Temple gave him a stern look. "The airport? What's wrong?"

"My wife's in the hospital. I have to get to her."

"What's wrong?"

"She's dying!" Marvelli said, raising his voice. "Now will you please take me to the airport?"

"Sure. Of course." Temple put the car into reverse and backed out of the space. "But what about your partner?"

"Loretta can take care of herself."

"But—"

"But nothing," Marvelli snapped. "You've got five men

down here with you. You guys watch her. My wife is dying. I have to be with *her.*"

"Absolutely." Temple pulled out onto the highway and headed for Fort Myers.

"Hurry up, will ya, Lawrence? I'm worried." Marvelli was looking out the window, chewing on his bottom lip, thinking about Renée. "Come on, step on it."

"I'll get you there as fast as I can. Don't worry." He picked up his car phone. "I'll call the airport and see what flights are available. We'll get someone bumped if we have to, say it's a government emergency."

"Thanks."

As the strip malls gradually gave way to open fields of grass and ferns, Temple picked up speed. He spoke softly into his car phone as Marvelli stared out the window, worried sick.

"There's a Kiwi flight to Newark at seven-forty. We'll get you on that one. Okay?"

Marvelli nodded, half-listening. He was thinking about Renée, imagining her face the way it had been before chemo and radiation. *Oh, Christ,* he thought, clutching his stomach.

Temple was driving with the phone to his face, waiting for someone to get back to him. "Just tell me one thing, Marvelli. Is there anything I should know about Loretta being at the spa?"

Marvelli shook his head, biting his knuckle. Renée dead. He didn't even want to consider it.

"Don't worry then. We'll watch out for her." Temple went back to the phone, explaining to whoever was on the other end that this was a government emergency and he needed a seat on that plane to Newark.

But Marvelli wasn't listening to anything. All he could think about was Renée. And life without Renée. He closed his eyes, tilted his head back, and blew out a deep breath. A shudder gripped his chest and shook him to the core. *Jesus, no,* he thought. *No. . . .*

14

Rancho Bonita was deserted as Loretta moved through swishing ferns down a pebble path, heading for the big mirrored building where the WeightAway headquarters were located. She wasn't surprised that no one was around. Mealtimes at the fat farm were always like this. They didn't feed you much here, and there was no snacking allowed, so when chow was on, the guests flocked.

She walked as fast as she could, but it had suddenly gotten very humid, and it felt as if she were moving through Jell-O. But despite the heat and the sweat pouring down her face, she kept going. She was determined to finish this job and show all the wonderful men in her life that she didn't need them, that she could do it alone.

As she came toward a clearing where two paths crossed, Loretta slowed down. She knew Martha Lee's boyfriend was out gunning for her, but he didn't know who she was any more than she knew who he was. In all probability Martha Lee didn't know that Loretta was the one working undercover for the IRS; they'd never even met. But Lance was the one she was worried about. The little shit had remembered too much about her, and he had a big mouth. All she needed was for him to come bouncing out of the bushes, playing his guessing game within earshot of Martha Lee or her boyfriend, and that would be the end of that.

Loretta frowned as she cautiously entered the clearing and took the path to the left. Lance was probably out looking for her right now. He'd followed her into the sauna, talking her car off, then hung around doing back bends and squat thrusts as the masseuse gave her a massage, which actually would have been wonderful if Lance hadn't been there. Thank God the Jamaican dominatrix who ran the Scotch hose concession chased him out when he tried to follow them in there.

Loretta had managed to slip out a side door and escape the Scotch hose ordeal, going to the front desk at the main building to find a pay phone instead. She'd called Marvelli's beeper and left a number that ended in four ones, then waited in the lobby, keeping her eye on the front gate since that was the only way into Rancho Bonita. She pretended to be absorbed in *WeightAway* magazine, flipping through the personal testimonials and the obnoxious before-and-after photos of supposedly satisfied customers. It was all bullshit, and looking at all their smiling skinny faces in the pictures just aggravated her. They all looked scrawny and old to Loretta, like people wasting away from some killer disease. A little fat filled in the wrinkles, kept people looking young and healthy. Didn't these morons realize that?

The way Loretta figured, these people were only smiling because they'd spent so much money to get skinny, they had to convince themselves that they were happy and that this was what they'd wanted all along when, in fact, being skinny was not all that it's cracked up to be.

She'd gone through that stupid magazine cover to cover, waiting for Marvelli to show his chipmunk face. Almost half an hour she'd waited, and she was getting nervous. She looked suspicious just hanging around. All the other guests had places to go, things to do, forms of torture they had to endure before they were allowed to even look at food. Loretta decided she'd better look like she was hanging out in the lobby for a reason, so she went back to the pay phone and called her father in Arizona.

Big mistake.

"You're where, Loretta? Doing what?" His voice was like a madeleine caught in her throat, bringing back all those "wonderful" memories of her childhood. She could imagine him sitting out on the patio in Scottsdale, his snowy white hair set off by a deep desert tan.

"I'm in Florida, Dad," she said, cupping the receiver with her hand and keeping her voice down. "I'm on assignment. Investigative work. I've got a new job."

"Investigative work? You're a private eye now? What are you, crazy? I swear, Loretta, I think you do these things on purpose."

"No, I'm not a private eye, Dad, and I *do* do these things on purpose."

She closed her eyes and swallowed back a sob. *Thanks for the vote of confidence, Dad.*

"Christ, if you want to do detective work, why don't you do it for your sister? She must use private investigators all the time."

"Good idea. I'll give her a call." She didn't even bother to correct his mistaken impression. It wouldn't be worth explaining. He'd always hated the fact that she'd chosen to work in corrections, and if he knew she was with the Jump Squad, he'd have a fit.

"You sound sad, Loretta. What's wrong? Do you need money?"

She closed her eyes and shook her head. "No. I'm fine, Dad." He always said the same thing whenever she called: "You sound sad. Do you need money?" As if a handout from him would fix everything.

"Loretta, I was just on my way out the door. Can I call you back tomorrow?" He made it sound like a chore.

"No, I won't be near a phone, Dad," she said. "I'll call you soon, though. Bye."

"You take care of yourself, Loretta. And don't do anything stupid."

Loretta hung up the phone and would have laughed if she weren't so disappointed in him. *Don't do anything stupid.* What a laugh. According to her father, *everything* she'd ever done was stupid. The fact that she wasn't born her sister was the first stupid thing she'd done, and it had been downhill ever since. There was no pleasing him.

The path to WeightAway headquarters wound down a slight grade where the foliage was thick and the heavy air didn't move. It curved to the right, then to the left, then suddenly came out on a wide marble patio that bordered the ultra-modern three-story building. The late-day sun reflecting off the mirrored glass was so intense it was hard to look at. Loretta shielded her eyes and stayed in the shade at the end of the path. A small parking lot was at the front of the building by the road. There was only one vehicle in the lot, a white Jeep Cherokee. The WeightAway International logo was painted on the door—trim block lettering encircling a can of WeightAway Super-Thick Diet Shake and a steaming WeightAway Micro-Fast Complete Frozen Dinner. She remembered their tastes all too well. They both sucked.

Loretta eyed the Cherokee, figuring it went with a security guard who most likely was posted inside. She was going to have to sweet-talk her way past him somehow, but she wasn't exactly sure how. She could say she was related to Martha Lee and that Martha was meeting her here. Or maybe she could quickly flash her New Jersey Department of Corrections ID and say she was from Florida Corrections, running a background check on someone. Security guards are all wannabe cops, and a lot of times they'll bend over backward to cooperate with real law enforcement personnel. *That might work,* she thought. But who could she be seeing at this time of day? It was after five, and from the looks of the parking lot, everyone had gone home. Maybe she could just say she was checking up on someone in the accounting department, ask for the guard's help, and bring him into the caper. Make him her Dr. Watson, then make him some bullshit promise about helping him get a job with the state. It would sure save her a lot of time if she had someone who could show her around.

The side door of the building suddenly swung open, and Loretta stepped back into the foliage to hide. Three short, squat women in flower-print housedresses came out onto the patio, all of them looking guilty. They all had long, straight bangs that covered their eyebrows, and they were speaking Spanish. Loretta watched as one of them took a rock from a flower bed and propped the door open a crack. They went over to a stone bench at the edge of the patio, pulled out packs of cigarettes from the pockets of their housedresses, and all lit up. Their eyes darted around nervously, as if they were afraid they'd get caught. No doubt Roger Laplante, supreme leader of the body Nazis, forbid smoking anywhere in his domain. The cleaning ladies didn't dare sneak a butt inside, and even doing it out here was apparently risky.

Loretta stared at the door being held open with the rock. Getting in wasn't going to be so hard after all, she thought as she stepped out into the sunlight and crossed the patio, walking purposefully, as if she belonged there. The cleaning ladies dropped their hands behind their backs as if that would hide the smoldering evidence of their vice. Loretta nodded to them and kept walking, going right up to the door that was propped open and letting herself in. The cool, dry air-conditioned air was an instant relief as her eyes adjusted to the dim light inside. *That was easy,* she thought.

"Can I help you, ma'am?"

Loretta cringed. Crap!

"Yes, you can," she said without missing a beat. "I'm looking for the accounting department."

A tall white guy in a blue polyester blazer was walking toward her. He had a walkie-talkie in his hand but no gun or cuffs that she could see. "The building's closed, ma'am."

Loretta said the first thing that popped into her head. "I'm with the movie company." She left it at that, as if that should explain everything.

"Excuse me?" He was a young guy, twenty-five at the most. Blond crew cut, a lot of pimples, and very serious. Skinny but not wimpy—maybe lifted weights in his spare time. "I'm going to have to ask you to leave, ma'am. This building is off-limits."

Loretta ignored what he said and pretended to check her watch. "Has Mr. Schwarzenegger arrived yet?"

He furrowed his brow at her.

Loretta smiled at him. "No one told you we were coming, did they? I'm not surprised. We asked for as much privacy as possible."

"Mr. Schwarzenegger?"

She smiled again. "Yes. *That* Mr. Schwarzenegger."

"No one told me anything about this." He allowed himself a small smile. "Are you serious, ma'am? He's really coming here?"

"He'd better be." She looked at her watch again and craned her neck over his shoulder as if Arnold might be standing right there.

He turned around, just in case. "Nobody told me," he said. Somebody was squawking on the walkie-talkie in his hand, but he ignored it.

"Nobody told you because they probably didn't know anything about it themselves," she said. "Arnold doesn't like a big fuss when he's working."

"He's making a movie here?"

Loretta scrutinized him for a few seconds. "Unofficially? Yes."

"What's it called?"

"Oh, I really can't say."

"Well, what's it about?"

She smiled and shrugged. "Sorry. You know how it is."

He looked disappointed.

She checked her watch again and mumbled to herself, "Damn! They said he might be late." She touched the guard's forearm. "Would you be a doll and show me where the accounting offices are? Maybe we can save some time here."

He frowned. "Why do you want to go up there?"

"The scout's report said it would be a good location for a

particular scene in the movie, but I have to check the light and the view from the windows. It might not work with the special effects."

"Special effects?" The guard was suddenly a wide-eyed fifteen-year-old. "What special effects?"

She shook her head and shrugged.

"Oh, come on. Can't you just give me a hint?"

She sighed, mildly annoyed. "Take me to the accounting office first."

"You promise?"

"We'll see."

"All right." He led the way to the elevators, looking back at her and grinning as he walked. "It's up on 3."

An open elevator was waiting for them. They stepped in, and the guard pressed the "3" button. He was doing all he could to contain himself he was so giddy. But as the elevator doors closed, Loretta started to worry. What if there was someone up there who wasn't so gullible?

The elevator stopped on the top floor. "What's he like?" the guard asked as they got out. His walkie-talkie crackled again, and she clenched her fists, praying he wouldn't reach for it.

"So what's he like?" the guard repeated as they headed down a long corridor.

"Arnold? Oh, he's very sweet. Usually."

"Oh. Sure, I'll bet." The guard stopped at a doorway and pointed down to the end of the hall. "The accounting department starts here," he said, nodding toward the nearest office. "All the offices from here on are accounting."

She nodded, wondering how the hell she was going to get rid of him. She started mumbling to herself, wandering down the hall and glancing into all the small offices she passed. "Now which one were they talking about? The report said it had a nice view of palm trees."

"Well, they all have pretty much the same view, I think." The guard wanted to be helpful.

"Yes, but . . ." She kept looking, pretending to be looking

for something technical. "The special effects people need certain conditions—the angle of the light, the amount of sky in the shot, things like that."

All the offices were nearly identical: beige metal desk, posture chair with oatmeal upholstery, computer, printer, phone; a few had fax machines. Only the plants and the pictures set the rooms apart from one another.

She passed one that had a travel poster for Sun Valley with a skier schussing down a powdery sun-drenched slope.

The next one had a Grateful Dead poster on the wall and a dancing bears bumper sticker on the file cabinet.

The one after that had a framed photo of a little girl on the desk. On the bulletin board there was another photo of a fat woman wearing a silver cardboard birthday hat with a pink feather glued to the front. Loretta stopped and stared at it. She leaned into the doorway to get a better look. *My God,* she thought. It was exactly who she thought it was, Ricky Macrae, Martha Lee Spooner's ornery sister-in-law.

"You said you were going to tell me." The guard came up behind her.

"What?"

"You said you were going to tell me about the special effects," the guard reminded her. He'd done his part; now he wanted her to live up to her end of the bargain.

She pressed her lips together as if she had to give this some serious consideration. "All right," she finally said. "But do you promise to keep it to yourself?"

"I won't tell a soul."

"I don't want to see you blabbing on *Hard Copy* or any of those other shows. It'll mean my job if you do."

"I promise. I won't tell a soul."

She hesitated. "I don't know. . . ."

"Please?"

"Oh . . . all right. Dinosaurs."

His eyebrows shot up into his hairline. "Dinosaurs? Really?"

"Don't tell *anyone* I told you. Please."

But he wasn't listening. "Dinosaurs . . . wow! Hey, I'm just gonna take a wild guess, okay? With all the palms and stuff around here, I bet you're doing *Jurassic Park 3*. I know you're not gonna tell me, but I bet that's the movie you're making. I'm willing to bet."

She sighed and shook a finger at him. "You're very clever. You know that?"

"Yes! I knew it! I knew it!" He was very proud of himself.

The walkie-talkie crackled again with that distant, disembodied voice, and Loretta's stomach jumped.

"Listen—I didn't catch your name," she said.

"Craig."

"Craig, would you mind doing me a big favor?"

"What?"

"Would you go down and bring Mr. Schwarzenegger up when he arrives?"

"Sure. No problem."

"I want to start taking light readings. If that's okay with you."

"Sure, sure. Go right ahead." He was already on his way down the hallway, heading back to the elevators.

Thank God, Loretta thought.

As soon as he was out of sight, she went back into the office that had Ricki Macrae's photo pinned to the bulletin board. Loretta studied it for a second. Ricki was heavier in the picture than she had been at her mother's house the other day, but the bitchy expression was the same.

Loretta looked around the small office, trying to figure out what she could take that would make Lawrence Temple happy. Next to the computer there was a clear plastic file box full of computer diskettes, backups of Martha Lee's work no doubt. Perfect.

But as she reached for the box, intending to stuff her pockets with diskettes, she remembered something. She couldn't take anything because that would be theft, and any evidence gained that way couldn't be used in court. She could make copies if she could find some blank diskettes, but making copies took time. What if her buddy Craig came back and found her in there with the computer on? She'd have a hard time explaining that.

There was a small desktop copier on a side table. If she could find something good in Martha Lee's files, she could make copies. That would be better, she decided.

She glanced at the tall file cabinet, then spotted the upright files on Martha Lee's desk next to the framed picture of the little girl. Loretta sat on the edge of the desk and dragged her finger along the tabs, reading the labels: "Waitford, Inc.," "Tolliver & Sons," "M&B Foods," "Frankfurt Dairies," "Dennison Group." The names didn't mean anything to her, so she pulled out a file at random, "Lexington and Myers."

There wasn't much in the file, but the top sheet was an invoice, dated a few weeks back. It was for 5,000 pounds of "Beef Product." Loretta made a face at the euphemism. She was sure "Beef Product" meant all the parts of the cow that were left over after they took the good stuff. She remembered the hard gristly bits she'd always find in the WeightAway Micro-Fast Salisbury Steak Dinner.

She put the file back and pulled out another one, "Sullivan-Davis." She found invoices for tons of cod and was immediately reminded of the WeightAway frozen breaded fish fillets, which had the consistency of sandpaper but tasted like nothing.

The next file she checked was marked: "Caxton Farms." This one was for truckloads of peas. All the WeightAway frozen dinners had peas. She hated peas.

As she put this file back, her eye caught the first one in the line, "Alvarez Cocoa Co." She pulled it out and found another invoice, this one on fax paper. It was for $210,000 for . . . ninety tons of cocoa?

No way! she thought.

Loretta remembered the piss-poor excuse for chocolate that WeightAway used in their foods, and there was no way in hell it was the real thing. Maybe they used a little to give you the hint of chocolate, but it was mostly artificial. Christ, she'd read the ingredients listed on the sides of enough packages to know real from bogus. The Chocolate Creme Sandwich Cookies tasted like chalk. The Double Dutch Choco-Shake tasted like more chalk. The strip of chocolate frosting on the Almost Sinful Eclair had the consistency of an oil slick and tasted about the same. And the Black Forest Cake was a chemical mirage. It looked like the real thing, but it tasted like whipped mud.

Ninety tons of cocoa? Never! She had no idea how much chocolate could be made out of this much cocoa, but it seemed like an awful lot, a lot more than WeightAway would ever use. She decided to make a copy of this invoice. This was definitely fishy. It had to be some kind of scam, billing for nonexistent supplies, something like that. And either Roger Laplante was getting rooked or else he was taking part in it, pocketing money he claimed as a business expense.

She switched on the copier and listened to it grind as she waited for it to warm up. This would definitely give Lawrence Temple's mechanical pencil a hard-on, she thought.

But just as the copier quieted down and the green ready light flashed on, she heard the elevator doors opening down the hall. *Must be Craig,* she thought. She quickly switched off the copier and put the Alvarez Cocoa Company file back in the uprights. She'd have to get rid of him again. Maybe send him out for Evian for "Mr. Schwarzenegger." She moved over to the window and stared out at the treetops, pretending to be studying the view.

"Can I help you?"

Loretta looked over her shoulder, surprised to hear a female voice instead of Craig the guard's. Then she saw who it was.

Crap!

Martha Lee stared at the porker in her office, working hard to keep the pleasant Welcome-to-Rancho-Bonita smile on her face. "I'm afraid this building is off-limits to the guests, ma'am. The guard downstairs should've told you that."

"Oh, well . . . you see, I was hoping that I might, you know, maybe perhaps run into Mr. Laplante. I watch him on TV all the time. I was just hoping . . . well, you know."

This chubbette was full of shit, Martha Lee thought. The Roger Laplante groupies gushed, and they weren't shy about what they wanted. Roger was their guru, and they wanted to touch him. They needed to *connect* with him, as Roger said. This one was not a groupie.

Martha Lee stepped into the room and noticed a warm, vaguely chemical smell. She knew that smell; her copier had been on. *Shit!* she thought. *This little blimp is the spy from the IRS. She has to be.*

"I'm afraid you won't find Mr. Laplante here," Martha Lee said, holding the smile and extending her arm toward the door. "But I may be able to arrange a short meeting for you. If you'll come with me."

The little fattie came out from around the desk. "Oh, that would be wonderful," she said.

Oh, it sure will be, Martha Lee thought, her face aching from the smile. *Don't you worry about that.*

Loretta felt a little queasy as Martha Lee held the door open for her and they stepped out of the jungle humidity into the spa's air-conditioned main building. She couldn't figure out if Martha Lee was on to her or not. She was a pretty good actress if she did know. As they walked past the front desk, Loretta wondered where Martha Lee was leading her. Not to her boyfriend, Loretta hoped.

"I was thinking we might have dinner first, Mrs. Marvelli," Martha Lee said, leading the way. "Then we can go find Mr. La-plante. If he's not too busy."

"Fine." Loretta smiled at Martha Lee, wanting to put her in a choke hold and arrest her on the spot. But even if she could get Martha Lee to the airport, she knew Temple and his men would stop her.

"Are you on the intensive plan, Mrs. Marvelli?" Martha Lee asked.

"Excuse me?" Loretta wasn't listening.

"Are you staying with us on the intensive plan or the stan-dard plan?"

"Oh . . . the standard plan." The "intensive plan" was Rancho Bonita's deluxe package. The standard plan was for the plebes.

"Well, don't worry about it," Martha Lee said as she picked up her pace to get the next door ahead of Loretta. It was the smoked-glass door of the "restaurant," as they called it here. In fact, it was the private dining room where the guests on the intensive plan had their meals. Everyone else had to eat in the cafeteria in another building.

The restaurant's decor was old Me-hee-co, grand hacienda style, the kind of place Zorro was always escaping from. The floor was made of large terra-cotta tiles, and the walls were flan-colored stucco. The legs of the dark wood tables and high-back chairs were carved like fusilli. Blue-glazed urns held gracefully arching palms, strategically placed to give each table a discreet amount of privacy.

A slinky young woman in a sleeveless floor-length black shift and trendy chunky heels sauntered over to them. Her bowl-cut was so black and close to her head it could have been painted on. Her brows were hidden under her bangs, so Loretta couldn't tell what her attitude was.

"Two for dinner, Jasmine," Martha Lee said.

"And how shall I . . . ?" Jasmine eyed Loretta's shorts and left her question unfinished.

"Special guest account," Martha Lee said, smiling at Loretta.

Loretta smiled back. She wanted to smack this Jasmine kid.

"Right this way," Jasmine said, snatching up two menus from an antique side table as she sauntered into the dining room, swinging her nonexistent hips. Jasmine had no butt, and her breasts were melted-down single scoops of ice cream. She circled an empty table, trailing her hand like a game-show bimbo indicating the grand-prize washer and dryer. Loretta and Martha Lee chose their seats, and Jasmine handed them the menus. "Enjoy your meal," she said, trying to smile—but not very hard—before she sauntered away.

Martha Lee opened her menu. "The fish is always excellent here. Actually, everything is excellent here."

I'll be the judge of that, Loretta thought as she scanned the menu. Whenever she got nervous, she got hungry, and she was starving now.

But as she read the menu, she looked for anything that had chocolate in it, still wondering about that ninety tons of cocoa. Unfortunately, desserts weren't listed on the menu, which wasn't a big surprise, since every item had its fat, sodium, and calorie content listed right beside it. They probably didn't serve desserts other than fruit. So what was WeightAway doing with all that cocoa? She glanced at Martha Lee over the top of the menu, determined to get back to Martha Lee's office, so she could go through the rest of those invoices. She just wished she knew where Martha Lee's boyfriend was.

"Good evening, ladies." Their waiter arrived. He was a good-looking guy, trim and in his twenties, wearing a blousy white collarless shirt and black jeans. His dark hair was pulled back tight in a ponytail. "Can I get you something from the bar?"

Loretta knew he meant the juice bar. Liquor wasn't served at Rancho Bonita. Loretta had a yen for a glass of red wine, a zinfandel or a pinot noir, anything to calm her nerves. She also had a yen for penne à la vodka, a big piece of chocolate layer cake, and a cappuccino. That would really soothe her nerves. But she wasn't going to get that here.

"May I suggest the avocado daiquiri? It's our special tonight."

Loretta stared up at the waiter. He'd actually said it with a straight face.

"I'll have a cranberry cooler," Martha Lee said.

"And for you, ma'am?"

"A large orange juice."

The waiter lifted a clipboard and wrote down their orders. Loretta couldn't figure out why he had a full-size clipboard until she noticed that there was a calculator attached to it.

"Shall I take your orders now so you can tally, or would you like your drinks first?"

Tally? Loretta thought. *Tally what?*

"I'm sort of hungry," Martha Lee said to Loretta. "Shall we order now?"

"Sure." But Loretta still wanted to know what this tally business was all about. "You go ahead. I'm still deciding."

"All right." Martha Lee pointed to the menu as she ordered. "I'll have the mushroom pâté . . ."

The waiter scribbled in his pad, then punched numbers into the calculator.

". . . the arugula salad . . ."

More scribbling, more punching.

". . . and the pasta primavera."

The waiter scribbled, then punched. When he got the tally, he smiled down at Martha Lee and nodded approvingly. He turned to Loretta, who couldn't for the life of her figure out why he was adding up their bill at the beginning of the meal, especially since Martha Lee had already told Jasmine that they were eating on Roger Laplante's tab.

"And for you, ma'am?" the waiter asked.

"I'll have the shrimp bisque . . ."

Scribble, punch.

". . . the Caesar salad . . ."

Scribble, punch.

". . . and the vegetable lasagna."

Scribble, punch, *beeeep!* The calculator went off like a mini-car alarm. Loretta could see heads turning behind the palm fronds, people murmuring, coughing into their fists.

What the hell's going on? she wondered.

The waiter bent forward and whispered, "I'm afraid you've gone over."

"What?"

Martha Lee leaned over and pointed to the calorie counts in Loretta's menu. "You've gone over 600. That's all you're allowed."

"What do you mean that's all I'm allowed?"

"I take it no one explained our policy to you," the waiter said.

"It's my fault," Martha Lee intervened. "I apologize, Mrs. Marvelli. Intensive guests get a video when they first check in that shows them how to order. You see, how it works is, the calculator beeps whenever you go over 600 calories. Mr. Laplante came up with this idea himself."

The waiter elaborated. "It's an incentive to teach our guests how to order sensibly when eating out, ma'am."

"Like negative conditioning," Loretta said, struggling to keep a lid on her temper.

"I'm not sure what you mean, ma'am."

"It's like giving a rat an electric shock when you don't want him to eat the food pellets."

"Oh. . . . Well, I wouldn't know anything about that, ma'am."

"It's no problem," Martha Lee said quickly. "Why don't we just start all over again?"

Loretta watched her face, looking for signs of ridicule.

"Ma'am, may I suggest you substitute the mushroom pâté for the bisque and take a half-portion of lasagna?"

"I don't like mushrooms." Loretta was getting angry.

And I want a whole *portion of lasagna,* she thought.

"All right then," he said, reading the menu over her shoulder. "How about starting with the celery tart, then the Caesar salad—but without the dressing—and the whole-portion lasagna?"

"How about *with* the dressing?"

"Very well. We'll give it a try." He punched in the calories.

Beep!

More murmuring behind the palms.

Loretta could feel her face burning.

"How about if we—?"

Loretta overrode him. "How about if we just skip the appetizer?"

"All right." He went to work on the numbers.

Beep!

Louder murmuring. Loretta wanted to die.

"You do realize, ma'am, that your orange juice is included in the tally?"

At the next table an incredibly fat man with a shiny bald head was stuffing spinach leaves into his mouth as he peered through the potted palms, staring at her. He wasn't the only one staring.

Loretta wanted to walk right out, but everyone was looking at her now. "All right," she said, struggling to control her voice. "Let's try this: the miso soup . . ."

She hated miso soup. Dirty water with slimy tofu cubes floating in it.

". . . the spinach salad, no dressing . . ."

To Loretta, having salad without dressing was like driving a car without oil. It just didn't go.

". . . and the red-pepper-and-kale stir-fry on quinoa."

She wasn't even sure what the hell quinoa was.

He tallied it all up, smiled, and nodded.

Humpty Dumpty at the next table stopped staring at her. Loretta glanced up at the other diners. No one was paying attention anymore, thank God. She knew this would work. If she ordered the most disgustingly nutrocious foods on the menu, things that would normally have been her absolute last choices, she'd stay under the limit. She knew from experience.

I wonder if I have enough calories left for a plain cup of tea, she thought. *Maybe a hair shirt and a whip to go with it.*

"I'll be right back with your drinks," the waiter said before he left.

Loretta and Martha Lee smiled pleasantly at each other, sipping from their water glasses, but mentally Loretta was painting vertical bars over Martha Lee's face. She had to get back to Martha Lee's office to Xerox that cocoa invoice.

The other diners started to murmur again, and Loretta immediately thought she'd done something else wrong. But Humpty

Dumpty at the next table wasn't staring at her this time. She followed his gaze to the maître d's station. A tall man in a peacock blue sports jacket was standing with Jasmine. He had his back to the dining room, but when he turned around, Loretta found out what all the whispering behind hands was all about. It was Roger Laplante, Mr. WeightAway himself.

He looked weirder in person than he did on TV, she thought. His skin was an unnatural caramel color, and his peaked hairdo looked like well-browned meringue. The weirdest thing about him was his eyes—they were too close together. It made him look like a dog that couldn't be trusted.

Suddenly Loretta remembered the $2,800 this place had rooked her out of the last time she was here. That figure was permanently imprinted on her brain, like a cattle brand.

Across the room Jasmine was pointing to their table, and Laplante fixed his beady eyes on them. His expression was hard to read as he approached. It was somewhere between urgent concern and where-have-you-been-all-my-life. Loretta remembered that about him from his infomercials. His facial expressions never quite matched what he was saying.

He came up to the table and looked at Loretta but talked to Martha Lee. "I got your message, Martha."

"Good," Martha Lee said.

Loretta's heart was thumping. *Message about what?* she wondered.

"This is Mrs. Marvelli, Roger. She's a guest here, and she's been dying to meet you."

Loretta tried to act awestruck and hoped she was convincing. "Mr. Laplante, this is a real pleasure. I see you on television all the time."

And I always turn you off, she thought.

"It's very nice to meet *you*, Mrs. . . ."

"Marvelli," Martha Lee prompted.

"Yes," Laplante said. He was giving her a funny look. Loretta couldn't read him at all. Was he on to her, too?

"Mrs. Marvelli was over at the cube, hoping to find you there," Martha Lee said. "That's where I found her."

"Really." His beady eyes widened as much as they could. "That was awfully naughty of you, Mrs. Marvelli. Guests are asked to stay out of the office complex. Only because there are no classes or beauty treatments there," he added quickly.

"I know," Loretta said, trying to be contrite, "but I am a big fan of yours, and I just thought—well, you've been such an inspiration to so many people, I was hoping maybe a little of that would rub off on me if I got to meet you."

She couldn't believe she'd said that.

Laplante pulled up a chair and sat on the edge of it, getting up close to Loretta's face. "I understand how you feel, Mrs. Marvelli. I really do. But you're not alone. You do understand that, don't you?" He laid his hand over hers. She fought the urge to pull it away.

"I do understand, but sometimes—you know—it's hard."

Loretta looked into his face, pretending to be fascinated with him, but the only thing she could focus on was the overpoweringly minty smell of his breath and the touch of his hand on top of hers.

The waiter returned, poker-faced now because the big boss was at the table. He set down the drinks and appetizers, and Loretta was miffed as soon as she saw the portions. Her orange juice was in a regular-size glass. She'd expected a tall glass. After all, it was dinner. And her miso soup came in a gorgeous hand-painted blue-and-white bowl that was about the size of a teacup, and it wasn't even full. She looked over at Martha Lee's mushroom pâté. It was a gray-brown square, smaller than a Chunky.

"Can I get you something, Mr. Laplante?" the waiter asked.

"Yes. The carotene cocktail, Caesar salad, and lasagna."

"Yes, sir." The waiter went back to place the order without writing it down.

Loretta glared at his back. Why hadn't he used his little bleeping calculator for Laplante's order?

She stared down into her soup. There was a odd-looking green thing in it. It looked like a leaf, but it was perfectly square.

"Please don't wait for me," Roger Laplante said. "Go ahead and eat."

Loretta picked up her soupspoon and noticed that it was was half the size of a normal soupspoon. The forks and knives were small, too. She'd forgotten about that. Another WeightAway innovation. With smaller utensils, you had to take more bites, creating the illusion that you were eating more than you actually were. "Feel full on half the intake." That's what it said on the box that WeightAway flatware came in. She'd bought a set when she first went on the program. Another goddamn rip-off.

Martha Lee picked up a tiny knife and spread some pâté on a pale, brittle cracker. She took a bite and raised her eyebrows. "Very rich," she said. "I don't think I can finish all this. Would anybody like to try some?" She lifted the edge of the plate.

Roger gave her a disapproving scowl and waved it off. "No sharing. It makes the tally meaningless."

"You're right; you're right," Martha Lee said. "It's just that I hate to see good food go to waste."

"Better to throw it out than carry it around on your body for the rest of your life," Laplante declared.

"You're right, Roger. You're right," Martha Lee agreed.

Loretta looked at skinny little Martha Lee out of the corner of her eye, a minispoonful of miso broth poised in front of her lips. She wanted to throw up on the two of them.

She took a sip of miso soup, trying not to stare at that green thing floating in her bowl. She wondered how the hell she was going to get away from these two.

And how she was going to get back to Martha Lee's office.

And how she was going to survive this meal.

After dinner Martha Lee went back to her office and booted up her computer. She'd left "Mrs. Marvelli" with Roger to let them get acquainted over roasted-grain coffee substitute. When dear

Loretta had gone to the bathroom, Martha Lee told Roger that she was pretty sure Loretta was an undercover agent from the IRS and that he should keep her busy while she did some checking. Roger started to hyperventilate, but she convinced him to chill out and just keep Loretta occupied for a while.

After leaving the restaurant, Martha Lee had gone straight to the front desk to get Loretta's husband's MasterCard number from her registration. She was checking with an on-line credit agency now to see if she could get a history on the Marvellis.

Staring at the screen, she picked out two more cheese curls from the open cellophane bag in her lap. *You could starve to death on the portions they serve around here,* she thought as she crunched down on the curls. She felt as if she'd only had a half—hell, a *third* of a meal. Thank God she kept a private stash of real food in her desk.

As she stared at the blank blue screen, she wondered how Roger and Loretta were doing. Roger had poured on the charm during dinner, but Martha Lee hoped he didn't go overboard. If he paid *too* much attention to Loretta, she'd know that they'd figured out who she was.

She glanced over at the upright files on her desk and frowned. She still hadn't paid the Alvarez bill yet, and now she was afraid to. What if the IRS had some way of tracking wire transfers? They might block it, thinking that Roger was siphoning money out of the country. She could overnight a check to Luis, but it would take a week for the check to clear. A lot could happen in a week. The IRS could barge in and freeze their assets. Even if they didn't come crashing through the doors with their guns drawn, they would examine the books, and they'd find a recent payment for ninety tons of cocoa. Roger would hit the ceiling when they confronted him with it. He'd deny ever having authorized such a purchase, which was true.

Then the shit would really hit the fan. The finger would be pointed right back at her. And if she knew that little worm Roger, he'd swear he didn't know anything about anything, that it was all her doing, that if anything illegal was going on at Weight-

Away—and there was plenty—ole Martha Lee must be the one who was responsible. And knowing Rog, she knew he could make that story fly. He was very persuasive that way. And it wouldn't take the feds long to figure out that Martha Lee "Sykes" was really Martha Lee Spooner, ex-con and current parole violator. The feds would nail her ass to the wall, and ole Rog would slide on by, slick as ever.

The computer screen suddenly came to life, words appearing behind an invisible cursor racing from left to right and back again. Martha Lee crammed two more cheese curls into her mouth and let them dissolve on her tongue as she read the credit history, wading through the unfamiliar abbreviations.

It gave Frank Marvelli's Social Security number and his address in Point Pleasant Borough, New Jersey. It said he was married, but it didn't give his wife's name.

Damn! She shoved two more cheese curls into her mouth and scrolled down.

According to the credit history, this Marvelli guy wasn't real quick about paying his bills. He was a month or two past due on his Sears and Macy's accounts, his Sunoco card—she scrolled down again—Exxon, Mobil . . .

Hang on.

She leaned forward and read the Mobil listing more carefully. There were two cards listed on that account, the second one to a "Marvelli, Renée."

Who's this Renée? Martha Lee thought. It should be in Loretta's name. Unless this Renée was a daughter. But was Loretta old enough to have a daughter who could drive? Doubtful, but maybe the kid was from a first marriage.

Martha Lee scrolled back up to the top of the file, to the abbreviations she didn't understand. She took a closer look and found "Dep/ F 11." Dependents/ Female, age 11?

An eleven-year-old wouldn't have a gasoline credit card. So who was this Renée?

Martha Lee scrolled back down to where she'd been and kept reading. There were two more department store accounts.

She scrolled down again, and her eye caught an unusually high dollar amount: $8,989.13. The creditor was Shore Medical Center. She kept reading. "Marvelli, Renée/ int cr 3/ sem-pri 16."

This Renée had been in the hospital. Three days in intensive care, sixteen in a semiprivate room.

Martha Lee scrolled down to the next entry. "Atlantic Anesthesiology Group—prep rad mas—20% co-pay, $277."

The woman had had a radical mastectomy. Jesus.

Martha Lee read the next entry: "Fine and Douglas, Radiologists—18 ses—20% co, $1,787.58."

Radiology treatments. Martha Lee scrolled down again. More unpaid medical bills. And all for Renée Marvelli. She clutched her own breast at the thought of a radical mastectomy. Poor woman. She was one sick puppy.

But what about Loretta the chubbette? Even if Loretta was a nickname, there was no way she could be Mrs. Renée Marvelli. They didn't make implants that big. People on radiology waste away to nothing. This Loretta was a long way from wasting away. A *long* way.

Martha Lee crunched down on another cheese curl. Loretta was the spy, all right. She had to be. Shit. . . .

She glanced over at her uprights, biting her bottom lip. She was going to have to risk wiring the money to Luis. Loretta had been in here. The copier had been turned on. No telling what she'd made copies of. The ledgers that Martha Lee was supposed to have fixed for Roger were in her desk drawer. That's probably what Loretta wanted. But there was no telling how much she'd Xeroxed. Loretta could hide a goddamn phone book in her cleavage.

"Martha! Martha! Are you here?"

Shit! It was Roger. He was coming down the hall, yelling for her like a maniac.

She glanced at the photo of Becky on her desk, and her heart sank. When the hell was she going to get a chance to wire that money? Oh, Jesus. . . .

"Martha!"

Oh, frig you, you big douche bag, she thought, glaring at the doorway. She crumpled up the bag of cheese curls and shoved them under her desk, wiping her fingers on the seat of the chair.

"Martha!" Roger appeared in her doorway, white as a ghost. "Is she the one? Is it that Loretta?"

"Where is she? What did you do with her?"

"I sent her off for a seaweed wrap. On me. But is she the one?"

"Yes, I think she is."

"What're we going to do, Martha?" He looked like he was going to wet his pants.

She put her finger to her lips, then picked up a pen and scribbled on a scratch pad: "Don't talk. Room may be bugged." She handed the pad to Roger.

He chewed on his fist, staring at the pad, shaking his head.

"Don't panic," she mouthed silently, then wrote another message on the pad: "Go down to patio. I'll meet you in 5 min."

He read it and nodded. "I'll meet you," he mouthed, pointing down at the floor.

She nodded and waved him off, then waited until she heard him get on the elevator. This was bad, she thought. This bitch Loretta was screwing everything up. She had to be stopped.

Martha Lee reached into her purse on the floor and pulled out her wallet. There was a scrap of paper with a phone number and a room number on it. She picked up the phone and dialed. It rang five times.

"Yeah?"

"Is this the Sunny Days Motor Court?"

"Yup."

"Room 6, please."

"I'll see if they're in."

Martha Lee frowned. *They? Joe's not by himself?*

The phone rang three times before someone picked up.

"What do you want?" It was a woman's voice. Real nasty.

"Is Joe there?"

"And who wants to know?"

The blood drained out of Martha Lee's face as her gaze rose to her "fat" picture pinned to the bulletin board. It was Ricky.

"Who is this?" Ricky demanded. "Say something."

Martha Lee hung up, her heart slamming in her chest. Torpedo Joe Pickett was here with Ricky Macrae. Ricky must be the one who'd hired Joe, not Tom Junior, because Ricky hated her guts. And if Martha Lee knew Ricky, she'd make sure Joe did the deed. Shit! Martha Lee knew she had to get out of there fast.

But then she looked at the framed picture of her daughter. *What about Becky?* she fretted. *What about the cocoa money?* Banks were closed now. She couldn't wire the money until tomorrow. If she was still alive tomorrow.

Unless the IRS got her first. Thanks to Loretta. A shooting pain zinged through Martha Lee's stomach. Her chest felt tight.

Her heart was pounding out of control. She leaned over the side of her chair and pulled out her bottom drawer all the way, reaching past the bag of rubber bands and the box of staples, past the bag of Junior Mints, the Pepperidge Farm Chocolate Chunk Cookies, and the can of Planter's Mixed Nuts, to the very back of the drawer. She burrowed her hand under a messy stack of loose plain envelopes and pulled out a chrome-finish .22 Browning automatic. It was just like the one she kept in her night table.

She put the gun in her handbag, covering it with some used tissues. Her hands were shaking. The gun made her nervous, but if she had to, she'd use it on anyone who got in her way.

She picked up her bag and stood up, a lump in her throat as she stared at the photo of Becky. *Don't worry, sweetheart,* she thought. *No one's gonna stop me. No one.*

"Joe! Joe!" Ricky was in the other room, yelling her head off.

"What?" Torpedo Joe was sitting on the toilet, reading the "For Sale" ads in the Fort Myers paper, looking at the motorcycle listings.

"Do you know who just called?" she yelled through the door.

He rubbed his stubbly neck. *Can't even take a shit in peace with this woman,* he thought.

"Are you listening to me, goddammit?"

"Yes, I'm listening."

"That was Martha Lee on the phone. She wanted to talk to you." Ricky banged the door open and glared down at him from the doorway. She wasn't wearing a thing. All he had on were his underpants, but they were down around his ankles.

"How'd she know to call you here?" Ricky demanded. "And what the hell's she want with you anyway? You said you didn't see her when you went over to that Rancho Bono place."

Joe rubbed his neck again. He had told Ricky that, hadn't he? Well, he couldn't exactly tell her the truth, which was that

Martha Lee had the sweetest little titties he'd ever seen, and that for such a little bitty person she sure knew what she was doing in bed. He couldn't tell Ricky *that,* now could he? She certainly wasn't going to be able to appreciate his circumstance. You had to have a man's unique perspective to understand why he'd slept with Martha Lee instead of killed her the way he was supposed to.

"You're not answering me, Joe."

All Ricky needed was a rolling pin in her hand, Joe thought. That's the way she'd been acting ever since they got down here. Why, why, why? She questioned everything he did and even wanted to know everything he was thinking. It was a bad frame of mind for a woman to be in.

"Joe!"

"Ricky," he finally said with a sigh, "we just performed an act of beauty back there in that bed. My feelings for you were solid and positive until you started yakking at me. Why're you trying to ruin that oh-so-beautiful mood?" He wished she'd close the door, so he could finish his business.

"Don't give me any of your bullshit, Joe. Why is that bitch calling here looking for you? What're you up to?"

Joe dropped the newspaper and showed her the innocence of his open palms. "Do you mind if I have a little privacy while I take care of my sanitary needs? I'll be right out, and we can discuss it then."

Ricky sneered at him before she slammed the door shut. Joe stood up and pulled out an arm's length of toilet paper. *Shit,* he thought as he wound the paper around his hand. Why'd Martha Lee have to call here? Women were nothing but complications. They *liked* to make things complicated. Men liked to keep things simple.

He bent over and thought about that some more. This wasn't a complicated situation, he told himself. But Ricky and Martha Lee wanted to make it complicated. Basically, he had just two things to do: kill this IRS person for Martha Lee, then kill Martha Lee. Only thing complicated about it was that he had to make sure he got paid from Martha Lee for the first killing before he turned around and killed her to get his second fee from Ricky. That was the only tricky part. Except for the fact that Martha Lee was awful sweet to him and Ricky was being a bitch on wheels. Martha Lee may be a liar and a cheat, but she sure was a honey pie. To his mind, eliminating such a superior specimen of femininity would be a damn shame.

Of course on the other hand, there was biker honor at stake here. Ricky had hired him first, and she was representing her brother, Tom Junior, a true brother of the open road. Joe wasn't taking care of Martha Lee for just Ricky; it was for a fellow biker.

But Martha Lee was awful nice, the kind of woman he'd like to look up whenever he happened to be in the area—

But see? This was how women made things complicated. Well, dammit, it wasn't complicated. He was gonna stick to his plan. Two hits, two fees, simple as that. Get himself a decent hog, then head west. Simple.

He threw the toilet paper in the john and flushed it.

"What the hell you doing in there?" Ricky yelled through the door.

"Put your stopwatch away, Ricky. I'm finished." He washed his hands and dried them on a facecloth, the only unused towel they had left. "Now what's the big deal?" he said, coming out of the bathroom.

Ricky was lying on the unmade bed, still naked, pouting at the TV set. He was about to get in with her so they could talk when he suddenly noticed something on the sheets on her side. It was a goddamn pistol-grip shotgun. *Holy shit,* he thought.

"Ricky," he said, holding his position, wishing he weren't in his skivvies, "what's bothering you? Let's talk about it." First move she made, he was gonna dive for the shotgun.

She didn't budge, though. Just pouted at the TV with her arms crossed over those big jugs of hers. He didn't dare take his eyes off her, but he could hear what she was watching on TV. One of those true-life cop shows. People getting arrested, crying and whining, kids in their underwear balling their eyes out, people making each other miserable, and the cops just making it worse. He hated those shows.

"I bought it for you," she mumbled, not looking at him.

"What?"

"I bought the goddamn gun for you. I thought you'd like it."

He inched closer to the bed. "You bought it for me? Where?"

"There was a guy out in the parking lot this morning selling stuff out of his trunk. You were still asleep."

He moved a little closer and got a better look at the weapon. It was a twelve-gauge pistol-grip Mossberg 500. Not new, but nice. He wondered if it was the six-shot model or the eight. He looked at pouting Ricky and suddenly felt like a real piece of shit. See? This was what women did. They made things complicated.

He picked up the shotgun and got into bed, leaning against the headboard. He wanted to check out the shotgun, but he knew he'd better pay attention to Ricky first.

"Thank you," he said.

She didn't say, "You're welcome."

On the TV set some dickhead highway patrolman was hassling a kid for speeding, browbeating the kid because he'd smelled pot in the car. He was wearing one of those dickhead Smoky the Bear hats.

"I said thank you, Ricky," Joe repeated. "I really mean it. I'm not used to getting presents, but this is one mighty fine weapon."

No response.

He held the shotgun by the barrel and circled her big boobie with the butt of the pistol grip. "I might even use this on Martha Lee. If you want me to."

She huffed her shoulders and moved her tit away. It jiggled real nice.

He reached for her tittie again, but she buried it under her crossed arm. "Look, Ricky," he said. "I gave Martha Lee this phone number for a reason. How'm I gonna shoot her over there with all those people around? I was thinking I could lure her out here and do it out in the woods where no one'll hear nothing."

"Bullshit," she grumbled, still staring at the TV.

"I swear to Christ, honey bun. That was my plan. Lure her out here, then do the deed—"

"Don't lie to me, Joe." She unfolded her arms and finally showed what she was holding, pointing it in his face. "I'm not in the mood for your crap, Joe." She had that itty-bitty two-shot derringer in her hand, the one she'd pulled on him up at her mama's farm, two itty-bitty barrels right in front of his face.

"Now, Ricky, why're you pulling a gun on *me?* I thought we were like *amigo* and *amiga* in this thing here."

"Shut up."

"I thought you had left your little popper home. Don't you think I can protect you?"

She just glared at him.

"So why'd you bring it? You're hurting my feelings here."

"I brought it because of that parole-officer bitch who pulled her gun on me at my mama's house, that's why. I'm not gonna let that ever happen to me again. She just better hope I never run into her. From now on, anybody screws with me, they're gonna be sorry. Including you, Joe." She jammed the little thing into the braid under his lip.

He backed away from it slowly, knowing he couldn't get the shotgun up fast enough. Besides, he didn't even know if the shotgun was loaded. "Baby doll," he said, "the only screwing around I want to do is right here with you in this bed." He tried to get to her tit again, hoping he could soothe the savage beast, but he could just barely reach her with the very end of his middle finger.

She jammed the derringer back under his lip. "I'm not kidding, Joe."

"I don't believe you are, honey bun," he said, trying to talk normal with that little gun pressed up against his lip.

Complicated, he thought, wishing he could get his hands around her neck, but not daring to try with that itty-bitty, mother-loving derringer still pinned to his face. *That's the way women always have to have it. Complicated.*

"You planning on staying like this all day?" he mumbled, frozen in place.

Marvelli sat on the edge of the hospital bed, trying to hold onto Renée's hand, but she kept pulling it away.

"Will you cool it?" she scolded. "I'm not gonna die."

But Marvelli wasn't so sure about that. She looked terrible. Her cheeks were sunken, and her skin was yellow-gray. Her voice was just a raspy whisper, and her eyes kept going in and out of focus. They cleared up and focused whenever he aggravated her, though, so he tried to keep it up just to keep her going, but he was having a hard time kidding around. He was worried sick that this might be the end of the line. He'd never seen her this bad.

He took the plastic glass of water from the night table and held the straw to her mouth, but she turned away and made a face. "Will you stop?" she said. "You're forgetting all your lines. You're supposed to tell me not to die or else."

His throat was tight. "All right"—he took a sip of water—"don't die or else."

"Or else what?"

"Or else . . . I don't know." If he said another word, he knew he'd break down and start blubbering, and he didn't want to do that, not in front of her.

"Hey"—she took his hand—"you better buck up, pal. I can't do everything, you know."

"Yeah . . . I know."

He stared at the IV bag hanging from a pole next to the bed, a long tube leading down into Renée's skinny arm. He thought of it as an hourglass, time running out.

The woman in the next bed started to cough, a deep, wet cough that went on for a full minute or more. Marvelli couldn't see her because the curtain was drawn. "What's her story?" he whispered to Renée.

"Lung cancer," Renée said, shaking her head gravely. "And she still smokes."

He could tell from Renée's expression that she wasn't giving her roommate long to live. That was the amazing thing about Renée—she could distance herself from other sick people. They were sick, but she wasn't. She just wasn't feeling particularly well, that's all. Marvelli had never been able to figure out if this was extreme positive thinking or an elaborate system of denial.

Suddenly he noticed the wallpaper. It was a pattern of tiny bouquets of red, blue, and yellow flowers, thousands of them, and suddenly it made him mad. The whole room with its comfortable chairs and its cheery curtains made him furious. He would've preferred a regular sterile hospital room where they treated the patients like broken clocks—fixed 'em up and got 'em out. But this homey decor was bullshit. It was for the terminal patients, the ones who would be checking out soon. The hospital was trying to make the last days a little nicer for the hopeless cases. Like the lady with lung cancer behind the curtain.

"Stop," Renée said.

"Stop what?"

"You're driving yourself crazy. I can see it in your face. Just stop."

"What're you talking about?"

She closed her eyes as if she were suddenly dizzy and waited until it passed. "I'm not going to die. It's *my* goddamn body, *my* life. Okay?"

He touched her cheek with the backs of his fingers. "Don't get upset."

She turned away from his touch. "Don't baby me. I know what's going on. It's not my time. I'll know when it is, and I'll let you know."

"But what if—?"

"Trust me. I know. It's my body. It lies and it cheats, but I know how it operates." She squeezed his hand. "Trust me."

Can I really? he wondered, circling her knuckles with his thumb.

His beeper suddenly went off in his pocket. He reached for

it automatically, then stopped himself before he looked at it. He shouldn't be worrying about work, not now, not here.

"Go ahead, look at it," Renée said, reading his mind. "Stop being so gooney."

He looked at the readout on his beeper and didn't recognize the number at all. *What area code is 305?* he wondered. Then he saw the last four digits—1111. Shit! It was Loretta. She was in trouble.

"What?" Renée's eyes were suddenly sharp and focused.

"It's Loretta," he said. "Something's wrong."

"Where? In Florida?"

"Yeah." He reached for the beige phone on the bed table. "I gotta call this IRS guy down there and tell him to go check—"

"No, *you* go." Renée held onto his sleeve to keep him from putting the phone to his ear. "*You* go."

"But I gotta call this guy Temple and tell him—"

"Call him, but then *you* have to go. How could you just leave your partner on the job in another state all by herself? Are you crazy?"

"I came back to see *you*, Renée."

"I don't care. You shouldn't have."

"But I was worried about you."

"You're always worried. What else is new? Call this IRS guy, then you get yourself back down there."

"But—"

"I'm okay. *I will not die.* Trust me, will you? If this were really serious, I'd tell you. In two days I'll be back home."

"But—"

She looked him in the eye. "Do you trust me or don't you?"

Her eyes were sharp and intense. There was even a little color in her cheeks now.

"Of course I trust you."

But what if you don't *know?* he thought. *Death doesn't call ahead. It just shows up. Right?*

"Get your ass down there."

He thought about Loretta down there on the fat farm, wondering what the emergency could be. Then he remembered that Torpedo Joe was down there.

Shit.

He squeezed Renée's hand and glanced down at the four ones on his beeper.

"You promise you're not gonna die?"

Renée turned away and coughed into her pillow. "I promise. . . . Now don't ask me again."

Marvelli looked into her sallow face, then looked at the phone. He didn't know what to do.

17

Loretta was getting worried. *Where the hell is Marvelli?* she wanted to know as she followed Martha Lee through the indoor gym where dozens of guests were grunting and groaning, jiggling their arm fat to lift barbells and hand weights, risking their spinal disks to move stacks of iron bricks on Nautilus machines, heaving their haunches as they climbed Stairmasters, huffing and puffing and racing to nowhere on stationary bicycles. Just watching this sweaty circus of false hopes made her anxious. *Come on, Marvelli,* she thought. *Stop fooling around.*

"Don't you have to work today, Martha?" Loretta asked, straining to remain pleasant while hoping Martha Lee would fall in a hole. She was wearing a pair of skin-tight black bike shorts and a snug-fitting fuschia T-shirt tied in a knot at her waist.

"I'm taking the morning off," Martha Lee said. "I thought I'd work out a little. I'm feeling a little fat today."

Loretta glared at Martha Lee's shapely little butt as she walked ahead. If she was feeling a little fat today, what was Loretta supposed to be feeling? A little global?

Loretta's stomach growled, and not just because of the paltry breakfast—a quarter of a cantaloupe, two wafer-thin slices of toasted bagel with WeightAway fat-free cream cheese (which looked *and* tasted like Spackle), and a half-cup of the dishwater they called coffee. She still couldn't figure out whether Martha Lee was on to her or not. If she was, she was taking her time doing something about it. The woman had shown up at Loretta's bungalow early this morning, taken her to breakfast, and then arranged it with the body Nazis to get Loretta released from the boot-camp schedule that all the guests were supposed to follow. Martha Lee said she wanted to give Loretta a personal tour of Rancho Bonita, so that she could "take advantage of everything the spa had to offer." Martha Lee was sticking to Loretta like glue, but Loretta couldn't figure out why. If she'd figured out that Loretta wasn't here to lose weight, wouldn't Martha Lee just sic her boyfriend on her? Unless Laplante had ordered Martha Lee to stay close, so Loretta couldn't go snooping around the cube again.

Across the gym someone started counting out loud, and instinctively Loretta stopped and turned away, fearing that it was that goddamn Lance. She listened for a second, then realized it wasn't him, but that was no relief. The little pest could pop out of nowhere, and he'd already remembered too much about her. All she needed was for him to show up with Martha Lee around. He'd start in with his guessing-game crap, blabbing about her being in Corrections. That's all Martha Lee needed to hear. She'd be out of here in a heartbeat, and that would be the end of that. Unless her boyfriend the killer ended it first.

"Loretta?"

"Hmmm?"

Martha Lee had her hand on Loretta's forearm. "Honey, you look like you're a million miles away. Is something wrong?"

"No. Nothing." But Martha Lee was still staring at her, obviously not believing that there was nothing wrong. "I . . . I just don't think this will work for me," Loretta added with a sigh.

"What won't work for you, honey?"

"You know. All this." Loretta waved her hand at the exhausted exercisers. "I know WeightAway works for some people, but I just don't think I can . . ." Loretta let her words trail off.

"You don't think you can what, Loretta?"

Loretta wanted to smack that concerned look right off Martha Lee's face. She didn't want to say it.

"You don't think you can what, honey?"

Loretta gritted her teeth. "Lose weight."

"Oh, sure you can. I did it. So can you."

Loretta's eyes narrowed. She didn't know what she hated more—bullshitters or cheerleaders.

"What you need is to change your frame of mind. You're thinking of this as an ordeal, and that's bad. You need to think of this as a vacation. A vacation for your body."

"Hmmm . . . maybe. . . ."

"You know what would be good for you?"

"What?"

"A full-body salt scrub."

"Really?" Loretta tried to keep from making a face, but on the inside she was screaming at Marvelli for not rescuing her. A full-body salt scrub sounded like state-sponsored torture.

"Yes," Martha Lee said with a sharp nod. "A salt scrub and then a Dead Sea mud bath. That is the most *soothing* thing."

"I don't know, Martha. . . ."

But then she heard a loud voice behind her, and this time she was certain it was Lance. "Okay, people, are we motivated today?"

"YES!!!"

Loretta looked over her shoulder. Lance was standing on a treadmill, facing a small band of the brainwashed, all of them on similar treadmills. Unlike the others struggling with machinery around them, this group looked like they wanted to be here.

"Are we going to burn away some of that nasty old fat?"

"YES!!!"

"We've got one empty treadmill here," Lance shouted across the gym. "Who wants to join us? Who wants to walk all over their nasty old fat? Anybody?"

"Okay," Loretta quickly muttered to Martha Lee. "The mud bath sounds great."

"All right!" Martha Lee said. "I'll take you over right now. I'm sure they can fit you in."

"Great, let's go." Loretta headed toward the nearest door without waiting for Martha Lee. She had to get out of there before Lance spotted her.

Marvelli, where are you? she screamed in her head.

Martha Lee stood over Loretta, who was on her back and up to her neck in hot mud, a towel wrapped in a turban around her head. She was smoothing the last few glops of cucumber-avocado masque over Loretta's forehead with a wooden tongue depressor. It was like icing a cake. But for all the pampering, Loretta did not look happy. She was frowning bright green through the masque. They were the only ones in the terra-cotta-tiled mud room. Most guests waited till the end of the day for their mud baths, after they were through working out.

Martha Lee could feel the weight of her pistol in her fanny pack, her pulse racing, wondering how she was going to do this. She could do it now, she thought. Shoot Loretta in the tub, smooth over the bullet holes, put some cucumber slices over her eyes, and just leave her. It would give Martha Lee at least an hour, maybe two, before anyone tried to wake Loretta up. Everybody falls asleep in these yucky things. If anybody saw Loretta, they'd just think she was catching some *z*'s. It would give Martha Lee time to wire the money to Luis and head for the airport. If Roger didn't get in the way.

Loretta looked like she was sucking on a lemon, her face was so puckered. "This is incredibly icky."

"Relax, honey. You're not letting yourself enjoy this."

"I thought dirt was bad for your skin," Loretta said. "What am I doing sitting in mud? I'll get blackheads in places I can't even look at."

"No, no, no. This cleans *out* your pores."

"Are you sure?"

"Trust me, sweetie. Now I'll be right back."

Martha Lee went into the next room where Ida, the Jamaican lady who ran the baths, kept her supplies. Ida didn't get in for another hour or so. Martha Lee opened the refrigerator and looked for a cucumber, so she could cut some slices for Loretta's eyes. The shelves were full of all kinds of creams, lotions, and masques, but the two vegetable drawers were full of lemons and cucumbers. She pulled out a cucumber that was already cut open and went looking for a knife, thinking she better not leave any fingerprints on the knife. Or the cucumber for that matter. She put the waxy vegetable on the counter. *Shit.* Now she was going to have to wipe it down. And the refrigerator-door handle. And the drawers. *Shit!* she thought again, getting more nervous than she already was. She should've worn gloves. Why didn't she think of that?

She used the tail of her T-shirt to open counter drawers, looking for a knife, telling herself that this wasn't impossible as long as she didn't panic, this could be done. But in her gut she wasn't sure she could go through with it. She'd been around a lot of guns, but she'd never fired one, not once. Tom Junior used to tell her all kinds of weird stories about guns jamming and bullets missing from just a couple of feet away. Real guns don't always behave the way they do on TV, he'd told her, and now she couldn't stop thinking about that. What if she tried to shoot Loretta and the mud sent her bullets off course? She could miss Loretta completely. But what if she did shoot her, and blood started gushing out of the bullet holes in the mud, and she couldn't plug them up? She'd be found dead too soon. Then what?

Maybe it would be better to strangle her? Martha Lee thought. Might look like she died of natural causes, a heart attack, something they wouldn't call the cops for right away. Christ, that's all she needed—a bunch of cops all over the place when she was trying to get the hell out of there.

But no matter which way she figured it, she still didn't like the idea of killing Loretta herself. Just thinking about it was making her queasy. If goddamn Torpedo Joe weren't under the influence of that little witch Ricky Macrae, he'd have already done it by now. Martha Lee had promised him fifteen grand, and he'd believed her. He didn't know she intended to stiff him. And he'd never think of looking for her in Costa Rica after she disappeared. But goddamn Ricky, she had Joe out gunning for *her*, and unless Ricky had changed a whole lot since Martha Lee had last seen her, Joe would do whatever she wanted because if he didn't, she'd bug him to death. Ricky was real good at bugging people.

Martha Lee kept looking through drawers for a knife, but she couldn't find one. *To hell with the cucumber slices,* she thought in frustration. Maybe a wet washcloth over Loretta's eyes would do just as well. But where the hell were the washcloths? She looked around the room, her heart thumping, ready to forget about the whole thing—at least the killing Loretta part—when suddenly she spotted a magnetic knife rack on the wall over the counter. Right under her goddamn nose, she thought. Jesus! She wasn't thinking straight. She was gonna screw this up. She knew it.

She reached over the counter to take a knife down, and suddenly she realized something else. She was leaving fibers all over the room—her fuscia T-shirt, her bike shorts, her socks. And her hair. The cops would find her hair all over the place. People got convicted on this kind of stuff all the time. Cops didn't need fingerprints. She backed away from the counter and crossed her arms tight, afraid to touch anything now.

A handwritten note taped to the refrigerator door caught her eye. "MORONS!" it said in big block letters. "DO NOT GET THE SALT WET. IT GETS LIKE ROCK. TOO HARD TO USE!" At the end of the note an arrow pointed to the other side of the refrigerator where an open twenty-pound bag of rock salt was on the floor, propped against the wall. Martha Lee bent down and took a closer look. The salt had hardened so badly she couldn't break the crust with her fingers. She stood up and kicked the bag with the toe of her Reebok. It was as hard as dried cement. This was the kind of salt Ida used for the salt scrubs. Martha Lee kicked the bag again. A stack of twenty-pound bags sat on a wooden pallet in the corner. She went over and kicked one of the bags on the pallet. It crunched.

She stared down at the stack of salt bags, thinking.

"Martha? Did you forget about me?" Loretta called in from the mud room.

"Nope," Martha Lee called back. "I certainly have not."

"I thought you might have abandoned me."

"No, no, no. I'm gonna fix you up with something special."

"What's that?"

Martha Lee went back to the counter to get a knife. "You'll see, honey."

Loretta woke with a start. She must've dozed off, she thought. This mud was so warm and relaxing—actually warm verging on hot. The cucumber-avocado masque had dried tight on her face, and the cucumber slices were still on her eyes, right where Martha Lee had put them. She turned her head from side to side. Neon squiggles drifted behind her shut eyelids. She felt a little light-headed from the heat.

"Hello," she called out. "Martha?"

No response.

She wondered how long she'd been asleep.

"Hel-lo-o."

Silence.

Lying prone in the thick mud, Loretta worked her hands to the bottom of the tub. She tried to push herself up, but she had almost no energy. She tried again, but she couldn't budge herself.

"Hello." She cleared her throat and raised her voice. "Martha. Anybody."

Nothing.

She worked one hand through the mud, intending to take the

cucumbers off her eyes, but she couldn't break the surface. She tried again, but it was solid. Suddenly her heart started to pound.

Loretta shook her head back and forth and wiggled her brows until the cucumbers fell from her eyes. The light blinded her for a second as she kept trying to break through the hardened mud. But it was no use. She was stuck.

When her eyes finally adjusted to the light, she could see an expanse of tiny white salt crystals spread before her. It had hardened to an impenetrable crust. She looked around the room, puzzled by the wooden plank walls and the rows of wooden benches. The room she had been in was tiled. How'd she get here? Then she noticed the smell. She knew that smell. It was like hot baked underwear. She was in a sauna.

"Hello!" she called out. "Is anybody there? Hello!"

A single naked lightbulb glared down at her from the ceiling. To her right was the door, but the tiny window had been covered over with a piece of newspaper. She could hear music on the other side—that nouveau disco stuff they played at all the aerobics classes around here.

"Hello! Hello!" she yelled.

Sweat was pouring off her face, melting the masque and getting into her eyes. The more she squirmed, the hotter the mud felt. She turned her head as far as she could and strained to see the thermostat on the wall. It was too far away for her to make out the temperature setting, but the timer was set for the maximum, whatever that was.

Could it be an hour? she wondered. She could slow-cook to death in that time. Murder by Crock-Pot.

She struggled again, trying to push though the salt crust, but it was no use.

Martha Lee was on to her. She had to be. This was no "special treatment." The little bitch was trying to kill her. And she'd even had Loretta convinced that this salt treatment would help her lose a few pounds. Martha Lee had had the nerve to say that when the salt mixed with the mud, it formed an enzyme that conditioned the body for weight loss. "Passive weight loss," she'd called it. And like a dumbbell, Loretta had believed her. How stupid! Just goes to show that people believe what they want to believe, even people who should know better, like her.

Loretta tried to punch her way through the salt crust, but she only ended up mashing her knuckles. The crust had to be at least three or four inches thick. Martha Lee had poured two big kitty-litter-size bags into the tub and spread it out nice and even before she turned a sprayer on the whole thing and hosed it down. All the while she kept yammering on about this special enzyme and passive weight loss, and Loretta was only half-listening because the warm ooze was making her sleepy. Loretta had noticed that all the mud tubs were on wheels, so that guests could be brought out to bake in the sun when the weather was nice. Martha Lee must've waited for Loretta to doze off before she wheeled her into the sauna. *Goddamn her!* Loretta thought as she punched the salt crust again.

"Help!" she shouted. "Help! I'm in the sauna!"

But the only reply she heard was the incessant beat of the mindless dance music outside.

Marvelli, you son of a bitch, she thought, fighting back tears, *where the hell are you?* She'd beeped him last night from her room and left the 1111 code. He'd promised that he'd come running if she beeped him. So where was he?

She pushed on the salt crust again, banging it with both fists, kicking it with her knees and feet, cutting her skin on the sharp crystals. She struggled and strained, not wanting to cry, not wanting to admit that she was trapped and that she couldn't get herself out of this. But she *was* trapped, and the mud was getting hotter, and the more she thought about it, the more panicky she became. She started struggling in a frenzy, thrashing at the mud, when suddenly a sharp pain zinged through her chest. She froze, scared to death, hoping it would pass. But it didn't.

I'm having a heart attack, she thought. *No one can hear me. No one will find me. I'm going to die.*

"Help me!" she screamed. "Please help me!"

She tried to force herself to calm down, knowing that panicking would just make things worse. But she couldn't help herself. Her mind was racing faster that her pulse. She thought about using her back to break the crust, but she'd have to pull her head into the hole and get all the way into the mud to do it. What if that didn't work and she couldn't find the hole again? She could drown. Even if she did find the hole, there'd be thick mud all over her face and in her nose. She couldn't get her hands out to clear it away. She could suffocate.

Her heart started to hammer, pain throbbing through her chest, hot mud and salt chafing her neck, sweat pouring into her eyes.

"Marvelli!" she screamed through her sobs. "Marvelli, where are you? Marvelli!"

"I'm afraid we don't have any economy models in the lot right now, sir." The squeaky-clean kid behind the Hertz counter at the airport was very serious. He was wearing a starched short-sleeved white shirt and a yellow tie, and his pin-straight hair was plastered down and lacquered in place. "I can give you a Mustang, though, at no additional cost."

"Fine," Marvelli said, glancing at the clock behind the kid's head. He was worried sick about Renée, but he was worried about Loretta, too. He'd tried to call Loretta from the airport in Newark earlier that morning, but there had been no answer at her room.

"Would you prefer a convertible, sir?" The kid had a permanent furrow between his brows.

"Sure, whatever." Marvelli wasn't even listening. He just wanted a car, so he could get to Rancho Bonita.

The Hertz kid put the paperwork on the counter and showed Marvelli where to sign, which Marvelli did without reading anything. He then tore off Marvelli's receipt, laid in on the counter, and put a set of keys on top. "It's a blue car, sir, and you'll find it in Space 238 in the parking garage. Go right out this door, cross the street, and the garage is straight ahead. Enjoy your stay in Florida, sir."

But Marvelli was already on his way, crumbling up the receipt and sticking it in his pocket, the keys dangling from his teeth. *Loretta,* he thought. He had to find her. She'd beeped him last night. She was in trouble. Renée was right. He should never have left.

As he jogged up to the automatic doors, he had to slow down and wait for them to open. He dashed out into the sunshine, cars and minibuses lined up at the curb. He cut through a rush of pedestrians on the sidewalk, squeezed through two bumpers, and waited for a break in the traffic so he could run across.

"Two thirty-eight," he repeated to himself as he slipped out of the sun and into the shade of the parking garage. He scanned the lines of rental cars and the white numbers painted on the black floor. Two-thirty-eight, two-thirty-eight—

"Marvelli. *Que pasa?*"

Marvelli looked up and saw Lawrence Temple coming toward him. He didn't like the sound of Temple's Spanish. It was phony friendly. Flanking Temple in a tight V formation was his IRS goon squad—four dark suits with RayBans over their eyes. Two were average in size but grim of face, one white, the other Hispanic. There was something ominous and gnarled about these two. The other two were strapping, no-neck, Southern Methodist linebacker types, just as grim but somehow slightly less threatening because they didn't seem as bright. Temple stopped walking, and the goons broke out of the V formation to form a loose circle around Marvelli.

"How'd you know I'd be here?" Marvelli asked.

Temple laughed. "We're feds."

The goons were smiling.

"Loretta beeped me. She may be in trouble."

Temple started shaking his head before Marvelli had even finished. "She's all right."

"How do you know?"

"We saw her."

"You went to the spa?"

Temple shook his head. "There was a DEA plane in the area. They did some air recon for us. Loretta was spotted early this morning walking with Martha Sykes—"

"Spooner," Marvelli corrected.

Temple shrugged. "The important thing is Loretta's all right."

Marvelli had a gut feeling that Loretta's safety wasn't job one in Temple's playbook. He kept his gaze leveled on Temple, the goons in his peripheral vision, as he pocketed the car keys just in case he needed his other hand. The two big meatballs moved farther behind his shoulders, out of his range of vision, as if they could read his mind.

"Maybe it's time to call it a game with this thing," he said to Temple. "If Loretta doesn't have anything for you by now—"

Temple cut him off. "She's not in any trouble, Marvelli. Let's just leave her in place and give her a chance to dig up something good for us."

"Hey, Lawrence, Loretta's not a fed and neither am I. We can't stay here forever. We gotta bring this Spooner woman back to Jersey."

"You have until Monday."

"Says who?"

"That's what Loretta told me."

"Well, that's true, but it doesn't mean we're authorized to be down here in Florida all that time."

"Don't worry about it. We'll pay your day rate. You are helping us, after all."

The gnarly goons were smiling as if they knew something.

"I know you're worried about her, Marvelli, but believe me, she's all right. Let's just give her a little more time. Okay?"

Marvelli glanced back at the Bubba goons who were covering his back. They were both young. And strong. But it was the gnarly ones who bothered him more. They looked like they'd been around. Temple was a wuss. He'd trip over his own feet trying to get away if anything happened. But these other guys Mar-velli wasn't so sure about. And there were four of them and one of him.

"All right," Marvelli finally said. "Let her stay a little while longer. See if she can do something for you." He leaned forward and whispered in Temple's face, "But just tell me something."

"What's that?"

"Are these guys really accountants?"

Temple smiled at his question but didn't answer it. "I'll ride with you," he said to Marvelli, then turned to his troops. "Follow us."

The goons moved on command.

Loretta's face was a tear-streaked avocado green mask of torture and anguish. She was kicking the inside of the tub, sounding a monotonous dull gong as she called out for help over and over and over again. But she was so exhausted, she didn't realize that her pleas were no more than pathetic squeaks and murmurs. Her knuckles were raw and stinging from banging on the salt crust. And even though her chest pains weren't as bad as they had been, they were still there. But her primary fear wasn't that she'd had a heart attack. It was that Brenda Hemingway would come back and start up the clothes dryer again.

In Loretta's mind Martha Lee had become Brenda, and the specter of Brenda was haunting her—Brenda wearing her clothes, Brenda cackling in her face, Brenda determined to burn her to a crisp until there was nothing left.

When Loretta had been in that clothes dryer, going round and round, the gas burner roaring in her ears, the perforated metal getting hotter by the second, the fear of death merged with her fear of failure and became one and the same. An assault on her body was an assault on her very being. If Brenda had marked her for death, it had to have been her fault, something that she had done wrong that had made this happen. If she couldn't live, she couldn't succeed, and that was the crucial thing for Loretta—success, not just survival.

"Help me please!" she squeaked. "Please, help me!" She broke down into sobs, finally realizing that her voice was gone.

Suddenly the wooden door of the sauna swung open. "Martha, are you in here? They said you were here. Marth—oh, my God!"

It was Roger Laplante, and his beady eyes were bugging out of his head. He was wearing a raspberry-colored sports jacket and pale yellow pants, holding the door open with his fingertips and standing stiffly as if he were afraid he'd get dirty.

Do something! she shouted at him, but it was only in her head. Her mouth was moving, but nothing came out. He moved closer and partially blocked the glare of the overhead light bulb, sharpening the light so that she had to squint.

Do something, you big douche bag. Please! But she was yelling only inside her head.

Roger touched the salt crust with his index finger. He leaned on it with his palm, gradually bearing down on it. It held his weight. "Oh, Jesus!" he muttered to himself under his breath. "Don't sue! Dear God, don't sue!"

He rushed to the thermostat on the wall, then changed his mind and went back to the tub. He unlocked the wheels with his foot. "Have to get you out of here," he said, talking to himself. "Have to cool you down." But when he touched the edge of the plastic tub, he immediately retracted his hand, burning his fingers.

"She's gonna sue," he muttered in a tizzy. "She's gonna sue. Oh, God!"

Damn right I'm gonna sue, she thought. *Get my 2,800 bucks back.*

He took off his shoe, hopping around on one foot, and started to bang his heel on the crust, but that didn't do any good.

Loretta winced. Her face was being pelted with bits of salt. "Stop," she managed to get out.

Roger was startled by the sound of her voice.

"All right, okay," Roger said, patting the air over the tub. "I'll get you out. Don't worry. Don't sue. I'll get a hammer. Yes, a hammer. We must have a hammer here."

He rushed out of the sauna, then suddenly he stopped in his tracks at the doorway. "You!" he shouted. Loretta could see that he was pointing to someone down the hall. "Yes, you," he called out. "Come here quick. I need a hand. Quick!"

Dazed from the heat and still fighting the glare of the light-bulb, Loretta saw a second shadowy figure coming toward her.

"We have to get her out of here," Roger said. "I don't know what to do."

Help him. He's an idiot, Loretta tried to say, but she was so weak she couldn't move. She tried to kick the tub again, but her legs wouldn't respond. She was dizzy and totally exhausted. It was a struggle to keep her eyes open even a slit.

"What should we do?" Roger asked in a panic.

The other person didn't say a word.

Torpedo Joe looked at the guy in the faggy pink jacket, then looked at the poor fat woman trapped in the tub.

"Do something!" the big faggot yelled at him. "Do something!"

But Joe didn't say squat, not wanting to give himself away. This guy probably figured he was one of the geeks who worked here since he was wearing black shorts and a white polo shirt just like all the other workers around here. Joe had snitched them from the men's locker room—the fools didn't use locks at this place. He kept his hand over his chin as if he were thinking hard about how to handle this situation when in fact he was hiding his soul-patch braid. Job or no job, he wasn't about to shave that off. He needed *some* hair.

"Come on, come on! Do something! Don't just stand there."

Joe glared at the guy but held his tongue. The faggot was probably somebody important around here. Nobody wore clothes like that unless they were somebody and they knew no one would give 'em shit about it. He touched the crusty stuff in the tub. It was rock-hard.

"Can you break through that?" the big dumb peacock asked. He was crazy as a chicken.

Joe just grunted at him. Then he looked at the poor woman rolling her head from side to side, her eyes half-closed and out of focus. She was moaning something, but Joe couldn't understand her. The towel around her head came undone and fell to the floor, and Joe saw that she had long, wavy dirty blond hair.

"Take it easy, dear," the peacock said, picking up the towel and wiping her brow with it. "What's your name, dear? Tell me your name."

"Loretta . . . ," the woman slurred.

Loretta? *Loretta?* Joe had heard that name recently. He took a closer look at her face, and suddenly he realized where he'd heard it. *Goddamn!* he thought. It was that woman from the parole office back in Jersey where Marvelli had brought him. Shit! It looked like somebody had tried to cook her to death. He wondered if this was the broad Martha Lee wanted him to do, the "spy" she'd talked about. It was possible, Joe thought. This Loretta woman was the law.

But then he thought about it some more. Jesus H. Christ, he thought, what the hell did that little bitch Martha Lee do? Hire somebody else? Hey, nobody was gonna do him out of a job. They had a deal.

He looked around the sauna and found another towel hanging from a rack on the wall. He whipped it down, folded it over the salt crust where this Loretta's legs should be, and started to pound with his fist. She wasn't gonna die. No way. No one was gonna screw him out of a fee. He was gonna save her, *then* kill her, then give Martha Lee the bill.

He pounded away, pounding as if he were pounding in the

head of the asshole who'd tried to take his job away from him. Finally the crust started to crack near the edge of the tub. Joe rearranged the towel and kept pounding, stopping now and then to press all his weight on the crust. Finally he was able to pry loose a chunk the size of a boulder. He tipped it over the edge and let it drop. It cracked one of the floorboards and left a pretty good gouge in the wood it was so heavy.

"Hey," the peacock complained, frowning at the damage. "Be careful."

"You want her out or not?"

"Of course, I want her out."

"Well, then. . . ."

The peacock just made a face at him as Joe went back to work, breaking the salt with his bare hands, letting the boulders crash to the floor just to spite the big faggot. When Joe got to her neck, he tucked the muddy towel under her chin so that it looked like she was wearing a bib and pounded out the last piece that was holding her in.

"Get her out. Quick," the peacock ordered.

Don't sweat it, pal, Joe thought. *I'll get her out.*

He fished around in the mud until he found her arm, then pulled her up to a sitting position.

"Get her out!"

"I'm *getting* her out."

"You don't have to get testy about it."

I don't get testy, Joe thought. *I get mad.*

It was hard to get a purchase on her, she was so slippery. She was also buck naked, it seemed. He got her to lean over the side of the tub, though, then managed to lift her onto his shoulder. She made a noise like a toilet plunger as he pulled her out.

"Take her back to the mud room," the peacock ordered. "Hose her down and give her a rubdown. I'll go get the nurse."

"Will do," Joe said.

But a nurse won't do no good, he thought. *Not when I get through with her.*

He walked out into the hallway with Loretta on his shoulder, heading in the direction that the peacock had indicated. She squished as he carried her, mud plopping on the floor, and he had to hold on tight to the backs of her knees so he wouldn't drop her. He thought he could feel a boob on his back, but he wasn't sure with all this goddamn mud. She was a hefty one, just like Ricky. Mud spattered his calves as he moved down the hall, looking for this mud room the peacock had talked about. He'd better find it soon and do what he had to do, he thought. Holding Loretta's squishy-slick flesh was making him awful horny.

Loretta was still groggy when the big guy with the buzz cut laid her down on a massage table. He turned her over facedown and started working on her neck. He was rough, but she was too weak to resist. She hadn't gotten a good look at his face, but she imagined that he was a big strapping Swede, a Viking masseur. He dug his fingers into her neck, kneading her muscles like bread dough, then suddenly he slipped his forearm under her throat and flexed his bicep. She figured this must be some kind of chiropractic adjustment, but she groaned to let him know that it was a little too much.

"Easy," she moaned.

"Uh-huh," he said, but he didn't let up.

Maybe he didn't understand English.

"Too much," she said.

He didn't let up.

Suddenly Loretta heard brisk footsteps on the tiles as someone came into the room. "The mud, the mud, get the mud off first." She thought she recognized the impatient voice. It sounded like Roger Laplante.

She tried to push herself up from the table, not wanting to be naked in the same room with that bastard, but she was suddenly so dizzy she had to lie back down and close her eyes, afraid that she was going to pass out. *Thank God the big Swede is here,* she thought. She didn't want to be left alone with Laplante, not like this.

A spray of warm water crossed her back. Muddy water trickled off the table and coursed to the center of the tiled floor, where it swirled around the drain.

"That's it," Laplante said. "Get all of it. Her legs, her feet. All of it."

The masseur did as he was told, washing the mud off her entire body. Finally he went to work on her hair, laying it out flat on her back and squeezing the mud out with his hand. The warm water was making her sleepy.

"Okay, okay, that's enough," Laplante said. "Give her a rubdown now."

The masseur's strong hands went to work on her neck and shoulders again, but he wasn't so rough now. It felt so good. She had to fight to stay awake.

"Are you feeling better, ma'am?" Laplante asked. "Are you all right?"

"Yes . . . I'm okay," Loretta murmured, aggravated by the sound of Laplante's voice but too tired to open her eyes and tell him off. "Nothing wrong with me."

"Good. I'm so glad to hear that you're all right."

"No you're not," she mumbled, half in a dream.

"Pardon?"

"You're full of shit. You don't think I'm all right. You think I'm too fat."

"Ma'am, I *never* said that."

"You've been saying it for years. . . . You say it on TV every day. . . . You tell me I'm too fat, but I'm not. . . ."

The masseur went to work on her lower back. She felt like jelly. Loretta kept babbling to keep herself awake.

"We're all too fat . . . all of us. . . . That's what you think. . . .

So what's wrong with being fat? . . . It's not like being stupid. . . . Fat and lonely, fat and lonely," she sang, "goes together like a horse and carriage. . . ."

"Ma'am, I sympathize completely with how you feel," Laplante said. "I've dedicated my entire life to helping people—"

"Bullshit," she said, rotating her hips and arching her back with the pressure of the masseur's hands. "You don't understand shit. . . . I know what it's like. . . . You don't. . . ."

"But I do—"

"*Not*. . . . Third grade . . . Mrs. Hancock . . . skinny witch . . . I ripped my dress in the playground . . . really bad . . . could see my underwear. . . . Wanted to go home and change, but she wouldn't let me. . . . Made me wear a crossing-guard slicker, a big yellow one. . . . Had to walk home that way. . . . The other kids said I was so fat I had to wear a tent. . . . Boys went woo-woo and ran around me, like Indians. . . ."

"I understand what you're saying, ma'am. When I was a boy in New Hampshire—"

"Shut up. . . . I've heard that story a million times. . . . Don't want to hear—ooooo, that feels good."

The big Swede was doing long strokes up and down the length of her back, putting his back into it. God, it felt good.

"Ma'am, are you sure you're all right? Is there anything we can get you?"

"Like what?"

"Whatever you'd like?"

"How do you know what I like? You don't know shit." She tried to push herself up, wanting to tell him off to his face, but her head started to spin again. She flopped back down and closed her eyes. When she opened them again, the room was still spinning.

"Frig you, Marvelli," she muttered, swiping the tear from her nose.

"Excuse me?" Laplante asked.

"Shut up."

"Who's Marvelli?"

She paused and frowned, realizing where she was. "My husband," she said.

"And you call him 'Marvelli'? That's his last name, isn't it?" She didn't answer.

"Continue with the massage," Laplante told the masseur. "I'll be right back."

Loretta heard the snippy click of Laplante's departing footsteps. The masseur kept working on her back. As soon as he was finished, she was getting the hell out of there, she thought. To hell with the IRS and to hell with Marvelli.

"I'm gonna crack your back now, okay?" the masseur asked.

"Sure . . . I guess." She turned her head to look up at him. He had something odd under his lip. It looked like a braid.

"Lie still," he said. "This'll just take a minute." He got up on the table, straddling the small of her back on his knees, then linked his fingers over her forehead and started to pull back.

"Hey, wait a minute! Wait a minute!" she said.

He stopped pulling. "What?"

"You're not into Rolfing or anything like that, are you?"

"No," he said. "I've got my own style."

Marvelli was suspicious as soon as he walked into the room. It was a conference room at an IRS office somewhere outside of Fort Myers, but there were deli platters full of cold cuts and cheeses and all kinds of salads on the table, loaves of rye bread and pumpernickel, hard rolls, a cooler full of soda on the floor, and a coffee urn and big plate of cookies wrapped in pink cellophane on the sideboard. Lawrence Temple and his four attack-dog accountants were smiling at him, waiting for his reaction.

"What is it, Christmas?" Marvelli said.

Temple shrugged. "We're gonna be here for a while. Might as well eat."

Marvelli nodded to himself, scanning the plates of food. "Why are we gonna be here for a while?"

"To monitor Loretta," Temple said.

"Oh. . . . So this is like . . . command central?"

"Yeah, you could say that."

"Uh-huh. . . ." Marvelli nodded. "So how are we monitoring her from here?"

"I've got two men parked outside Rancho Bonita, watching."

"*Outside* Rancho Bonita," Marvelli said.

"Right. And that DEA plane I told you about? It's still in the area. I asked them to keep an eye out for her if they pass over the spa."

"If they pass over," Marvelli repeated.

"Right."

"Uh-huh."

"You want something to eat?" Temple asked. "Go ahead. Help yourself."

The attack dogs were already filling their plates, two Dobermans and two Rottweilers chowing down. One of the two big guys didn't even bother to make a sandwich; he was stuffing a slice of rare roast beef right into his mouth. The skinny guy with the dark thinning hair tore open a hard roll and started spreading mustard on it, but he was keeping his eye on Marvelli.

Marvelli scanned the platters, but he didn't have much of an appetite. He was worried about Loretta. And Renée.

"*Mangia,* Marvelli," Temple said, heaping potato salad onto his paper plate. "Come on. Don't let the taxpayers' money go to waste."

Marvelli went over to the coffee urn and poured himself a cup. He looked at the cookies through the pink cellophane, but nothing appealed to him. He poured milk into his coffee and took a sip. Loretta was over there by herself, he kept thinking. She could be in trouble—real trouble—and he'd never know it. These guys didn't know what the hell they were doing. You don't send someone out undercover and just leave her there. All these guys cared about was nailing Roger Laplante. They didn't give a shit about Loretta.

They didn't care about Renée either. They didn't care that she was back in the hospital. They didn't care that she could be dead by now.

Marvelli swallowed a quick gulp and told himself to calm down. Nina and his mother-in-law had his beeper number. If anything happened to Renée, they'd call. And they hadn't called, so that meant nothing had happened.

But what if something did happen? he thought. *What if Renée did die? Then what?*

Everything goes down the toilet, that's what happens, he thought.

It was Nina he was most worried about. His mother-in-law, Annette, was a good person, but she wasn't going to be much help raising a teenager. Grandmothers don't tell teenagers what they need to know. They just try to make nice with their grandkids when they get to that age. They never set kids straight about the stuff that matters. He couldn't imagine Annette giving Nina the birds and the bees, giving her advice about boys and dates and sex and stuff. Annette didn't talk about that kind of stuff. She thought it was "filthy."

Loretta would probably be good at that, he thought. She was hip, and she put things straight. No bullshit with her. She called a spade a spade.

She wasn't delicate about anything as far as he could tell, but there was something about her attitude and her sharp tongue that he kind of liked. There was something about *her* he kind of liked. She was real. Yeah, she could be nasty, and she was a little on the heavy side, but she was okay. Not bad-looking, either. Not at all. Very pretty face. Beautiful eyes. . . .

He stared into his paper coffee cup. What the hell was wrong with him? Why was he thinking this? He had Renée in the grave and Loretta taking her place, just like that. What was he, crazy?

"You sure you don't want anything to eat, Marvelli?" Temple was tipping up a cold cut platter, like the old hag offering Sleeping Beauty the poisoned apple. This was crazy, too, Marvelli thought. What the hell was he doing, hanging around with these sons of bitches when—?

But then he spotted something on the platter—rolled slices of olive loaf. He hadn't had olive loaf in God knows how long. His mother used to put it in his sandwiches when he was a kid.

Olive loaf with white American cheese. . . . He stepped toward
the table. Maybe he'd just have a little.

"Go on. Make yourself a sandwich," Temple urged as Marvelli reached for a slice of olive loaf. "I know you're worried
about Loretta, but come on, she's a bruiser. Who's gonna mess
with her?"

The attack dogs snickered behind their sandwiches.

Marvelli put the olive loaf back and leveled his gaze on Temple. "What's that supposed to mean?"

Temple looked surprised. "What?"

"That Loretta's a 'bruiser,' that no one's 'gonna mess with
her'?"

"Well, you know. . . . I mean, isn't it obvious?"

Marvelli shook his head. "Not to me."

"Well, she's a big girl," Temple said. "She can take care of
herself."

"Oh . . . I still don't get it."

One of the Dobermans piped up. "What he means is, she's
too big to hurt and too fat to worry about guys hitting on her."

The dogs snickered in agreement.

Marvelli just looked at them in silence. "So what you're saying is, I don't have to worry about her because she's fat." He
stepped toward Temple. The dogs instinctively stopped smiling
and went into formation beside their boss, one Doberman and
one Rottweiler on either side of Temple.

"Look, Marvelli, I know she's your partner," Temple said,
"but I didn't mean anything by it—"

"Yes, you did. You said exactly what you meant. She's out
there doing your dirty work for you, but you don't think she's
worth the time of day. She's just some fat bitch who's expendable
to you. Like a paper clip. Well, that's all over now."

"What do you mean?"

"What I mean is, I'm going over to the spa and I'm getting
her out of there. Forget about interagency cooperation. That's
crap."

Temple's smiling face suddenly turned grave. "Sit down, Marvelli. Let's talk about this."

"There's nothing to talk about, Lawrence. You're not helping us any, so we're not helping you. End of story."

The dogs put down their plates.

"I think you're forgetting something, Marvelli," Temple said. "We're a *federal* agency. You're state, and you're out of your jurisdiction. When push comes to shove, fed trumps state."

"Really?"

"Yes, really."

"Forget about it, Lawrence. I'm outta here."

Marvelli moved toward the door, but the dogs rushed around to get in his way, blocking the doorway. They stayed in the same formation, all four facing him, the two skinny guys on the inside, the two linebackers on the outside.

Marvelli gave them a withering look. "Are we gonna play games here or what?"

"Sit down and have a sandwich," the skinny guy with the thinning hair said. He didn't say it very nice.

"Get out of my way . . . please."

The skinny guy shook his head.

"I'm asking you nicely," Marvelli said, his voice rising.

"Sit down, Marvelli."

"I don't want to have to ask you again. Now move."

The skinny Doberman nodded sharply, and the Rottweilers knew what he meant. They lunged to grab Marvelli's arms, but Marvelli was quicker, and he grabbed their neckties first, dropping his weight and dragging the big guys down. He kicked up while he was down low and caught the two Dobermans under the chins, sending them both to the carpet. When he pulled himself back to his feet, the Rottweilers were able to stand up, but Marvelli took the opportunity to take their balance by pushing them both in the face simultaneously. The Rottweilers staggered back and tripped over the Dobermans, falling into a moaning heap.

Marvelli stepped over them and opened the door. Before he left, he stared back at Temple, who was standing there with his plate in his hand, still trying to figure out what he'd just seen.

Marvelli pointed at his face, and Temple's eyes widened. "You've got mayonnaise in the corner of your mouth, Lawrence."

"Hold it! Hold it! Stop! You're hurting me!"

Loretta struggled to break free from the masseur, but she was facedown on the massage table, and he was straddling her back, fingers linked around her forehead, pulling her head back.

"Stop, I said!"

"Just calm down and sit still," he said. "This is good for your health."

"The hell it is." She managed to push his hands off her sweaty brow, but in the process her breasts nearly fell out of the towel that was wrapped around her. "That's enough. I don't want any more," she yelled. She tried to wriggle out from under him, but he was too heavy.

"Just give it a chance, lady," he said with a grunt as he latched onto her forehead again. "This'll just take a minute."

"No!" she protested, struggling to break his grip. "No more! You're going to kill me."

"Now who went and told you that?" he asked. There was a mean grin in his voice.

Suddenly Loretta was petrified. He *was* trying to kill her. She strained to keep him from snapping her neck. This was Martha Lee's boyfriend, she thought. It had to be. A picture of the braid under his lip and the stubble on his shaved head flashed in her mind. She'd only caught a glimpse of him, but he seemed familiar. She wondered if he'd recently been hairier. She fought to turn her head a little, so she could see his face, but then she spotted the tattoo on his forearm. It was a red torpedo. That biker Marvelli had brought in the other day, she thought, Torpedo Joe Pickett. Oh, God!

"Let go!" she screamed. "Let me go!"

"Be still, woman. This here 'adjustment' won't take but a minute." He pulled back harder, and she could hear something cracking in her neck.

"Let go!" she screamed, but she could barely form the words. He had her stretched back so far she couldn't close her mouth.

Oh, God! she thought, trying not to panic. *Oh, God!*

But she was panicking, and she knew it. It was the same feeling of dread and terror that she'd felt in the clothes dryer at Pinebrook.

Fight back, dammit! she thought. *Fight back!*

Loretta struggled and strained under Torpedo Joe's weight and managed to get to her knees.

Joe was tottering on her back. "Hey! What're you doing? Whoa!"

She lifted him up and dumped him over the side.

"You bitch," he hissed from the floor, holding a sore hip.

She scrambled off the table, clutching the big white towel around her, but Joe got to his feet fast and blocked the doorway.

"Get out of my way," she demanded.

He smiled at her. "Yeah, sure. Just for you, sweetheart." He took a step forward and cracked his knuckles. "Come on, darling. This is your destiny. Let's just get it over with."

Destiny, my ass, she thought.

She pulled off the towel and thrust her chest out, letting him get a good look. "You ever see hooters like these, Frankenstein?"

He stopped short, slack-jaw dumb, startled by her bobbling boobs.

While he was distracted, she twirled the damp towel into a rat's tail.

He was drooling into his braid as he reached out for a cheap feel. "Maybe we can arrange for a temporary stay of execution," he said.

"Think again, Frankenstein." She snapped the towel in his face and scored a direct hit.

"Ooowww!" He clutched the side of his face and dropped to one knee.

The loud smack had startled even her, and she thought she may have put his eye out, but she wasn't going to stick around to find out. If he lost an eye, he deserved it.

"Bitch!" he snarled, trying to snatch her bare legs as she passed by.

She dashed around him and out the door, stark naked, the towel trailing behind her in her hand. She could hear him muttering and cursing behind her as she ran down the tiled hallway. Glancing back, she could see that he was limping, holding onto his hip with one hand, his face with the other.

Suddenly he roared, "Come back here and face your destiny, bitch."

"I'll figure out my own destiny, asshole," she murmured as she kept running, huffing and puffing along.

At the end of the hallway, there was a fogged-up glass door with WOMEN'S STEAM ROOM painted on it in white letters. *Hallelujah,* she thought. *Maybe I can lose him in there.*

But when she pushed through the door, she was immediately disappointed. She'd hoped for rolling clouds of steam to hide in, but it wasn't nearly as steamy as she'd imagined it. Just sort of misty. The long wooden benches were empty; no one else was there.

Joe burst through the glass door. "Where are you, darling? I'm gonna catch you sooner or later."

Loretta had ducked behind the door as Joe came in, and now she was right behind him. As he hobbled into the room, she looped the big towel over his head as if they were skipping rope together, caught his ankles, and tripped him. He fell forward, sliding on the wet tiles, and crashed headfirst into one of the benches.

"Goddamm it!" he roared, squeezing his eyes shut as he clutched his head.

Loretta dropped the towel and grabbed an abandoned muumuu hanging on a peg by the door. It was big as a tent and in a horrible orange-and-green banana-leaf pattern.

Fat-lady drag, she thought with a scowl as she threw it over her head and ran out of the steam room. She headed down the hallway, adjusting the muumuu as she went, and burst through a metal door with a red-lit EXIT sign above it. Suddenly she was outside in the sunlight, and immediately her face turned red. She felt ridiculous in this getup.

"Loretta! Loretta Kovacs!"

Loretta spun around, trying to locate the whiny, singsong voice. Lance the aerobics instructor was standing by a bank of low palms, doing some kind of semaphore with hand weights Velcroed to his wrists.

"It finally came to me," he announced for all the world to hear. "Loretta Kovacs! From New Jersey! And you're a prison warden! Or something like that. Am I right?"

If she had had the wet towel, she would have rat-tailed him to death, the little jerk, and there was no time to strangle him because Joe was going to be out here any second. She turned her back on Lance and raced down the dirt path, running as fast as her bare feet would take her.

"Hey, Loretta! Wait! You didn't tell me if I was right or not? Am I?"

"Bet you can't catch me," she called over her shoulder, mimicking his singsong.

"Oh, great!" he squealed with delight. "You're on."

He took off after her, sprinting down the winding path. "Is

this a game I don't know about, Loretta?" he asked, coming up behind her.

"Yup." She was huffing and puffing, the stupid muumuu slowing her down like a wind sail.

"But don't you think we ought to warm up a little first?"

"Nope."

"It's really not very good for you to start exercising from a cold start. Strains the muscles, the heart, the knees . . ." He caught up with her and kept pace, running by her side.

"It is good, cardiovascular-wise," he blithered on, "but you should build up to it. Especially if you're not used to running in this heat. You could dehydrate in no time out here if you're not careful."

"I'm . . . fine," she grunted, struggling to keep up the pace.

"Oh, my God! You're not wearing any shoes, Loretta. You could tear an Achilles tendon, especially if you haven't stretched."

The path wound to the right and suddenly went downhill through an isolated stretch of dense waist-high ferns. "What about the hips?" she panted.

"Your hips? Well, yes, I supposed you could do some damage there—Hey!"

She bumped him hard with her hip, knocking him off the path and into the ferns. When she looked back, all she could see were swishing ferns.

Maybe an alligator got him, she hoped.

She slowed her pace but only a little, not knowing where Joe was now. She'd already made up her mind: She was getting the hell out of there. Duty is one thing; stupidity is another.

The path came out near the main building, where there was a lot of hustle and bustle, people checking in and out, staff members rushing here and there, groundskeepers tending to the plants. She slowed down to a fast walk. The front gates were just beyond the circular driveway. She worked on catching her breath, breathing in through her nose and out through her mouth. She was going to walk right out those gates and keep on going, she told herself. She'd hitch a ride if she had to. Anything to get out of here.

She kept walking, afraid to look back, afraid that bigmouth Lance was back there or worse, Torpedo Joe. She heard crunching footsteps coming off the path, but she kept her eyes straight ahead and kept on going. If Joe was back there, he wouldn't dare try anything with all these people around.

When she made it through the black iron gates, she kept on going for a few more steps, still not wanting to look back. She felt as if she were crossing a border, sneaking out of hostile territory. Finally, when she got to the edge of the road, she peered through the high wrought-iron arch. Joe was in the visitor parking section, looking all around for her, trying to be inconspicuous. She backstepped until she was out of his line of view, hidden behind the bushy hedges that lined the driveway.

She laid her hand over her heart and felt it thumping as she finally let out a long breath.

"Nice dress," someone said behind her.

Startled by the unexpected voice, Loretta started to turn around, but a sharp jab in the back stopped her.

"Don't turn around, and don't make a peep."

Loretta turned her head slowly. Out of the corner of her eye she could see Martha Lee in a sleeveless black cotton shift. She was holding a gun to Loretta's back. A lipstick red Chrysler Le Baron convertible was parked ten yards away down toward the end of the driveway.

Martha Lee prodded Loretta with the pistol, aiming her toward the car. "Get in, tubby," she said. "You drive."

Loretta was behind the wheel of the convertible, driving down a deserted two-lane road, heading for the highway, the big muumuu fluttering all around her in the breeze. Martha Lee was holding the little chrome automatic in her lap pointed at Loretta. Loretta kept looking to see if Martha Lee's hand was shaking; she seemed nervous. When Martha Lee saw what she was doing, she snarled, "Just drive. Keep your eye on the road."

"So what are you going to do?" Loretta asked. "Kill me?"

"Shut up and drive."

"Are you going to kill me?" Loretta insisted. "Just tell me."

"If I have to, I will."

Loretta's throat was dry. "I'm a parole officer," she said. "Now that you know that, it'll go harder on you if you do decide to kill me."

Martha Lee shot her a withering look. "As if I care."

"What *do* you care about?"

"I told you to shut up."

"Why should I?" Loretta wasn't going to just sit there and take orders the way she had with Brenda Hemingway.

Martha Lee lifted the gun and jabbed the air with it. "I told you to shut up." Her hand was shaking.

Loretta pumped the brake as she approached the highway intersection. "Which way?" she asked as she pulled to a stop at the stop sign.

"Turn right." Martha Lee was looking all over the place. She was a nervous wreck.

Loretta flipped the directional and waited for a break in the traffic before she turned onto the four-lane highway. She quickly picked up speed but stayed in the slow lane. *No use rushing to my own execution,* she thought, her long hair blowing in the wind.

As they drove, the swampland gradually gave way to dry scrub followed by a series of strip malls. Loretta couldn't help but notice the proliferation of fast-food restaurants on this stretch of road—Burger King, Wendy's, McDonald's, KFC, IHOP, Popeye's, Pizza Hut, Little Caesar's, Bob's Big Boy, HoJo's—and her stomach started to growl.

"What do you say we stop for drive-through?" Loretta shouted over the rushing wind, hoping to buy time.

"What?" Martha Lee shouted back.

"Chicken nuggets and fries. Pizza. Pancakes. A grilled cheese. Anything. I'm hungry."

"Shut up."

"There's a Stuckie's up ahead. How about a pecan roll?"

"Forget it."

"Come on. Doesn't a dying woman get a last wish?"

"Shut up!"

Loretta glanced down at Martha Lee's shaking gun hand, wondering if she really had the guts to kill her. The woman was hard-core, but she was no Brenda Hemingway. Of course, Martha Lee seemed pretty unstable with that gun. She might kill Loretta by accident. Most shootings did happen that way. Loretta glanced at the gun, wondering if she could grab it fast without getting shot *and* keep control of the car. What if the stupid muumuu got in the way?

But the more restaurants and supermarkets Loretta passed, the hungrier she got, and the more desperate measures she considered. Maybe if she hammered Martha Lee in the nose with her hand hard enough to stun her, Loretta could get the gun away from her. Or maybe yank her hair and bang her head against the dashboard. Or rip her ear off. But each plan Loretta considered had the same drawback. No matter what Loretta did, Martha Lee would still have the gun.

But she wasn't going to sit back and just let it happen. Not this time.

"You really gonna kill me?" she shouted to Martha Lee over the racket of the wind. "If that's your plan, I want to know. You owe me at least that."

Martha Lee's eyes bugged out of her head. "If you don't shut up right now, tubby, I'll do it right here. I swear to God."

Loretta's heart leaped, but she was determined not to be intimidated. "So what's the scam, Martha Lee? Why didn't you hit the road when you found out we were here looking for you? You must have something going, or else you wouldn't have stayed."

"I said, *shut up.*"

"Does it have something to do with the Alvarez Cocoa Company?" Loretta pressed.

Martha Lee jammed the gun into Loretta's stomach, and it growled back. "*I said, keep quiet, tubby.*"

Loretta glanced down at the gun in her side. "I guess I hit a nerve. So let me guess. You were scamming your boss, paying for nonexistent chocolate with WeightAway money. Don't get me wrong—I'm not shedding any tears for Roger Laplante. He can go to hell. Of course, bamboozling men is your specialty, right? You did it to Tom Junior and his biker pals."

"*Shut up!* You don't know shit about shit." Martha's voice was as shaky as her hand.

"Hey, you can cry on my shoulder. I don't care. It must be something sad for you to be acting this way. What is it? Your mother's in the hospital?"

Martha Lee transferred the gun to Loretta's neck, sinking the barrel into her flesh. "Look, I don't need any more of your lip. I got my reasons for what I did, and I don't need you or anyone else to judge me. I'm doing what I *have* to do, and it's none of your business. It's between me and God what I do."

"Well, don't let me get between you two." Loretta straightened her back, holding her head stiffly, wishing Martha Lee would put that gun somewhere else. She didn't want to get shot in the neck. She could just see the headlines: "Parole Officer in Ugly Muumuu Gets Shot in Double Chin."

She glanced in the rearview mirror. *Where the hell are the cops when you need them? Don't they patrol this road? Doesn't anyone see this? We're in a convertible for chrissake.*

Martha Lee dropped her hand and stuck the gun in Loretta's side again. Loretta looked in the side mirror, praying for a police cruiser. The traffic light at the next intersection turned red. As Loretta slowed down, she noticed a big billboard on the right-hand side of the road that showed a potbellied alligator smacking his lips and pointing toward a grocery store on the other side of a huge parking lot. It was called Gator Mart. Loretta pumped the brake and pulled to a stop behind a pickup.

"Excuse me. Miss? Excuse me." A man's voice came from Loretta's left. When she looked, she saw that a deep blue Mustang had pulled alongside their car.

"Excuse me? Do you know if there's a Ramada Inn somewhere around here?" It was Marvelli. She could've killed him. Finally he shows up.

"Don't get cute," Martha Lee said under her breath.

"I'm sorry. I'm not from around here," Loretta said to Marvelli, signaling him with her eyes.

"Me neither," Marvelli said. He gave her a meaningful look, but with that greaseball haircut of his, he looked like an otter who'd been caught in an oil spill.

She knew she should be happy that he was here, but she wasn't. With Brenda, she had to be rescued. This time she wanted to rescue herself.

She glanced over at him and shrugged. "Sorry," she said.

Just follow me, she thought. *I'll do the rest.*

When the light turned green, Loretta hung back and let the pickup truck pull away.

"What're you waiting for?" Martha Lee snapped. "Go!"

"You're the boss." Loretta stomped the accelerator, putting her bare foot to the floor. Martha Lee was thrown back in her seat. Loretta took a sharp right, tires squealing, and raced into the Gator Mart parking lot.

"What're you doing?" Martha Lee screamed.

Loretta ignored her, determined to get herself out of this.

Straight ahead a bag boy was gathering up shopping carts, pushing a train of at least twenty. Loretta leaned on the horn and steered toward the middle of the train, like a kamikazi honing in on a destroyer.

"Stop!" Martha Lee screamed, bracing herself against the dashboard.

Loretta narrowed her eyes and kept on going. The bag boy ran for his life as a woman in a big station wagon jammed on her brakes to avoid a collision, and other shoppers just pointed in stunned surprise.

The red convertible plowed into the shopping carts, bending the train into a U, pushing them forward in a squealing, crunching mass of bent metal.

On impact, Loretta banged her chin on the steering wheel, and Martha Lee was thrown forward. The gun flew out of her hand. It sailed over the windshield and hit the crumpled hood with a loud *thunk*.

Loretta grabbed Martha Lee's wrist. "You're under arrest."

Martha Lee snatched it back. "The hell I am." She leaped into the backseat and scrambled over the trunk, then started running toward the supermarket.

"Come back here!" Loretta yelled, trying to open her door. But she couldn't budge the tangle of shopping carts pinning the door closed, so she clambered into the backseat and went over the trunk the way Martha Lee had, high-stepping over the hot blacktop in her bare feet, the jungle-print muumuu flying all around her as she ran. "Get back here!" she yelled. "You're under arrest, you skinny little shit! Get back here!"

Jesus! Marvelli thought as he pulled his car up to the front of the store. *Look at her go.* He'd never thought Loretta could move *that* fast.

He threw the transmission into park and shut off the engine, then jumped out of the car and ran into the supermarket to help Loretta with the arrest. He didn't have a gun, which he never liked to carry anyway, and he didn't have any cuffs, but he figured they could improvise something to keep Martha Lee on ice. It was a pretty big supermarket. They could get some clothesline or duct tape or something.

He stepped on the black mat in front of the automatic double doors, but the mechanism was too slow, so he pushed his way in before it opened on its own. The temperature instantly dropped thirty degrees as he dashed into the air-conditioned store. An elderly couple in Bermuda shorts and oversize sunglasses stood right in his path, scowling at him. A disapproving cashier stared at him over her glasses, clearly annoyed.

"How you doing?" he said to them with a smile and a wave, then tore off down the cereal aisle, looking for Loretta.

"Loretta!" he shouted. "Loretta! Where are you!"

Loretta's voice came echoing back over the cornflakes. "Produce!"

"I'm coming." He turned around and went back the way he'd come, passing the Wheaties, the Lucky Charms, and the Count Chocula in a blur. "Hang on, Loretta, I'm com—"

But as he rounded the aisle, a deafening mechanical roar burst through the automatic doors, shattering one and flattening the other. The scowling old couple abandoned their cart and fled to save themselves. Shoppers and clerks screamed and scattered into the aisles.

A blood red motorcycle screamed to a halt in front of a ceiling-high Sprite display. A tattooed monster in black shorts and a white polo shirt with a stubbly bald head and a reddish-blond braid under his lip was glaring at Marvelli, revving his engine.

"Marvelli!" the man roared.

Marvelli squinted at him. "Joe? Is that you?"

Joe clenched his fist and shook his blue-torpedo arm. "You are fucking dead, Marvelli! You are dead!"

Marvelli smiled and opened his arms in welcome. "How you been, Joe?"

Torpedo Joe glared at him. "I'm gonna kill you, Marvelli. I'm gonna squish you like a bug." He popped the clutch, and the motorcycle jerked forward, turning around in a tight circle until it was aimed straight at Marvelli.

Marvelli sprinted back down the cereal aisle, Joe right on his tail. He took a sharp left at the end of the aisle, but Joe stayed with him, even as he wove his way into the meat department. At the ground-beef cooler, Joe reached out to grab Marvelli by the collar, but Marvelli stopped running and ducked, and Joe whizzed by, going all the way down to the cheese and yogurt section before he could turn the big bike around and make another pass.

This time Marvelli stood his ground as if he were just waiting for Joe to mow him down. Joe bared his teeth, picking up speed as he raced toward his target. He leaned over the handle bars, bracing for the sweet impact that would transform Marvelli into hamburger.

But at the last moment, Marvelli took one step to the side, and Joe whizzed on by again. He braked hard, but the bike skidded sideways and crashed into a seven-foot floor display of six different kinds of Keebler cookies.

"Watch out for the elves, Joe," Marvelli shouted to him.

Joe revved his engine, struggling to right the bike, his tires slipping on smashed cookie packages, crunching chocolate chips and Grasshoppers, oatmeal raisins and S'mores. He was too angry to put his thoughts into words, but it was written all over his bulging, purple-red face: *Kill!*

Marvelli cupped his hands over his mouth. "You haven't been working on that rage thing we were talking about back in

Jersey, have you, Joe? I bet you haven't cut down on your sugar intake, either. I can tell."

Joe let out an animal roar—primal and mindless—as he finally maneuvered the bike out of the crumbled cookies and took off after Marvelli again.

"You want to talk about it, Joe?" Marvelli shouted as he ran.

"No!" Joe yelled as he was about to run Marvelli down.

But at the last second Marvelli stepped out of the way again, and Joe thundered all the way down to the prepackaged cold cuts before he could screech to a halt.

"Don't you want to help yourself, Joe? Are you just giving up on yourself? Is that it? You're not even gonna try?"

"Frig you, Marvelli!" Joe circled around the gourmet cheese case to make another pass.

"All right for you," Marvelli said. "You're forcing my hand." He ducked into the nearest aisle, frozen foods, which was lined with tall glass-doored freezers from one end to the other. Marvelli opened as many as he could as he ran, but Joe barreled right through them, ripping them off their hinges. They smashed to the linoleum one right after the other—*bam! crash! bam! crash! bam! crash!*

Marvelli turned back, and the sight of such senseless destruction disappointed him deeply. Joe had no respect for anything. This had to stop.

Marvelli reached into the nearest freezer and pulled out a Mamma Russo's Extra Large Frozen Pepperoni Pizza. He took aim and flung the box like a Frisbee, aiming for Joe's front tire.

"Yes!" Marvelli hissed as the pizza lodged between the floor and Joe's front tire.

The tire wobbled, and the motorcycle went into a skid, sliding sideways down the aisle, like a ballplayer sliding for home, Joe's face frozen in shock and fury. The bike slid out of the aisle and crashed into a magazine rack between two checkout lanes. Joe groaned and cursed, hurling copies of *Bride, People,* and the *National Enquirer* off his chest as he struggled to get his leg out from under the fallen bike.

"Last chance, Joe," Marvelli said, running over to him. "I don't have time to screw around with you right now. Are you gonna behave or what?"

Joe sneered at him, climbing to his feet, his hands out like claws, ready to pounce. "What do *you* think, asshole?"

"That's pretty much what I thought, Joe."

A frozen Butterball Turkey Breast in a yellow plastic net came out of nowhere and clobbered Joe over the head. He went down like a palooka, crashing into a heap on top of the magazines.

Marvelli held the frozen turkey by the net, swinging it by his side like an oversize sap as he stared down at the unconscious biker. "I hate it when guys like you make me do things like this."

He trotted back to the freezer case where he'd found the turkey and put it back, then cupped his hands over his mouth and called out, "Loretta! Where are you? Loretta, you still here? *Loretta!*"

ALL BAKING DONE ON PREMISES, the sign over the bakery department said. Loretta had chased Martha Lee into the back room where the ovens were, but the aromas were making her weak-kneed. Metal racks on carts six feet tall were laden with all sorts of baked goods. Chrome worktables were groaning with sugary confections. She was surrounded by birthday cakes, carrot cakes, angel food cakes, devil's food cakes, apple pie, peach pie, pecan pie, Boston cream pie, key lime pie, black-and-white cookies, sugar cookies, gingerbread men, hazelnut biscotti, iced coffee rings, babkas, pounds cakes, cupcakes, bear claws, elephant ears, cheese danish, prune danish, corn muffins, bran muffins, blueberry muffins, twelve different kinds of bagels, cannolis, rum-cake pastries, cream puffs, eclairs . . .

Eclairs!

Her nemesis and her comfort. Cream custard on the inside, a shell as light as air, a thick stripe of rich chocolate on top. It had been so long since she'd had one. Her stomach was pleading like a dog under the table. But she knew she shouldn't. This was no time to eat. Besides, she shouldn't be eating these things anyway. But she'd been subsisting on grass and twigs for the past two days. She needed something to keep her going. She needed her strength. She needed support.

She reached out for an eclair, pinching the sinful delight between her thumb and index finger. This was necessary, she told herself. She'd been through a lot. She needed sustenance. If she were back in the produce aisle, she would've taken a carrot. But she wasn't in produce, she was here, in the bakery department . . . thank God.

The eclair floated toward her lips on cherub's wings. She took a bite, light-headed, anxious, totally justified. Her eyelids fluttered in ecstasy. Salvation.

"Oouufff!" A sharp blow to the kidneys knocked the air out of Loretta, dislodging the piece of eclair from her mouth before she even started to chew. It flew across the room and hit the wall. Loretta wheeled around, furious.

"Eating again, huh, tubby?" Martha Lee was brandishing a long metal oven paddle, slicing the air in front of her as if it were a scythe. "Get out of my way, fat stuff. I'm getting out of here."

"The hell you are," Loretta snarled. She was about to hurl what was left of the eclair at her attacker when she stopped to take another bite, then threw the rest at Martha Lee, hitting her in the chest.

Martha Lee lunged with the paddle, going for Loretta's throat. Loretta ducked and suddenly spotted a squadron of cannolis lined up in formation on a bottom rack. She snatched one and took a quick bite. Sugar shot through her limbs like the bullet train to Tokyo. She was Popeye the sailor man.

Martha Lee lifted the paddle over her head. "I'm gonna chop your big fat head off. I swear to God."

"Go ahead. Try it," Loretta said, defying her to attack again.

The sharp edge of the paddle came rushing down toward Loretta's head, but she quickly picked up a large pumpernickel loaf from the counter and held it up in front of her face. The blade of the paddle sank into the loaf but didn't touch Loretta.

She let go of the pumpernickel and grabbed the end of the paddle, doing a tug-of-war with Martha Lee for control of the weapon.

"Let go, fatso." Martha Lee shouted as she strained to keep the paddle.

"Give up. You're under arrest." Loretta wouldn't let go.

Martha Lee pulled. "I'm not going back to prison."

Loretta yanked. "Oh, yes, you are."

Martha Lee yanked back. "Oh, no, I'm not."

"Yes, you are."

"No way!"

"Yes way!"

Loretta stuck out her butt and put her bulk behind it as she pulled back hard.

"Whoooa!" Martha Lee hung on like a monkey in a hurricane. She slammed into the oven doors. But as soon as she turned around to flee, Loretta had the paddle to her throat, pinning her against the ovens.

"You're under arrest," Loretta shouted, leaning her weight on Martha Lee's throat.

"It's hot," Martha Lee croaked, flailing her arms. "I'm getting burned."

"You gonna come quietly?"

"Let me go! It's hot!"

"You gonna come quietly? Answer me."

"Yes! Yes!"

Loretta let up on the paddle and grabbed a fistful of Martha Lee's dark hair, forcing her down to the floor and dragging her along on all fours. "You're going back to Jersey," Loretta declared.

Martha Lee was making a fuss, crying and shouting and carrying on, but Loretta couldn't understand a word of it as she hauled the prisoner out to the front of the store.

Marvelli was already there, standing over Torpedo Joe's motionless body. He was holding a fresh roll of duct tape. "Where were you?" she said, still pissed at him. "I was looking all over for you."

Martha Lee was squirming like a cat under Loretta's grip. "Let me go! Let me go!"

Loretta nodded at the duct tape. "What're you gonna do with that?"

"I was gonna tie up Joe before he wakes up."

She shook Martha Lee by the scruff. "Tie her up first. Before I kill her."

Loretta hauled Martha Lee up and held her arms behind her back while Marvelli taped the wrists together. When he was through, Loretta used her foot to bend Martha Lee's knees and get her down on her belly, then sat on top of her to keep her still while Marvelli taped the ankles.

"Let me go, you big fat slob! Get off me!"

Loretta grabbed the the roll of tape from Marvelli's hand, ripped off six inches, and plastered it across Martha Lee's mouth. "There. Chew on that for a while."

"Okay, let's do Joe now," Marvelli said.

They crouched over the unconscious biker, Marvelli turning him over and crossing his wrists behind his back while Loretta scratched at the roll of tape to get the end.

"You think duct tape will hold this monster?" she asked.

"It better," Loretta said.

"Marvelli! Loretta! Where are you?"

They both froze, recognizing the voice. It was Lawrence Temple.

"Shit!" Loretta hissed.

"Ssshhh. Stay down." Marvelli pushed Martha Lee into a checkout lane.

Loretta followed them, peering over the conveyor belt. Temple and his IRS goons were coming into the store, and Roger Laplante was with them. In his raspberry sports jacket, he looked like a parrot surrounded by a pack of vultures.

He was yakking at Temple, all red in the face and righteously indignant. "Martha Lee is responsible for all of this. I'm telling you, Temple. You'll see. *You'll see.*"

But Temple was ignoring him. "Marvelli! Loretta!" he shouted. "We want Martha Lee Sykes. If you've already apprehended her, she's ours."

"The hell she is," Loretta grumbled.

"Ssshhh!" Marvelli gestured for her to shut up.

Martha Lee started humming frantically, her eyes popping out of her head.

Loretta pinched Martha Lee's nose, cutting off her air. "Quiet!" She looked at Marvelli, her jaw set. "We're not giving her up."

"Damned straight we're not," Marvelli whispered. "She's ours."

Loretta could've kissed him. Finally they were in agreement about something.

"*Marvelli! Loretta!*" Temple shouted, then he turned to his men. "Find them," he said. "Hurry up."

"Quiet!" Loretta shouted over the backseat of Marvelli's rented Mustang. Martha Lee was in the trunk, kicking the lid, making a racket.

Marvelli was behind the wheel, doing a steady sixty-five on the interstate, heading for the airport. They passed under a big green-and-white sign that spanned all three lanes—FORT MYERS, NEXT FOUR EXITS—and Loretta let out a long breath. They were on the homestretch.

Martha Lee started thumping on the lid again.

"Quiet, I said!"

Marvelli glanced over at Loretta. "You think we should take the tape off her mouth? So she can breathe?"

Loretta frowned. "She sound weak to you?"

Marvelli looked in the rearview mirror. "Guess not." He checked the side mirror.

"Are they following us?" Loretta was worried that Temple and his crew were on their trail. "I don't think they saw us leave," she said. "I'm pretty sure they didn't."

Marvelli shrugged. "Who knows. They may not have seen us carrying Martha Lee out, but maybe they saw us driving away."

"Yeah, but wouldn't they have chased us down by now?"

Marvelli gave her a look. "These are IRS agents we're talking about, Loretta, not real feds."

"They carry real guns, don't they?"

"Doesn't mean they know how to use them. . . . Of course, that could be worse, couldn't it?" He was chewing on the inside of his cheek.

"Are you trying to make me feel better?"

"Oh, that reminds me." He reached into his waistband and pulled out a chrome-plated automatic. He handed it to Loretta. "Hold onto this, will you?"

Loretta inspected the gun. It was loaded. "Where'd you get this?"

"It's Martha Lee's. I found it in the parking lot after you crashed into the shopping carts. Take it. I don't like carrying a weapon. I always lose 'em."

She handed it back to him. "I don't have any pockets in this thing. Sorry." She plucked at the detestable muumuu.

Marvelli took back the gun and stuck it in his waistband.

"Uh-oh," he said a moment later. He was looking in the rearview mirror.

Loretta turned around. About a quarter of a mile back, a speeding gray sedan was lane hopping, passing on the right to get around cars in the fast and middle lanes. "Is that them?" she asked.

"Only IRS agents drive that bad."

"Crap."

Martha Lee started thumping in the trunk again.

"Shut up!"

"Calm down. They don't have us yet," Marvelli said. A funny little smile pushed its way into his cheeks as he gunned the engine. A loud *thud* in the trunk was followed by flurry of panicked thumping. "Sorry," Marvelli said, then turned to Loretta. "Remind me she's back there if I start driving crazy. We're supposed to bring 'em back alive."

But Loretta was too busy looking out the back window, keeping an eye on the gray sedan. "They're definitely following us. Crap! We'll never get Martha Lee back to Jersey."

"Positive mind, Loretta," Marvelli said. "Got to have a positive mind."

A sign up ahead said: AIRPORT, 1/2 MILE. Marvelli tailgated a minivan in the fast lane until the driver took the hint and moved over. Up ahead a trailer truck was doing seventy-five in the center lane. Temple and his boys were six car lengths behind and gaining on them.

"What're you gonna do?" Loretta asked.

"You know anything about basketball?"

"A little."

"You know what 'setting a pick' is?"

"No."

"When the guy with the ball is being chased, sometimes he'll use one of his teammates as an obstacle."

"I don't get it."

"Just watch. You'll see."

Marvelli inched up on the truck, running neck and neck with its cab.

Loretta spotted another sign: AIRPORT, NEXT EXIT. "You're gonna miss the turn," she said in a panic.

"No, I'm not."

Loretta looked back. The gray sedan was closing in on them. One of the skinny geeks was driving, blowing the horn and flashing the headlights. The other geek was sitting next to him up front, Temple by the door. He was holding a revolver on the dashboard, so that Loretta and Marvelli could see it.

The exit was coming up on the right, and they were over in the fast lane. "You're gonna miss the exit," she shouted at Marvelli over the roar of the truck right next to her window. "They're gonna get us."

"Positive mind," he repeated as he suddenly zoomed ahead of the truck. "Watch my right." He pulled ahead of the cab, then cut the wheel to the right, cutting in front of the honking truck and crossing into the slow lane in one move. They screeched onto the exit ramp, leaving sixty feet of rubber behind them. The gray sedan whizzed past, blocked from following by the speeding truck.

"Hey! It worked!" Marvelli said, glancing in the rearview mirror. "How about that?"

Loretta's heart was thumping louder than Martha Lee in the trunk. He'd almost turned the car over. "You could've gotten us killed," she gasped.

"Nah . . . positive mind. Works every time."

Loretta clutched her chest. She could feel the little globs of cholesterol that had been jarred loose by the scare coursing through her veins.

Marvelli zipped around a cloverleaf and followed the signs to the airport. As he took the exit for the airport access road, Martha Lee started kicking again.

As the terminal came into view, Loretta bit her bottom lip. "Now what do we do? You didn't get tickets, did you?"

"No."

"Have you arranged with an airline for transporting a prisoner?"

"No."

"Have you done anything?"

"I got us here."

"Great."

"Calm down. We'll improvise."

"This isn't jazz, Marvelli."

He didn't answer. At the cargo terminal, he pulled over and stopped at the curb. "Go in and find out when the next flight to Newark leaves."

"In this?" She plucked at the muumuu. "I can't go in there like this. I'm barefoot."

"Don't worry about it. This is Florida."

She made a face at him but did it anyway, watching her step and avoiding the hot blacktop as she got out. Fortunately, there were two TV screens right inside the automatic doors, one for arrivals, the other for departures. She ignored the Federal Express and UPS clerks staring at her from their respective counters. After scanning the departures, she rushed back out to the car.

"There's a flight on Wild Goose Air leaving in twenty minutes. The next one is a Continental flight that leaves at one-seventeen."

Marvelli checked his watch. "That's almost two hours from now. We'll take the Wild Goose flight."

"How?"

"Positive mind, Loretta. Keep telling yourself: positive mind."

As they drove away from the curb, Loretta wondered if this was what he told Renée when she was at her worst.

Marvelli drove out of the terminal and got back on the access road that circled the airport. He passed the exit for short-term parking and took the one marked: EMPLOYEE PARKING. A yellow automatic gate blocked the way. There was no guard, just a machine for inserting an ID.

Loretta frowned at him. "Now what, Mr. Positive Mind?"

"I dunno. Should I break it down?"

"Hang on." Loretta got out of the car and manually lifted the wooden gate. It wasn't hard to lift, but an alarm started ringing as soon as she did. Marvelli drove through quickly, and as soon as she dropped the gate to its former position, the bell stopped ringing. She jumped back in, out of breath.

"That was easy," he said.

"Positive mind," she grumbled. "Now go."

Marvelli drove to the end of the parking lot closest to the terminal. The tails of three jetliners were nearly hanging over their heads they were so close. One of them had the Wild Goose Air logo painted on it: silhouettes of three geese flying in formation into the sunset. The parking lot was surrounded by a high cyclone fence topped with barbed wire.

Loretta just looked at him.

"Keep thinking positive," he said, scanning the runways through the fence. "Just think positive," he mumbled to himself.

"I'm thinking positive," Loretta said, "but nothing's happening."

"Don't nag."

"I'm not nagging."

"And don't get mad. It doesn't help."

She wanted to strangle him. "I don't want to pressure you, but don't you think we'd better do something quick? Temple must've called the local cops to come looking for us."

"Doubtful," Marvelli said, still scanning the tarmac. "Feds don't like to get the locals involved unless they really need the muscle. They don't like to share."

On the other side of the fence, four baggage handlers in green coveralls were loading luggage into the cargo hold of the Wild Goose jet, emptying the first of two trolleys stacked high with suitcases, duffel bags, and boxes. Loretta focused on something on the second trolley. "If we could just get over that fence . . . ," Loretta said.

One of the baggage handlers, a young guy with long sunbleached hair tied back in a ponytail, went over to the fence, looked both ways, then pried back a section, sneaking into the parking lot. He walked quickly over to a parked car, slunk down behind the wheel, and lit up a crooked cigarette. Loretta didn't have to smell it to know that it was pot.

Marvelli smiled. "See? You gotta have positive mind."

She gave him a withering look. "Just pull the car up to the hole in the fence."

"What're you thinking?"

"Unlock the trunk and follow me."

"What're you going to do?" Marvelli insisted.

"I'm gonna get us home with Martha Lee. What do you think I'm gonna do?" *That and save my life,* she thought.

They got out of the car, and Marvelli opened the trunk. Martha Lee was drenched in sweat, blinking at the sunlight, humming like crazy. She was like a newborn, wet and cranky.

"Stand her up," Loretta said. "We've got to get her to that luggage trolley."

"What're you gonna do? Put her in a suitcase?" Marvelli asked.

"I'm not *that* cruel." Loretta grabbed Martha Lee by the upper arm and sat her up. She weighed next to nothing, so she was easy to move.

Marvelli took Martha Lee's other arm and hauled her out of the trunk. She tried to struggle, but they were both much bigger than she was. She squirmed and hummed and flailed her head as they lifted her off the ground and carried her to the fence. Marvelli backed through the flap, pulling Martha Lee through, Loretta coming last.

"Over there," Loretta said, high-stepping it across the hot pavement all the way to the shady side of the luggage trolley where the baggage handlers couldn't see them. "Go distract those guys. All I need is a minute or two."

"You sure you know what you're doing?"

"Just do it, Marvelli. Have some positive mind."

"Okay." He sounded dubious.

Marvelli went around the trolley and walked up to the baggage handlers. "Hey, any of you seen what's his name with the long hair?" he called out. "Security's looking for him . . ."

While Marvelli chatted them up, Loretta found what she'd spotted through the fence, a big beige plastic pet carrier. She forced Martha Lee down onto her stomach and kept a bare foot on the small of her back as she opened the door of the pet carrier. Inside, a groggy German shepherd looked at Loretta with forlorn eyes, barely able to lift his head. "All doped up for the trip, huh?" Loretta muttered. "Poor dog."

Martha Lee started struggling to get free. She stopped when Loretta put more weight on her back.

"Come on, King, Rex, Rin Tin Tin, whatever the hell your name is." Loretta found a leash inside and clipped it to the dog's collar. She tried to coax the animal out, but the dog was too woozy to move. "Come on, come on. Atta girl. Good boy."

The dog just looked at her, tongue hanging out, eyes out of focus.

"Crap." Loretta reached in and lifted the dog out, setting him down on the ground next to Martha Lee. Then Loretta picked up Martha Lee, who was screaming under the duct tape, flailing her head in a panic.

Loretta positioned Martha Lee's feet, aiming for the mouth of the pet carrier, and jammed her in. Martha Lee tried to make her body rigid, but she was no match for Loretta, who pushed on her shoulders until she folded. Finally only Martha Lee's head was sticking out. Loretta looked down and flashed a mean grin, remembering her ordeal in the mud bath. "Aren't you so glad you're a perfect size six?" she gushed, then shoved Martha Lee's head in and shut the door. "Have a nice flight."

Marvelli peered around the edge of the luggage carrier. "Where is she?" he whispered. Then he noticed the doped-up dog panting on the ground. "Where'd he come from?"

"Never mind about the dog. Martha Lee's ready for boarding. Let's worry about getting us on." She spotted a pair of sunglasses hanging out of Marvelli's breast pocket. "Let me have your glasses."

"What?"

She took the glasses herself and put them on, then picked up the dog's leash. "Just play along," she whispered.

She dragged the deadweight dog out from behind the luggage carrier. "My dog!" she cried out, rotating her head like Stevie Wonder. "Help! Help! My dog!"

The baggage handlers ran over to her. "What's the problem, lady?" one of them asked.

"My dog needs water," Loretta fretted. "Quick!"

Marvelli picked up on her cue, rushing up and taking her by the arm. "What's the quickest way back into the terminal?" he asked. "This lady needs help." He rolled his eyes as if to say he didn't need this headache, but he had it, so he had to deal with it.

"How'd she get out here?" the burliest baggage handler

asked. They were all stunned by the sudden appearance of a barefoot blind woman in a blindingly gaudy muumuu, dragging a half-dead Seeing Eye dog.

Marvelli shrugged helplessly. "I just found her out here."

"See that gray door over there?" the burly baggage handler said. "The one marked '14'? Go through there. It'll take you back into the terminal."

"Will the alarm go off?" Marvelli asked, assuming it would have one.

"Nope. That one's okay."

"Thanks." He started to lead Loretta toward the door. "This way, ma'am. And slow down," he said out of the corner of his mouth. "You're supposed to be handicapped."

She started walking, but the dog was like an anchor. "Come on, Bowzer. You can do it," she urged. "Come on, dammit. Move!" She jerked on his chain, and the dog lumbered into a half-hearted trot. Suddenly she felt terrible, treating the poor animal this way. "I apologize, Rover. Just make it to the terminal, and I'll make it up to you. Dog yummies on me. Whatever you want. Just don't stop."

The dog took his time, but at least he kept moving. When they made it to the door marked "14," Marvelli pushed it open and led Loretta and the dog into a short corridor. The cool marble floor was relief on Loretta's feet. The air-conditioning seemed to energize the German shepherd a bit as they ran to the stairway and bounded up the stairs. When they got to the next floor, they found another gray metal door marked "14."

"Hang on, hang on!" Marvelli stopped her before she pushed the crash bar. "This one's got to have an alarm."

"Why?" she asked, annoyed with him for being so cautious.

"Because they don't want terrorists going out where the planes are, that's why."

"What're you, the man from UNCLE? Get out of my way." Loretta pushed through the door, and an alarm did sound. The waiting area for Gate 14 was on the other side, passengers waiting to board filling the gray vinyl seats. She pulled Marvelli by the sleeve and shoved him into a chair, then stood there with the dog, rocking on her heels, doing her Stevie Wonder imitation. A heavyset black woman with a badge pinned to her navy blazer ran into the waiting area. She had handcuffs, a walkie-talkie, and a can of mace attached to her belt. "Did you open that door?" the woman barked.

"I was looking for the ladies' room." She yanked on the dog's leash. "Bad, Rufus! Bad!"

The guard pulled the door closed and stopped the alarm. She glared down at Marvelli in his seat. "Are you with her?"

Marvelli shook his head. "Nope."

The woman looked skeptical, but she didn't challenge him. "Do you want me to take you to the ladies' room?" she said to Loretta.

"I think we'll find it this time, thank you."

"Ask for help if you need it." The black woman stomped off.

When she was gone, Marvelli got out of his seat and went to the monitors hanging over the waiting area. "Our flight leaves in ten minutes, Gate 16, right over there." He nodded across the way. "You get rid of the dog. I'll get us some tickets. Pray this flight isn't booked."

"Right," Loretta said. As Marvelli trotted off to find the Wild Goose ticket counter, she wandered over to the waiting area at Gate 16. On the way, she passed a little dark-haired boy in knee-length shorts and a baggy T-shirt standing by the ladies' room, guarding a beat-up backpack and a sky-blue carry-on bag. Loretta guessed that he was about eight or nine.

"You by yourself?" Loretta asked the boy.

"No."

"Who are you with?"

"My mom." He nodded toward the ladies' room. "She had to go."

"That happens," Loretta said. "Your mom ever tell you not to talk to strangers?"

"Yeah."

"So why don't you listen to her?"

The kid rubbed his nose and shrugged.

"Don't talk to strangers," Loretta said. "They're not all as nice as me."

"Okay."

"You got any pets?" she asked.

"No."

"Then here." She handed him the leash. "All kids should have pets. Take it easy, Lassie," she said to the dog, and started to walk away.

The little boy's mouth fell open. He'd hit the kid lottery.

Loretta took off the sunglasses and wandered into the crowd of passengers at Gate 16. She found a seat over by the windows between a distinguished-looking man in his sixties wearing a dark suit without a tie and reading a newspaper and a woman in her twenties with long brown hair parted in the middle, listening to a Walkman. Loretta could hear the music, it was cranked up so loud, and she was surprised that it was classical music. Solo piano. A Bach fugue, she thought. Nice.

A woman's voice came over the intercom: "Wild Goose Air Flight 77, nonstop to Newark, New Jersey, will begin boarding passengers now. Please have your tickets out and ready when your seat number is called. Passengers holding seat numbers 29 through 40, please come forward."

As people started shuffling into line, Loretta looked for Marvelli to come running through the terminal with their tickets. *Come on,* she thought. *Come on!*

She sank down into her seat and tipped her head back, closing her eyes to rest for a moment. There was still time, she told herself. It would take ten, fifteen minutes to board the passengers.

But when Loretta closed her eyes, an unexpected wave of fatigue washed over her, and she could've fallen asleep right there, she was so exhausted—except for the fact that she was worrying about everything. Martha Lee was in the pet carrier, but would the baggage guys hear her frantic humming and see her through the grill? Marvelli had gone to buy tickets, but what if he didn't get back in time? Then there was Lawrence Temple. They'd lost the feds on the highway, but where were they now? And even if she and Marvelli managed to get Martha Lee back to New Jersey, could the feds legally throw their weight around and take her back? And if they did that, would Julius Monroe rescind his offer to give her a permanent job with the Jump Squad? And what the hell was she going to do if she lost this job? Where could she go? What would she tell her father?

The mantra started chanting in her head: *I'm fat; I'm single; my career is in the toilet. I'm fat; I'm single—*

"Hello, Loretta."

Loretta's eyes shot open. Lawrence Temple was standing right in front of her. She looked over her shoulder and saw the two skinny goons. The husky goons were behind Temple, one of them holding Roger Laplante by the elbow. It wasn't the smiling, feel-good, infomercial Roger Laplante. It was the pissed-off, frig-you, I-want-to-kill-somebody Roger Laplante.

"Where is she, Loretta?" Temple asked, grimly deadpan.

"Who?"

"You know who. Martha Lee."

Loretta could see all her worst nightmares coming true: going home empty-handed, losing the job, losing her last shot at putting her life back together.

"Where is she, Loretta?" Temple asked again.

"Where is she?" Roger Laplante echoed. He was seething. "That little bitch tried to screw me. She paid over two hundred grand to a dummy company in Panama. Thank God the bank called for confirmation and I was able to cancel the wire before it went through. But that can't be the only thing she's done. I know it. If my books are for shit, it's because of her." He was talking to Temple now. "Martha Lee Sykes—or whatever her name is—is the one responsible for any financial shenanigans at Weight-Away. I *know* it. *She's* the one you want, not me. Her."

"We've been through this, Mr. Laplante," Temple said, blowing him off. "So where is she, Loretta?"

Loretta didn't answer. She was trying to think of something to say.

"You're hiding a fugitive, Loretta. That's a federal offense. Now where is she?"

The IRS agents closed in around her.

"Well, I . . ."

"I *will* have you arrested," Temple said. "Don't think I won't."

"Well, ah—"

BOOM!

An explosion from down the corridor made everyone duck. The roar of an approaching engine came up fast.

BOOM! Another gunshot, closer this time. It sounded like a cannon blast.

"Die, Marvelli!" someone yelled.

Loretta stood up on her seat to see what was going on. People were scattering, running in terror as the sound of the engine roared closer. Suddenly Marvelli came running down the corridor full tilt followed by Torpedo Joe Pickett on his red motorcycle, a pistol-grip shotgun in his hand and Ricky Macrae hanging onto his waist. He was still wearing his black WeightAway staff shorts and white polo shirt, and Ricky was in skintight black jeans, a red tube top, and a black leather vest, showing off those massive arms of hers. Even from this distance Loretta could see that Ricky was furious, her raccoon eyes flashing. Loretta could feel her stomach tightening, and she hated herself for reacting this way. *Ricky Macrae is not Brenda Hemingway,* she told herself. *Ricky is not Brenda, and I'm not afraid of either one of them.*

But now she wished she'd kept Martha Lee's gun when Marvelli had offered it.

Temple's men had their guns out, but they didn't seem to know what to do with them. They seemed confused.

"Shoot the biker before he kills Marvelli," Loretta hissed at the IRS agents, but they ignored her, looking to Temple for their orders.

"Don't fire," Temple told them. "Too many people here."

"Well, then do something," Loretta snapped, but he ignored her, too.

By now Joe had corralled Marvelli into a corner of the waiting area, revving his engine threateningly as Marvelli struggled to catch his breath, his back to the plate-glass windows that overlooked the runways. The barrel of Joe's shotgun was leveled on Marvelli's chest.

Ricky screeched from the back of the bike, "Where is she, you limp little dickhead? Where's Martha Lee?"

Hearing Ricky talk to Marvelli like that gave Loretta an uncontrollable urge to go over there, grab her by that awful rat's nest of hers, and throw her through the glass, but Temple was holding her wrist, trying to get her to get down and take cover. Roger Laplante was already under her seat, cowering like a bad dog.

In the meantime Temple's goons had mobilized and were trying to do an end run around Joe to take him from behind, but Joe saw them coming.

BOOM! He shot through the plate-glass window three feet to Marvelli's side, then pulled a revolver from his shorts, training it on the IRS agents as they Grouchoed around the waiting area. "Freeze, assholes. Drop your guns, or I start shooting civilians."

Temple was on the spot, and he didn't look comfortable having to make a decision that couldn't be figured out with a calculator.

"Joe, Joe, look at me," Marvelli said. "Let's talk about this—"

"You shut up!" Joe kept the shotgun on Marvelli as he turned back to the feds. "Now drop your guns." He used the revolver to shoot through the window again.

Temple whispered to Loretta, "How many bullets do you think he has in the shotgun?"

"How the hell should I know?"

"Okay," Temple finally said to his men, clearing his throat. "Do as he says. Put down your weapons."

Reluctantly the IRS agents tossed their automatics into a pile on the carpet in front of the check-in counter. Loretta's knees were shaking. She couldn't keep her eyes off the shotgun pointed at Marvelli.

Ricky climbed off the bike and walked up to Marvelli, standing clear of Joe's shotgun. "Where is she, dickhead?"

Marvelli showed her his palms in a gesture of conciliation. "Can't we talk about this?"

"No!" she screeched, and spit in his face.

Loretta snatched her wrist away from Temple. That did it. This little shit wasn't going to get away with that. She marched over toward Ricky.

Ricky's brow arched when she noticed Loretta coming. "Well, if it isn't fatty Patty," Ricky said in a drop-dead voice. "Nice dress."

"Back off, bitch," Loretta shouted, getting in her face. She didn't give a damn. She wasn't going to put up with any more bullshit.

"*You* must know where Martha Lee is," Ricky said. "Tell us or say good-bye to your partner."

Loretta saw red. "Forget it. You're not getting squat."

"Oh, yeah?"

"Yeah."

Marvelli stepped forward and tried to get between them. "Easy, ladies, easy. Why don't we just sit down and—"

Joe jabbed the air with the shotgun, reminding Marvelli that it was aimed right at him. "Freeze!" He swept the room with his other gun, keeping everyone else at bay.

Ricky gave Loretta her Elvis sneer. "Now what're you gonna do?"

"I'm not giving up Martha Lee." And she meant it. She was not going to lose this time.

"Oh, you don't think so, huh? Well, what if I—?" Ricky reached between her blubbery breasts.

Loretta didn't wait to see what Ricky had in there. She snatched the chrome-plated automatic from Marvelli's waistband, wheeled around, and buried the barrel deep into Ricky's chin fat, tilting her head all the way back.

"Drop it," Loretta growled.

Something hit the carpet. Loretta glanced down and saw the Derringer.

Ricky's arms were out straight, arm fat quivering. "Joe!" she screamed. "Do something! Shoot her, goddammit! *Shoot her!*"

The barrel of Torpedo Joe's revolver was five feet from Loretta's head, looking right at her.

"Joe! Shoot her!"

Loretta's throat was tight. She still had the gun under Ricky's chin, but her hand was shaking. "I'm not backing down," she managed to get out.

Ricky was going nuts. "What the hell're you waiting for, Joe?" she screamed. "Do something! Help me!"

Marvelli was right next to Loretta. "Don't be stupid, Loretta. Do you hear me? Put the gun down."

Joe snarled at him, "Back off, Marvelli." He shook the shotgun, indicating that he wanted Marvelli to move away from the women.

Loretta was shaking her head, talking to herself as much as to Marvelli. "No. They are not getting Martha Lee. I'm not backing down this time. They can kill me if they want, but I am not backing down."

"Joe!" Ricky's lips were trembling, her double chin jiggling.

"Loretta, don't be stupid," Marvelli pleaded. "Let them have—"

"Shut up, Marvelli!" Joe growled.

"Joe!" Ricky wailed. "Do something! Shoot her!"

Joe narrowed his eyes and looked at the two women, his revolver aimed at Loretta's head, the shotgun in the general direction of the crowd that included Lawrence Temple and his men. Joe's eyes swept the crowd. It was dead quiet, except for Ricky hyperventilating. He stared at her for a long moment, then focused on Loretta and started shaking his head. "I can't shoot her, Ricky."

"Why not?"

" 'Cause she's a good person. I feel for her."

"Joe! What the hell're you talking about? She's got a gun to my neck, for chrissake."

"If you'd heard what I'd heard this morning, you'd feel the same as me, Ricky. Miss Loretta, when you were on that massage table telling me about all the crap you put up with because you were fat when you were a kid, even though I was trying to kill you, my heart went out to you. The story about having to wear the rain slicker when you'd ripped your dress? Pitiful, just pitiful. I was a fat kid, too, so I know what it was like."

Ricky screamed, "Shoot her, Joe!"

But Joe just shook his head again. "Ricky, I've seen your baby pictures at your mama's house. You've always been on the heavy side yourself. You should have a little understanding."

Ricky's eyes narrowed. "Shut up, Joe!"

"Well, Miss Loretta, I didn't realize what you were all about until just now. So even though you work with this ass-pain Marvelli over here, you're basically a very good person. You take Martha Lee back to New Jersey. The woman's just a two-timing 'ho' anyway."

Loretta kept the gun on Ricky. She didn't know whether he was being sincere or not. Maybe he was trying to trick her.

"Joe!" Ricky whined. "Martha Lee screwed me and my brother. You gave me your promise that you'd take care of her."

Loretta spoke up before Ricky could dissuade him. "There are a bunch of IRS agents here, Joe. They want Martha Lee, too.

If I say where she is, chances are they'll get to her before you do. And do you know what that means? They'll try to put her away on white-collar charges, which you know is nothing. Six months to a year at some federal facility that looks like Rancho Bonita—"

"I resent that," Roger Laplante yelled from under his chair.

"Anyway," Loretta continued, "if I take Martha Lee back to Jersey, she'll have to serve out the rest of her original sentence. Five and a half years in. Hard time. No chance for parole. Which would you rather see Martha Lee have? Hard time or the country club?"

Lawrence Temple spoke up. "Loretta, you're misrepresenting the case—"

"Shut up!" Joe snarled. "I've already made up my mind. She's yours, Loretta. I'll hold these sons of bitches here until you get where you're going."

A tear spurted from Loretta's eye. "Thank you, Joe. You're a good person. Basically." She looked over at Marvelli, keeping the gun buried in Ricky's baby fat. "Come on. Let's go—"

"Oh, no. Not him," Joe objected. "Marvelli and I have a bone to pick."

Loretta shook her head. "No good, Joe. He's my partner. We go together or not at all."

"Jo-oe!" Ricky wailed.

"I'll give you Ricky for Marvelli," Loretta said. "That's a fair deal."

Joe made a face as he thought about it. "Well . . . I suppose," he finally said.

Loretta took a step back from Ricky, keeping the gun trained on her.

"Thanks for nothing," Ricky grumbled, glaring at Joe.

"Don't give me any grief, woman," Joe barked.

Ricky turned her back on him in a huff. Loretta wasn't sure, but she could've sworn hard-ass Ricky was sobbing.

"Okay," Loretta called out to the crowd, "everybody with

tickets for Newark, get on the plane now." She and Joe kept their weapons out while scared passengers rushed to the door where two flight attendants quickly took their tickets and sent them down the chute.

"The passengers are boarded," one of the frightened flight attendants reported in a quavery voice after a few minutes.

"Did you get us tickets?" Loretta asked Marvelli.

"Yeah, I got 'em."

"Okay, let's go. Joe, you take care of yourself."

"You, too, Miss Loretta."

"Why're you being so nice to her?" Ricky complained with a sniff.

Joe grumbled under his breath, "We'll talk about it later."

Loretta and Marvelli backstepped toward the door.

Joe turned the shotgun on Lawrence Temple and his men.

"You two aren't going to get away with this," Temple called out. "This is just a waste of everybody's time. We'll get Martha Lee back in the end, Loretta."

"I'm sure you will," Loretta said, backing through the doorway that led to the plane. "After she serves her time in Jersey, she's all yours."

"It doesn't work that way, Loretta. You'll see that I'm right."

"Quiet down!" Joe shouted at Temple.

Loretta and Marvelli started running down the chute toward the plane. The two nervous flight attendants—a blonde and a brunette—were waiting for them, ready to close the hatch.

"Here," Loretta said to the brunette, flipping the gun's safety and handing it to her. "Have the pilot hold onto this for us."

The brunette held the gun as if it were a dead fish. "Your seats are right there," she said, nodding to two empty seats near the cabin. "Two C and D."

"First-class?" Loretta asked Marvelli as they took their seats and buckled up.

He shrugged. "That's all they had left."

"Julius won't approve this."

"Yes, he will. Don't worry. I'll take care of it."

The jet's engines revved to a high whine as the plane started to back away from the terminal. Loretta grabbed Marvelli's hand and started praying that they'd get off the ground without another glitch.

Please, God, please, she thought. *Please!*

"Ladies and gentlemen," the captain's voice came over the intercom, "we have received special clearance to take off immediately. Please have your seat belts buckled and your tray tables in the upright position for takeoff. And on behalf of the crew, we hope you enjoy the remainder of this flight and come fly with us again."

"Fat chance," someone behind Loretta muttered.

The engines whined higher as the plane picked up speed, rumbling down the runway.

Loretta linked her fingers through Marvelli's and squeezed. *Please, God, please! No surprises.*

The nose of the plane tipped up, and the rumbling tapered off. Loretta could feel the swoop in her stomach as the plane left the ground and started its ascent. She held her breath, holding Marvelli's hand in a death grip until the plane finally reached its cruising altitude and leveled off.

When the seat belt sign chimed off, she started breathing again. "Thank you, God," she whispered. Then she turned sideways and threw her arms around Marvelli. "We made it. I can't believe it. We made it!"

The brunette flight attendant appeared in the aisle, carrying a small bottle of champagne and two plastic tulip glasses. "Compliments of the captain," she said. "You really showed some guts back there, ma'am."

Loretta smiled. "Thanks."

The brunette poured the champagne, then left them alone.

"I assume they don't know about Martha Lee in the pet carrier," she said out the side of her mouth.

Marvelli reached for a glass. "I don't think so. While you were making a fuss about getting water for the dog, I loaded Martha Lee on myself."

Loretta picked up her glass and grinned. "To us," she said. "We deserve it."

Marvelli nodded. "To us," he repeated.

Marvelli took a sip, glancing sideways at Loretta. He'd never been jammed in so close to her before, touching elbows and drinking champagne. He was all hyped up, and hot and bothered.

This is bad, he thought. *This isn't right*. He shouldn't be feeling this way about Loretta. For a lot of reasons. Most of all because he was married.

"You think Martha Lee is all right in that pet carrier?" he asked, trying to start an innocuous conversation.

"Yeah. It was pretty big," Loretta said. "She had room to move."

"So I guess she'll be all right."

"Yeah. I'm sure she'll be okay. It's not a long flight."

"Right."

But Marvelli's stomach was jittery. It was going to be a long flight for him. Maybe he could go to the bathroom for a while, hide out in there. He couldn't just sit here. He was afraid of what might happen.

Then he noticed the in-flight phone in the seat back. "I think I'll call home," he announced, reaching into his jacket for his wallet. "See if they're all right."

He could feel Loretta's green eyes looking at him as he slid his credit card through the slot on the phone, carefully following the directions printed on the seat back. She shook out her hair and threw it over her shoulder, and he could feel the breeze it made and smell her smell.

Oh, Jesus, he thought as he dialed his home number. *Maybe*

I could get headphones or something after this, pretend to fall asleep.

The phone rang four times before anyone picked up.

"Hello, Nina? It's Daddy."

Loretta stared at his hand holding the empty champagne glass.

"What? No. . . . When did it happen?"

The pain in Marvelli's voice instantly alarmed her. It was like an arrow going right through her.

"Where's Grandma? Are you alone?"

Loretta's heart beat faster. She didn't have to ask. She knew.

"I'm on the plane right now. I'll be home in a couple of hours. Okay? Don't worry. I'll be there."

Marvelli was pale. He suddenly looked feverish. Loretta wanted to put her hand to his forehead. She wanted to help him. She wanted to do something.

His voice cracked as he spoke. "I'll be home as soon as I can, Nina. I'm sorry. I should have been there. I'm sorry."

Loretta felt awful. She felt helpless and out of place.

"I'm coming home. Just hang on, Nina. I'll be there soon. I love you. It's gonna be all right."

He hung up the phone and stared out the window, rubbing his forehead with his fingers.

Loretta didn't know what to say, but she had to say something. "Renée?" she finally asked.

He nodded, his face still turned away.

"Do you want to talk about it?" she asked.

He shook his head. "I have to think," he whispered. She could tell from quaver in his voice that he was crying.

Three days later the weather was gorgeous—perfect Indian-summer temperatures with horse-tail clouds painted over a light blue sky. The sun peeked through the leaves that were just starting to turn, reflecting off the shiny hood of the black hearse but considerate enough not to bear down on the mourners in their dark clothes. It was an absolutely perfect day, Loretta thought. But not for a funeral.

"Black crows in a stone field," Julius Monroe murmured under his breath as he stared at Marvelli and his extended family sitting on folding chairs in front of the open grave, an army of gray headstones covering the background. Renée's coffin was suspended over the open hole, supported by nylon straps.

Loretta was standing next to Julius, feeling very out of place. Julius was the only person she knew here other than Marvelli's mother-in-law and his daughter, Nina, and she'd only met them once. Julius was like a solemn penguin in his black suit and white skullcap, hands clasped behind his back. Annette was wearing a black dress and a matching hat with a wide ribbon around the brim. Nina's dress was a navy pinpoint polka-dot pattern with a pleated skirt and a rounded white collar. They were both sobbing, Nina more quietly than her grandmother, sitting on either side of Marvelli, who hugged them both, whispering to them, consoling them.

But who was consoling him? Loretta wondered. She knew he had to be hurting, but he'd been knocking himself out to keep everyone else together, shaking hands, holding hands, patting shoulders, hugging everyone. He was more like a master of ceremonies than a new widower. He'd probably fall apart later when it was all over and he was alone with his memories. Loretta wished she could do something for him, though. Like dress him up. That suit he was wearing was a nightmare—gray sharkskin, the kind of fabric that shines. *Who wears sharkskin anymore?* she thought. *And to your wife's funeral?* Maybe it was the only suit he owned.

At the foot of the grave, a balding priest in a long white tunic and tinted glasses stood holding an open Bible in one hand, a holy water sprinkler in the other. The instrument looked like a medieval potato masher with a perforated silver ball on one end and a black wooden handle on the other. The priest murmured prayers as he flicked holy water over the coffin in the sign of a cross. When he finished blessing the grave, he closed the Bible and turned to the family.

"I'm told that all throughout her illness, Renée often advised her loved ones that when she died, they should think of her passing as a beginning, not an ending; that her absence would open up a space that would allow for realignment in the family, like the kind of plastic puzzle that requires the removal of one tile, so that all the others can be slid into place to create a picture. . . ."

Loretta fuzzed out, staring at Marvelli. She wondered if he thought of Renée's death as a beginning. A beginning of what? Loneliness?

Julius leaned over and spoke in her ear. "So, have you come to your senses?"

She frowned at him. "About what?"

"Working for the Jump Squad. You still want the job?"

"Of course I still want it," she whispered. "I went crazy to bring back Martha Lee Spooner. She's back in prison now, and that was the deal. You said I could have the job if I brought her in on time."

"Chill, my dear, chill. I know what I said. I'm just wondering if *you* still want it, having seen what there is to see of it." The skullcapped penguin rocked on his heels, waiting for the right answer.

She glanced at Marvelli in his sharkskin suit, his fingers linked with his daughter's on one side, his mother-in-law's on the other. *Beginnings and endings,* she thought. Her hopeful beginnings always somehow turned into bad endings for her. Would the Jump Squad be the same thing all over again?

"Are you still here among us, Loretta?" Julius said. "Or are you conversing with the angels over this matter?"

She didn't answer him. Maybe she should ask Renée, she thought.

"Loretta?" Julius whispered.

"Ssshhh," she said.

The priest had stopped speaking, and a cemetery worker in dark green work clothes was turning the crank that let out the nylon straps, lowering the coffin into the grave. One of the undertakers held a big bouquet of red and white carnations, handing them out to the mourners as they lined up and came forward—some singly, some in pairs—to toss a flower onto the coffin. Julius went over and merged into the line, but Loretta didn't move. She felt funny doing something this intimate for someone she hardly knew.

Julius made his way to the head of the line, bowed his head, and tossed a white carnation on top of the gathering pile on the coffin's lid. The crowd soon dwindled down to the closest relatives—the cousins, the aunts and uncles, the nieces and nephews, the brothers and sisters, then finally Nina, Annette, and Marvelli. They stood together, the priest and the undertaker hovering nearby. Marvelli was practically holding his mother-in-law up, she was so distraught, and Nina was hanging onto his sleeve,

silent tears streaming down her face. Marvelli was doing his best
to be strong for them, but his chin was crumpling, too. They
threw their flowers in but didn't leave like the others. After a few
moments the priest stepped in and took Annette by the arm while
the undertaker ushered Nina and Marvelli away from the grave
and back toward the waiting limousine.

Loretta stared at Marvelli in his greaser suit with his junior
Mafioso haircut and remembered him eating all those cinnamon
buns the first day she'd met him. He's a real piece of work, she
thought. A wonderful person. A brick. But he was no beginning—at least not for her. He was a solid middle in the middle of
a family who needed him. Not a beginning.

Loretta started back toward the road where the other
mourners were getting into their cars, getting ready to go. She
walked slowly, not wanting to pass Marvelli and his daughter.

"No, Dad. Don't," she overheard Nina saying to her father.

"You sure?" Marvelli said.

"Don't. Grandma will get mad."

"But I brought the tape and the boombox and everything.
It's in the limo."

Nina shook her head. "Don't. It would be . . . weird."

"But your mother and I loved old rock 'n' roll. We used to
dance to "The Peppermint Twist" when we were in high school.
Come on, Nina," Marvelli persisted. "Mommy would want us
to do it. She was crazy like that. She didn't care what other people thought."

"I know, Dad, but just don't. Please."

Marvelli sighed. "You sure?"

"I'm sure," Nina said.

"All right. Maybe you're right." He didn't sound convinced,
though.

Shuffling behind them, Loretta was relieved for Nina. A
boombox at a funeral? Please. She stared at the back of Marvelli's
head as they walked, a sad smile on her face. It would never work
out, she thought. Never in a million years. Marvelli was definitely
not a beginning.

As they came up to the limousine, Loretta veered off toward the line of parked cars, intending to find hers and go home, but suddenly Marvelli glanced back and noticed her.

"Loretta," he said. "Hang on." He turned to Nina. "Get in the car. I'll be right there."

Loretta's stomach clenched. She had wanted to sneak away.

"Thanks for coming," he said, giving her a hug. "I appreciate it."

Loretta hugged him back, and the warmth of his body against hers suddenly made her a little light-headed. But at the same time she felt very guilty feeling what she was feeling, holding Marvelli when Renée literally wasn't even in the ground yet. "I'm sorry," she said into his ear, then pulled away.

"People are coming over to the house for coffee and sandwiches," he said. "Why don't you come?"

"No, I . . . I'd feel funny. I really didn't know Renée. . . ."

"No, don't be silly. Come."

She shrugged. "Okay. Maybe." She had no intention of going.

"Okay, I understand," he said. He seemed disappointed. "Look, I'm taking the rest of the week off, but I will see you back at the office next week, right?"

The blood rushed to Loretta's face. She didn't know what to say. She was having second thoughts.

"You did a good job down in Florida. You're tough stuff. I like working with you."

"Really?"

"Yeah, I think we worked pretty well together. Maybe Julius will put us together again sometime. If you don't mind putting up with me, that is."

"No, no, I wouldn't mind."

The back window of the limousine rolled down. "Dad," Nina called out. "They're going to be waiting for us back home."

"I'm coming," he said, then turned back to Loretta. He put his hand on her forearm. "Thanks for coming, Loretta. I gotta run now. I'll see you Monday." He rushed back to the limousine and got in. It pulled away from the curb as soon as he shut the door.

"So, what do you think?"

Loretta jumped at the sound of Julius Monroe's baritone coming over her shoulder. Her face was still flushed.

"What do I think about what?" she asked.

"Working for the Jump Squad. Yea or nay?"

The shiny black limousine was winding around the cemetery. She watched it until its directionals started blinking and it pulled through the tall iron gates, disappearing into the street.

"Well, Ms. Loretta Kovacs?"

She stared at the opening in the gate where the limo had just been. *Entrances and exits,* she thought. *Beginnings and endings.* Gradually she started to nod.

"Yes. I do want the job."

Beginnings are always better than endings, she thought.

"All right for you," her new boss said, shaking his head. "But don't say I didn't warn you."

"Don't worry," she said with a grin. "I've been warned."